DANCE FLOOR

BOOKS BY HELENA DIXON

Murder at the Dolphin Hotel
Murder at Enderley Hall
Murder at the Playhouse

HELENA DIXON

MURDER
on the
DANCE FLOOR

bookouture

Published by Bookouture in 2020

An imprint of Storyfire Ltd.
Carmelite House
50 Victoria Embankment
London EC4Y 0DZ

www.bookouture.com

ISBN: 978-1-80019-057-3
eBook ISBN: 978-1-80019-056-6

This book is a work of fiction. Names, characters, businesses,
organizations, places and events other than those clearly in the
public domain, are either the product of the author's imagination
or are used fictitiously. Any resemblance to actual persons, living or
dead, events or locales is entirely coincidental.

Murder on the Dance Floor is dedicated to my husband, who supplies me with coffee, helps with my research and knows when to disappear when I'm writing.

Torbay Herald – November 1933

Another success for Torbay Private Investigative Services
Captain Matthew Bryant of Torbay Private Investigative Services was today commended by the Chamber of Commerce in Torquay at their annual dinner. Captain Bryant, who has successfully assisted in solving several crimes locally, including the recent terrible murders in September of two young women in Torquay, was honoured by the Chamber. The head of the Chamber of Commerce, Councillor Harold Everton, said, 'Torbay Private Investigative Services is a real asset to the town. Residents and visitors alike are benefitting from Captain Bryant's hard work.'

Captain Bryant said he was honoured that the Chamber had recognised his business in this way.

Generous bequest for church of the Sacred Heart

The church of the Sacred Heart in Exeter was today announced to have benefitted from a generous bequest in the will of local man, Jack Dawkins. Mr Dawkins, proprietor of Jacky Daw's Emporium in Exeter has left the entirety of his estate for the benefit of the church. The estate is thought to be worth several thousand pounds. Mr Dawkins had no family.

CHAPTER ONE

It was a cold autumnal afternoon and Father Lamb of the church of the Sacred Heart leaned forward in his armchair to warm his aged hands against the fire blazing in the hearth. He had come at Kitty Underhay's invitation to take tea with herself and her grandmother in the salon of her grandmother's suite at the Dolphin Hotel in Dartmouth.

Captain Matthew Bryant was also present, having met the elderly priest from the train at Kingswear Station and had escorted him across the river on the ferry to the hotel. Matt was now seated on one of the bentwood occasional chairs near to Kitty, his long legs stretched out in front of him. Kitty knew her grandmother was anxious to meet Father Lamb since he might have some information about Kitty's mother who had been missing since June 1916.

Kitty and Matt had first met the priest a few weeks earlier when trying to trace Jack Dawkins, an old acquaintance of her parents. Sadly, Dawkins had been at the end of his life when Matt had tracked him down but Father Lamb believed he might have some news for Kitty.

'May I offer you some tea, Father?' Kitty's grandmother presided over the silver teapot.

'Thank you, that would be most kind. The weather outside is most inclement today.' A gust of wind blew the rain against the leaded panes of the large bay window as if in agreement.

Kitty noticed a slight tremor in her grandmother's hand as she poured the tea. The flickering light from the fire seemed to

accentuate the fine lines on her carefully powdered face and Kitty
knew she was finding the meeting difficult.

The priest accepted the delicate china cup and saucer, setting it
down carefully on the polished mahogany side table next to him.
He always reminded Kitty of a benign tortoise with his balding
head appearing too small above his white clerical collar.

Kitty offered him a cake from the selection on the tiered stand.
'Thank you, Miss Underhay.' He took a jam tart and settled back
in his seat.

'We appreciate you coming to see us, Father. When Matt and
Kitty said they were trying to discover if Mr Dawkins had any
recollection of my daughter, I must admit I did not hold out much
hope. Seventeen years is a long time.' Her grandmother replaced her
own cup on its saucer and appeared to gather herself as she spoke.

'Indeed. You will be aware, no doubt, that I cannot break the
seal of the confessional so I cannot disclose anything that Jack may
have shared during that time.' Father Lamb paused and looked
around at them all. 'However, at the very end of his life, Jack did
indicate that there were things he wished to say. Miss Underhay,
he sent you a letter, I believe?'

'Yes.' Kitty nodded. 'Please call me Kitty, Father.' She smiled
at the priest.

He looked at her grandmother. 'I believe that your daughter's
disappearance lay very heavily on his conscience, especially at the
end. He was in love with Elowed, I think all his life.' Father Lamb's
voice gentled and Kitty's grandmother dabbed at the corners of her
eyes with a lace-trimmed handkerchief.

Kitty blinked and Matt reached for her hand, giving a squeeze
of reassurance. 'We saw in the paper that Jack had made his will
in favour of the church. That was a nice thing to do,' Kitty said.

Father Lamb nodded and reached for the worn brown leather
satchel he had carried with him from Exeter, and which now lay at

his feet. 'It was a very generous bequest. It will be put to good use in the parish. I had to supervise the clearing of Jack's things and ensure everything was in order as part of the probate. When Jack was in his last days, he kept talking about a box and mentioning your mother's name. He kept muttering, "See she gets the box," and "Elowed's girl." He glanced at Kitty for a moment as he unfastened the buckles of his bag. 'I found this amongst his possessions and I'm sure this is what he wished me to give you.' He reached into the satchel and drew out what looked like an old wooden cigar box, battered with use and time.

Kitty accepted it from him as he passed it across to her. She was curious to see the contents, but fearful at the same time. Her gaze linked with Matt's and she drew courage.

'Thank you.'

She lifted the lid clear of the box, setting it aside on the arm of the sofa. A delicately carved ivory rosary lay on top of a sheaf of papers, many of which appeared to have been clipped from newspapers. The edges yellowed with age.

'I rather think that the rosary belonged to Jack's mother. I know that you are not a catholic, but I think he would have liked you to have it as a keepsake. He had no family, as you know.' Father Lamb looked at Kitty's grandmother as if seeking her permission.

'That is a kind thought, Father,' Mrs Treadwell said.

'I have not examined the remainder of the contents of the box so I don't know how helpful it will be in your quest, but Jack clearly felt it was important.' The priest's brow furrowed slightly, and Kitty guessed he must have been concerned about passing on Jack's box and the effect it might have.

Kitty ran the rosary beads through her fingers, the ivory cool against her skin. 'I shall treasure this, thank you.' She stirred the clippings with her fingertips wondering what secrets lay buried in the fragile pile of paper. The corner of a photograph appeared, and she picked it up to study it more closely.

'What is it, darling?' her grandmother asked.

'A photograph of Mother. It's like the one I have of her taken on the moor.' She frowned as she studied it. 'But she is standing slightly differently, I think. It must have been taken at the same time.' She passed the image across to her grandmother.

Mrs Treadwell took out a pair of spectacles from the embroidered case that lay next to her on the side table. Slipping them on, she then peered at the photograph. 'Yes, Kitty, I think you may be right.' A heavy sigh escaped her as she removed her glasses and carefully handed the picture back to Kitty.

Kitty showed the photograph to Matt. He had seen the other photograph before when Kitty had first told him of her mother's disappearance during the Great War. They had gone through all the documents from the time of Elowed's disappearance when Matt had first come to the Dolphin and they had been investigating a series of brutal murders in the town.

'Jack was fond of photography. He had several cameras and belonged to a club at one time, I believe,' Father Lamb said.

'I suppose this answers the question of who took the picture I have of Mother on the moor. I have often wondered.' Kitty accepted the photograph back from Matt and returned it to the box. She replaced the lid and set the box aside. She would examine the contents later.

'Father, when we last met you said that on his deathbed Jack Dawkins was rambling that he should have warned my mother about something, or at least gone with her somewhere. You thought it might have been to do with a criminal network in the city that used to gather at the Glass Bottle public house. You kindly offered to make some enquiries on my behalf. Have you managed to do so?'

'Yes, I have made some enquiries about the landlord of the Glass Bottle, you will recall he is the son of the previous landlord who was there in 1916, though they share the same name, Ezekiel Hammett.' Father Lamb peered over the top of his glasses.

'You thought he might have more information,' Matt said.

'Unfortunately, he appears to be away at the moment and the pub is closed. I have been unable to determine where he has gone. I have to be careful not to appear too curious. When he returns, I'll telephone you.'

'Thank you.' Kitty exchanged a glance with Matt. The priest had told them the Glass Bottle had a bad reputation so they would need to proceed with caution if they were to discover anything useful.

She could see by her grandmother's demeanour that, although she was trying hard to conceal her emotions, the box and its contents were distressing to her. They passed the next hour or so in an amicable fashion. Matt turned the conversation to the fundraising that Kitty had assisted with for the boys' orphanage in Torquay.

'The Davenport house is to be let. I doubt they will return anytime soon, if ever,' Matt said, referring to the large house next to his at Churston. The Davenports, a theatrical family from London, had been involved in Kitty and Matt's last case as well as driving the fundraising for the orphanage. Kitty suppressed a shudder. The case brought back bad memories for her. Matt had been mistakenly arrested for murder and she had almost been killed during that adventure. She had no desire to see any of the Davenports again anytime soon.

Father Lamb nodded his head gently; he was familiar both with the case and the family. 'A good thing, I suspect, although Miss Davenport will be much missed in the community.'

'Yes, Genny worked hard with a number of charities,' Kitty agreed.

'Millicent has missed her, I believe,' Kitty's grandmother remarked.

Kitty exchanged a glance with Matt. Millicent Craven, former mayoress of Dartmouth, and one of her grandmother's oldest friends, was Kitty's particular bête noire. Mrs Craven was on every committee of every charity and public body. She had taken a great interest in their last case, insisting she be kept informed of their progress. This had not sat well with Kitty.

Father Lamb declined the invitation to stay for supper and Mrs Treadwell insisted that he return to Exeter via taxi. 'The train will be dreadfully busy at this time of day and the weather is so wild.'

Matt escorted the elderly priest downstairs to the lobby and out to Mr Potter's waiting automobile.

'Are you all right, Grams?' Kitty asked as she collected up the dirty tea things and returned them to the trolley for the staff to remove. She was concerned that her grandmother appeared tired by Father Lamb's visit.

'Yes, my dear. I think I may have a cold coming, however. My head is aching rather.'

'Go and lie down for an hour before supper and I'll bring you some aspirin,' Kitty suggested.

'Thank you, I think I will.' Her grandmother gave her a small, weary smile and retired to her bedroom. Kitty finished tidying up and took her some aspirin with a glass of water.

'I rather think I would like supper on a tray tonight, Kitty. Can you ask chef for some soup for later? My appetite is diminished, and I feel quite exhausted.'

Kitty smoothed the pastel pink satin eiderdown over her grandmother. The older woman appeared pale and fragile in the large bed. 'Of course. Is there anything else I can get for you?' Anxiety prickled at her. Was this quest for information about Elowed too much for her grandmother?

'I shall probably feel better once I've rested, my dear.' The older woman closed her eyes and Kitty was forced to withdraw to the lounge.

She had just finished telephoning the kitchen with her grandmother's instructions when Matt returned to the lounge. He raised his eyebrows at discovering Kitty alone.

'Grams has retired to bed. She feels unwell,' Kitty explained.

'I noticed she looked quite tired while Father Lamb was here,' Matt remarked. 'It's turning into a foul evening out there tonight. The rain is quite heavy and there is already a mist rising from the river. I'm glad Father Lamb accepted the offer of a taxi.'

'Yes, the wind keeps gusting too. I can hear it around the chimneys.' Kitty crossed to the large bay window and drew the heavy dark green velvet drapes closed against the night. With the lamps already lit and the fire glowing in the hearth the salon had a cosy, intimate feel to it.

Kitty took her seat back on the sofa, her gaze straying to the small wooden cigar box. 'I hope she'll be all right. I can't help but feel somewhat responsible for all of this. That box is a little like Pandora's. I'm afraid almost to see what is inside.'

Matt took a seat next to her, his hand capturing hers. 'I understand. You and your grandmother have been searching for answers for so long, and this is the furthest you have come. There is still the chance too that the landlord at that public house in Exeter, the Glass Bottle, that Father Lamb told us about when we saw him at Jack's funeral, may have information when he returns.'

Kitty sighed. 'I know. I want to see what is in those papers, but I can't help but feel afraid.'

'Chin up, old girl. Remember, inside Pandora's box there was also hope.'

CHAPTER TWO

Tempting as it was to delve straight into the contents of Jack Dawkins' mysterious box, Kitty was kept busy caring for her grandmother and running the hotel. Her grandmother appeared to be suffering from a severe cold and Kitty couldn't help but worry that the renewed search into her mother's disappearance had triggered it.

'Darling, you must take my place at the hoteliers' annual dinner dance on Friday. It's very important that the Dolphin is represented. I'm sure Matt will be happy to accompany you,' her grandmother instructed from her sickbed.

'I don't know, Grams.' Kitty placed a fresh cup of tea next to her grandmother's bed and began to tidy the debris from the top of the cabinet.

Mrs Treadwell went to speak but a paroxysm of coughing prevented her for a moment. She held her handkerchief in front of her lips as Kitty looked on anxiously. Kitty passed her a glass of water. Once she had taken a sip and recovered her breath, she continued.

'It's important to attend. All the influential people from the council will be there, along with the proprietors from the premier establishments in Torbay.' She fixed Kitty with a steely gaze despite her watering eyes.

'Yes, but you are unwell and there is the hotel to manage,' Kitty started to protest.

'We are quiet at this point in the season; you can be spared for an evening. I have a suite reserved at the Imperial in Torquay, where they are holding the event this year. You can dine and dance and enjoy yourself without the worry of returning back across the river. I insist you go, Kitty.' She started coughing again as soon as she had finished speaking.

Kitty could see her grandmother had clearly made up her mind, and further discussion would not only be useless but would probably worsen her condition.

'Very well, I'll telephone Matt and see if he is free to escort me.' She picked up the tray and watched as her grandmother settled herself back against her pile of pillows.

'Take Alice with you, she can help you dress.'

Kitty raised her eyebrows. 'And ensure my reputation is maintained?'

'Thank you, darling.' A small smile played at the corners of her grandmother's lips.

Kitty rolled her eyes in mock exasperation; aware she had been manipulated into attending the dinner dance. She had not seen much of Matt since Father Lamb's visit. He had been engaged to solve a delicate case involving a well-known lady in Torbay society who tended to appropriate things that weren't hers. Matt had been tasked with restoring the objects to their rightful owners while preserving the lady's good standing.

She was pleased that his business had recovered and that he had not been swayed by his parents' pleas that he return to London with them and take up a post with the diplomatic service. However, she found she had missed his company, especially as they had grown much closer over the last few weeks.

The box of papers Father Lamb had given her sat next to her mother's photograph on top of her dressing table. The ivory rosary was hung on the corner of her mirror. She had lifted the lid of the box a few times to glance at the contents but, on each occasion, she had been disturbed and had been forced to place it aside. The cursory peeps she had taken had told her nothing that she did not already know.

Kitty took a seat at her pretty kidney-shaped dressing table and picked up the black candlestick-style telephone receiver to place a call to Matt.

'Hello, Kitty, how is your grandmother? Is she any better?'

'She's still unwell, I'm afraid. I've called to request a favour from you.'

'Oh, yes?' His voice was amused.

'Grams is insisting I attend the annual hoteliers' dinner dance in Torquay on Friday. She has a suite reserved at the Imperial Hotel where it's being held for myself and Alice. She suggested I ask you to escort me, if you're free.' She waited for his response.

Their friendship was back on track after a rocky time a few months ago and since then there had been signs it might blossom into something more. However, beyond a few kisses they had yet to go on any kind of formal date even though she was aware that their acquaintances appeared to view them as a couple. Quite how Matt saw their relationship, however, she was still unsure.

'I'd be delighted.'

She breathed a small sigh of relief and gave him the details of the event. After concluding their conversation, she opened the doors of her wardrobe to examine the contents. An important event such as the hoteliers' ball surely warranted expenditure on a new dress and maybe even some shoes.

Alice was quite excited when Kitty informed her about the dinner dance.

'A night at a posh hotel, miss? Our Betty is working there that night waitressing in the dining room.' Alice's eyes sparkled with delight. Kitty was sure that she would waste no time in taking the opportunity to crow over her cousin.

'My grandmother has a suite reserved, so, yes, we are to stay overnight. It will save us taking a night-time ferry crossing or coming back the longer way by road.'

Alice clasped her hands together in glee. 'And I shall be your maid again, miss? Help you dress and do your hair? There will be some lovely gowns there, I reckon. Will you have something new to wear?'

Kitty laughed. 'I did think my wardrobe looked a little sparse.'

'Will Captain Bryant be attending too, Miss Kitty?' Alice's tone was offhand, but mischief shone out of her eyes.

'You watch far too many moving pictures,' Kitty reproved. 'But, yes, he is escorting me, although I fear he may find it a rather dull affair. The last time I accompanied my grandmother I was saddled with this tiresome chap from a hotel in Paignton who rambled on all evening about the difficulties of engaging good kitchen staff.'

Alice giggled. 'You'll be dancing though, miss.' She waltzed around in front of Kitty, her white apron twirling. 'Like in the pictures, you in his arms.'

Kitty shook her head in mock despair. 'I'd better go shopping for a gown.'

'There's a lovely shop in Paignton. Miss Veronique it's called, in Winner Street. I saw a lovely frock in the window the other day. Dark red satin.' Alice sighed happily.

'Thank you, Alice.' She knew her maid was well aware of her penchant for red. Kitty always thought it warmed up her pale skin tones and showed off her naturally fair hair. She also had heard that Miss Veronique might be quite expensive.

'Don't worry if you find something that needs a bit of fitting, miss, I can titivate it up for you. They'll not have time to do it at the shop if the do is on Friday night. It's Thursday tomorrow,' Alice warned.

'That's very generous of you, Alice.' She appreciated the offer and Alice was a dab hand with a needle. When she had acted as Kitty's maid before during a visit to Enderley Hall, Alice had enjoyed acting as a lady's maid. Kitty's petite frame invariably involved having hems taken up to shorten her clothes and she was thankful for Alice's skills.

The girl flushed with pleasure and went off humming happily to herself.

It was well after lunch the next day when Kitty was finally able to set off on her shopping expedition. The weather was inclement with an icy chill in the air that held a hint of sleet. She had originally intended to go into Torquay, but lack of time meant that she found herself on the omnibus heading for Paignton.

She comforted herself with the thought that she at least had a fairly fat purse as she had not bought anything new since the summer's visit to Enderley and since then only a couple of hats. She alighted from the bus and made her way along Winner Street to Miss Veronique. The red satin gown was gone from the window, replaced by a chic evening dress in dark emerald chiffon.

The brass bell on the coiled mechanism jingled as Kitty pushed the door open. The shop was a little larger than she had expected. Dark red velvet drapes framed the entrance to the fitting area and two plush gilt armchairs upholstered in the same fabric stood either side of a dainty glass-topped table. The one wall held racks of gowns and behind the glass and gilt counter was a tempting display of evening shoes and bags.

Kitty had scarcely had the opportunity to check her windblown appearance in the large ornately framed full-length mirror when a woman in her mid-twenties, a similar age to herself, emerged from the dressing room area. Dressed in a plain serviceable black frock with her wispy mousy brown hair tied back with a ribbon, she was not what Kitty had expected to see in a shop such as Miss Veronique.

'Good afternoon, my name is Daphne. How may I help you?'
The girl was nicely spoken but her voice was as frail and wishy-
washy as her complexion.

'This is frightfully short notice, but I need a new dress and shoes
for the hoteliers' dinner in Torquay tomorrow night.'

The girl nodded. 'At the Imperial Hotel? Had you anything in
mind?'

'I do like red.'

The assistant showed her to one of the armchairs whilst she
looked along the racks, selecting a few gowns that she draped
carefully over her arm. 'Please come through to the fitting room.
I'm afraid at such short notice we will be unable to undertake any
alterations.'

'Oh, that's all right,' Kitty assured her. 'I have someone who
can assist me.'

The fitting room had some upright chairs and another cheval
mirror. The girl hung the dresses she'd selected on the brass hooks
that were attached to the wall. She assessed Kitty with a professional
eye as Kitty removed her coat and hat. 'You may find all of them
a little long on you.'

Kitty blushed. 'Yes, that's usually the case, I'm afraid.'

Together they selected the first gown and the girl assisted her
with the fastenings. The low back and front made her feel too
exposed and she shook her head when she saw her reflection in
the mirror.

As the girl helped her out of the first dress and into the second,
Kitty tried to make conversation. 'I expect you've probably had a
few ladies calling in for dresses for the hoteliers' dinner?' she said
chattily.

'Yes indeed, several ladies from the various hotels. I shall be there
myself this year.' She didn't sound terribly happy or enthusiastic
about attending.

Kitty turned around so the girl could help her with the buttons at the back of the second dress. 'Oh, I may see you there, then? I expect you'll have a fabulous gown working here.'

The girl had her head bowed as she concentrated on the buttons, but Kitty saw her frown in the reflection in the mirror. 'Father doesn't feel it necessary for me to have a new dress. I rarely go out.'

Kitty could see the girl's hands were bare of rings so guessed she must still reside at home. 'That's a shame, still I expect it would be easy to get carried away working somewhere like this with so many nice things to choose from.' She felt bad now that she'd mentioned the ball. Perhaps Daphne's father was one of those men who insisted on having the girl's wages paid directly to him, making a pocket money allowance back to Daphne to cover her personal expenses.

The girl straightened, having completed her task. A faint wash of colour tinged her pale face. 'There you are, miss.'

Clearly the conversation was at an end as far as the ball was concerned. 'Oh, this is lovely.' The dark red satin fabric of the gown fitted her well, flattering her slim frame. It was, as expected, a trifle long. 'Do you have some shoes I could try?' She told the girl her size and she returned a few minutes later with several boxes stacked one on top of the other.

She placed them next to Kitty and lifted the lid of the first box. A pair of shiny, high-heeled red and silver shoes emerged, nestled in cream silky fabric.

'I thought perhaps these?' The assistant lifted them out to show them to Kitty.

'Those are quite lovely.' She suspected this visit to Miss Veronique was going to be very expensive.

The shop bell tinkled, and an imperious woman's voice called, 'Daphne, have you finished putting away the new stock of handbags?'

The girl assisting Kitty with her shoes scrambled to her feet, her face flooding red. 'Almost. I'm with a lady, Miss Veronique.'

The curtains parted and a tall, thin, older woman with a generous aquiline nose and orderly curls entered the changing room.
Immediately Daphne became a bundle of nerves.

'I do hope Daphne is helping you find all you require, Miss…?'

'Underhay, Kitty Underhay, and, yes, thank you, Daphne has
been marvellous.' She took another look at her reflection in the
mirror, noting the look of relief on Daphne's face at her praise.

The dress would just need the hem raising slightly and the shoes
were perfect.

'I'll take the dress and the shoes, please.'

'The hem will need adjusting.' Miss Veronique frowned.

'That won't be a problem. I have someone who can make the
adjustments for me,' Kitty explained.

Miss Veronique's mouth compressed into a thin line.

'Miss Underhay requires the gown for the hoteliers' ball in
Torquay tomorrow, Miss Veronique,' Daphne hurried to assure
her employer. Kitty suspected that Miss Veronique had her own
seamstress who she used for alterations and she probably made a
nice profit there too.

'Oh, I see, something of a rush job then.' The woman's smile
didn't meet her eyes, which were as cold and beady as a snake. 'Has
Daphne shown you our range of evening purses, Miss Underhay? We
have a delightful silver one which would complement your gown.'

'No, that's quite all right, thank you. I already have one which
will match perfectly.'

Miss Veronique sniffed disdainfully and left Kitty to change out
of the gown. Daphne helped her with the buttons and re-boxed
the shoes as Kitty dressed.

'Please come through to the counter when you're ready, Miss
Underhay. I'll just go and pack your gown for you.' Daphne scuttled
away with the dress and the shoes as Kitty finished getting dressed.
She suspected the bill from Miss Veronique would make quite a

dent in her purse. Still, she would get good use from the gown over Christmas and New Year at the events at the hotel. Red was a nice seasonal colour.

Daphne had packed the dress with layers of tissue paper in one of the shop's distinctive pink and white candy-striped boxes and placed the shoebox in a matching bag. Miss Veronique added up the total and smiled ingratiatingly at Kitty as she paid the substantial bill.

'I do hope you'll be pleased with your purchases, Miss Underhay. Do call again.' She smiled at Kitty.

'Door, Daphne!' she commanded as Kitty tucked her dress box under her arm and picked up the other bag ready to depart.

Daphne sprang forward to open the shop door and Kitty made her exit into the already darkening street. She glanced back to see Daphne framed in the doorway of the brightly-lit shop with Miss Veronique watching over her. Kitty shivered in the cold wintery air and tried to shake off the feeling of foreboding that had suddenly enveloped her.

CHAPTER THREE

She had not gone many yards along the street when a familiar black car pulled to a halt beside her.

'Miss Underhay, I am headed back to the Dolphin, would you like a lift?'

'Mr Potter, that would be most kind.' Kitty smiled at the taxi driver. Mr Potter drove her and her grandmother regularly and they frequently called upon his services for their guests.

He jumped out and opened the door for her, helping her with her packages.

'There is a rug on the seat there, Miss Kitty, if you're cold,' he instructed as he closed the door on her and returned to the driver's seat.

She gratefully availed herself of the offer and snuggled down under the red tartan rug as Mr Potter pulled away.

'How is Robert's business faring? Is the Daisybelle doing well?' Kitty enquired.

Mr Potter's son had acquired the Daisybelle touring company at public auction earlier in the year after its owner had been brutally murdered in the spring during Matt's first case. The Potters intended to expand their business by running excursions to the moors and to the city.

'It's going very well, thank you, Miss Kitty. Robert is taking people to Exeter for the markets at present. He said as you'd put his leaflets in the Dolphin and recommended his business. It's much appreciated.'

'Not at all, Mr Potter. I hope he does well with it. You both work very hard.' Kitty relaxed back against her seat as the car began its familiar descent along the lane past the dark fields, many now empty except for stubble, hardly visible in the rapidly fading light, towards Kingswear.

The ferry across the Dart was busy with evening traffic, vans and cars and a couple of horse and carts. The horses surprisingly stoic when hemmed in with the other, noisier transport. Sleet started to fall as they crossed the water and Kitty was glad that Mr Potter had been passing. It would have been a cold, damp journey on the omnibus and then over the river as a foot passenger.

Mr Potter pulled his taxi to a halt outside the hotel, refusing Kitty's offer of payment.

'Not at all, Miss Kitty. I was on my way here to collect Mrs Craven.'

Kitty suppressed a sigh. She might have guessed that her grandmother's best friend would have been visiting whilst she was out. 'I'll let her know you are waiting for her.'

She collected up her parcels and entered through the heavy wood and glass front entrance door before making her way to the small brass cage elevator at the far end of the lobby.

Still carrying her packages, she managed to tap on the door of her grandmother's suite before entering. Mrs Craven was in the salon already dressed ready to leave in her navy wool coat and hat. Fox fur stole around her shoulders and diamond brooch gleaming on her bosom.

'Hello, Kitty, been doing some shopping I see?' The older woman eyed the pink and white candy-striped box and bag.

'It's for the hoteliers' ball at the Imperial tomorrow night. I needed new shoes and a dress.' Kitty smiled politely. She knew Mrs Craven did not really approve of her and had always disliked Kitty's mother, Elowed.

'Miss Veronique, gracious, your grandmother must be paying you far too well.'

Before Kitty could respond to that remark, Mrs Craven had collected her ivory kid gloves and bag and was calling her farewells to Kitty's grandmother who was still in bed.

'I presume my car is waiting for me. I expect I shall see you at the ball tomorrow. I, of course, am attending as part of the civic group on the mayoral table. Please take care of your grandmother, Kitty. I've left her with some grapes and a drop of Madeira.' With that parting instruction, she bustled out of the room.

Kitty scowled as she removed her coat and hat, patting her short blonde curls back in place before the mirror. She hadn't realised that Mrs Craven was to attend the dance, although since Mrs Craven was involved in everything in Torbay she shouldn't have been surprised. Satisfied she looked tidy once more, she crossed the salon to her grandmother's bedroom. Mrs Craven had left the door slightly ajar and her grandmother was sitting propped up by a mound of pillows, in her bed. A fluffy pastel pink knitted bed jacket covered her arms and shoulders and the bedside table next to her held an array of treats.

'Kitty, darling, I thought I heard you arrive. Millicent has just gone.'

'How are you feeling? Can I get you anything?' Kitty asked. Her grandmother looked tired and she hoped Mrs Craven hadn't overstayed her welcome.

'I'm all right, my dear, please don't fuss. Did you manage to find a suitable gown?' Grams pushed herself further up the bed and took a small sip from the crystal wine glass at her side.

'I ended up at Miss Veronique in Paignton,' Kitty said.

Grams snorted. 'Miss Veronique, my foot. Veronica Hayes she was before she married that Belgian chappie and started to give herself airs and graces. Still, I believe she has some nice clothes.'

Kitty smiled. 'I'll show you what I found.' She collected her parcels and snipped the string with a tiny pair of silver manicure scissors that her grandmother kept in her dressing table drawer.

'Oh, that looks divine, Kitty. Such a lovely colour, it will work for the festive season too. Will it need altering?' Her grandmother admired the dress as Kitty lifted it from the layers of tissue paper and held it up for her to see.

'Just the hem. Alice has offered to take it up for me. She's coming here when she finishes her shift. Are you sure we won't be disturbing you if we use your lounge?' Kitty asked.

'Not at all. I shall enjoy seeing you wearing it, and there is more room and better light in here than in your bedroom. Now, show me the shoes.'

Kitty returned her dress to its box and then passed the red and silver shoes over for inspection.

'Quite perfect, you'll look lovely. Matt will be very proud, I'm sure, to have you on his arm.' Her grandmother coughed discreetly into her lace-edged handkerchief as Kitty gave her a sharp look.

'She was a rather strange character, Miss Veronique,' Kitty mused. 'Her assistant said she would be attending the ball tomorrow too.'

Grams looked up from where she had been examining the buckle on Kitty's new shoes. 'Really? I had heard that Councillor Everton's daughter, Daphne, was employed there.'

'That must be the same girl. A pale little thing, seemed frightened of her own shadow?' Kitty asked.

'I don't know her myself, but I do know Councillor Everton, chair of the planning committee and head of the chamber of commerce too. Dreadful, bullish, overbearing man with very strong opinions. His wife, Marigold, is quite a timid soul, completely under his thumb, so I expect the daughter must be in the same mould as her mother.' Her grandmother passed her the shoe she had been admiring and settled herself back onto her white linen pillows.

'Are you absolutely certain we won't disturb you if Alice alters my dress in your lounge?' Kitty asked. Her grandmother looked tired and pale.

'Nonsense, I shall enjoy knowing you are close at hand. Now, run along and have something to eat before Alice arrives with her sewing box.' Grams smiled and waved her away. 'I shall have a little rest and enjoy this spot of Madeira before you return.'

Kitty sighed and agreed. She carried her dress and shoes back into the lounge and hung her new gown from the coat hook in the corner of the room so that it wouldn't crease.

Alice met her in the lobby as Kitty was walking back from the dining room. The young maid had changed out of her uniform into a plain grey dress and was carrying her sewing basket.

'Did you manage to find a frock, miss? I've got my workbox ready,' she asked as Kitty approached her.

'Yes, thank you, I shall need your sewing skills as even with a new pair of shoes, it is still a little long for me.'

Alice grinned. 'A bit of hemming will soon fix that, miss. Did you go to Miss Veronique?' She followed Kitty inside the elevator situated in the far corner of the lobby. Kitty pulled the metal cage closed and pressed the button in the small brass panel.

'I did, and thank you for the recommendation, although I think my purse may not be as grateful.' The elevator came to a stop and Kitty opened the cage and the mahogany door to allow them out onto the landing.

Alice's smile widened. 'She does have some lovely things though. I like to have a look when I go past.'

'I rather fear you are a bad influence on me,' Kitty told her as they let themselves quietly into her grandmother's suite. The radio was playing softly in the background and the gentle swell of big band music filled the salon lounge.

Alice switched on the standard lamp near the fireplace and pulled it forward a little while Kitty went to check on her grandmother.

'Hello, darling, have you eaten? I had a lovely rest while you were gone.' Grams smiled at her and Kitty was relieved to see the colour was restored to her cheeks.

She tidied up the bedside cabinet. 'Yes, I've had some supper. Alice is here too now. Are you sure we shall not disturb you?'

'Not at all. The company is very welcome and I'm looking forward to seeing you in your gown.'

Alice had set herself up nicely in the lounge when Kitty returned. The lamp threw off a good working light and the maid had positioned a low stool ready.

'All set, miss. Do you need a hand with the fastenings?' Alice asked as she surveyed her handiwork.

Kitty lifted her gown from its hook. 'Yes, please, I'll just slip it on.' She carried her dress into her grandmother's bathroom and changed. Alice helped her to fasten the buttons at the back as she slipped her new shoes on and secured the buckles.

'Oh, miss, that is lovely. Fits you a treat, it does. Just needs a little bit off the hem.' Alice examined her with a critical eye.

'Kitty, come and show me,' her grandmother called from her bedroom.

Kitty picked up her skirts so as not to trip herself up. 'Well, does it meet with approval?' She twisted and turned about.

'Perfect. The shoes are lovely too, just right for the occasion. Matthew will be dazzled.'

Kitty's cheeks flamed as red as her new frock. 'I did not choose this with Matt in mind.'

Her grandmother coughed discreetly into her lace-edged handkerchief. 'Of course not, darling.'

Kitty returned to the lounge and stepped up on the low wooden footstool Alice had placed ready for her. Her grandmother might be unwell, but she had the feeling that she was making the most of her illness to her own ends.

'Right, keep still, miss, or else I might stick you with a pin by mistake,' Alice instructed as she knelt on the Turkish rug next to the stool. She had a small tapestry pincushion strapped to her narrow wrist and was busy pulling out the skirt of Kitty's gown ready to commence the alterations.

Kitty stood in place as Alice crawled around her carefully pinning up the hem.

'I'm fair looking forward to tomorrow, miss. Did I tell you as our Betty is waitressing at the dinner?' Alice leaned back on her heels and eyed her handiwork.

Alice's cousin, Betty, was almost nineteen, some two years older than Alice. She was also, according to Alice's mother, 'a flighty piece'. During the last case that Kitty and Matt had worked on, Betty had been instrumental in providing information to catch the killer.

'Yes, Alice, you did tell me. I expect I shall see her then,' Kitty said.

There was a rivalry between the cousins as Betty considered Alice to be getting above herself, and Alice disapproved of Betty's appearance and manner.

Kitty had arranged for Mr Potter to take them to the Imperial the following afternoon. Satisfied that her grandmother was now recovering well from her cold, she felt somewhat happier about leaving her.

Alice assisted her in carrying her carpet bag to the lobby. She was dressed in her best coat with a new navy felt hat to match.

Her bright auburn hair was under control and a silvery brooch of marcasite in a floral design sparkled on her lapel.

'You look lovely, Alice,' Kitty said, sending a flush of colour into the girl's cheeks at the compliment.

'Thank you, miss.' Alice beamed and adjusted the bag containing Kitty's new gown on her arm.

Kitty bit back a smile as they waited in the line of traffic ready to board the ferry to cross the river. Her companion was clearly enjoying her elevated status as lady's maid and was nodding and smiling to her acquaintances through the taxi window.

It was a bright, clear day as they disembarked from the ferry at Kingswear and set off along the country lanes leading up towards Churston, then on past Paignton to Torquay. Once out of the town, Alice settled back in her seat.

'Is the Imperial as posh as the Dolphin, miss? I haven't ever been inside it before, and I never thought as I would ever stay there as a guest like.'

'It's been a while since I was last there myself. I attended a dance there about twelve months ago for someone's birthday. It's a much larger hotel than the Dolphin and has a nice position looking out over the sea. I'm sure we shall have a splendid time,' Kitty reassured the girl. 'We shall have tea and enjoy ourselves a little before I need to prepare for Captain Bryant's arrival.'

Alice's eyes grew round and sparkled at the mention of tea. Kitty suspected she would be crowing over poor Betty for quite a while about that.

Mr Potter drove at a steady pace along the coast road and into Torquay. A shiver ran along Kitty's spine as they passed the Pavilion theatre on the seafront. A place where she had almost met her end just a few weeks earlier.

The Imperial Hotel was situated a little further on past the harbour at a point where the road turned sharply upwards to climb

out of the town. Mr Potter turned a sharp right and drove his taxi
to the front doors of the large, white painted building.

The elderly concierge summoned a young uniformed bellhop
to the door of the car ready to offer his assistance with their bags.
His appreciative gaze when he saw Alice called a flush to that young
lady's face as he collected their luggage from the boot of the car.

Kitty paid Mr Potter and entered the hotel through the smart
brass and glass front entrance. The heels of her black patent T-strap
shoes clicked on the Italianate black and white marble floor tiles
as she headed for the polished oak reception desk.

As a hotelier she appreciated the fine white plasterwork and
elegant fluted columns in the open and spacious lobby. There were
two receptionists on duty, attired in neat navy-blue uniform dresses
with white collars.

'I have a suite booked in the name of Treadwell.' Kitty waited
while the girl found the booking. She knew the Imperial would
be pulling out all the stops to impress its fellow hoteliers. The
Dolphin had hosted the event a few years ago when her grandmother had been on the committee. It had been an enormous
amount of work.

Alice and the lad carrying their bags waited while the receptionist
found the key to the suite. Alice, gazing around her with wide eyes,
and the young bellhop sneaking peeps at Alice.

'Here you are, miss, please enjoy your stay.' The girl passed over
a key with a shiny brass tag attached bearing the room number.

'Thank you, room twenty-one. Oh, we would like to order an
afternoon tea for two, would that be possible?' Kitty asked.

'Certainly, miss, would you want it in your suite or in the public
room?' the receptionist enquired.

Kitty glanced at Alice. 'In the public room, please. I believe you
have a fine sea view here.'

'I'll organise that for you, miss.'

Kitty thanked her, and she and Alice accompanied the bellhop up the Italian marble staircase to the first floor. She tipped the boy after he had deposited their luggage onto the rack and Alice had taken Kitty's gown to hang it from the rail.

The suite was luxurious with a lounge area comprising two over-stuffed armchairs in front of an Adam style marble fireplace. Kitty had a comfortable bedroom with another smaller bedroom for Alice. A private bathroom with a claw-footed slipper bath completed their comforts.

Alice was at the picture window gazing out at the sea. 'Oh, miss, it's ever so grand.'

'Grams has certainly done us proud,' Kitty agreed. The suite was luxuriously appointed with polished mahogany chests and fine oriental style table lamps. Even with the now fading daylight she could see the rooms commanded a magnificent view of the sea.

'Come, Alice, leave the unpacking for now. Let's go and take tea downstairs while we can still appreciate the view before it grows too dark.'

To her surprise, Alice hung back, trailing a gloved finger over the edge of a delicate side table. 'I don't know as I should, miss. I mean, I ought to see to your dress.'

Kitty frowned, she had meant to treat her friend to a nice tea to show her appreciation for all the things that Alice did for her. She hadn't meant to make her feel uncomfortable.

'Oh, do please come with me, Alice. I would feel such a fool sitting there alone. Whatever would people think? You would be doing me a tremendous favour and I owe you for turning up the hem on my frock.'

Alice's brow creased, she was clearly considering Kitty's plea. 'Very well, miss. I know as your grandmother would want the Dolphin to be well represented.'

'Thank you, Alice.' Kitty beamed as Alice followed her out of the suite, locking the door behind them.

There were several public rooms on the ground floor of the hotel. Kitty selected a quiet corner with a view of the pleasure gardens and glimpses of the sea. A lamp threw off a comforting yellow light and the staff were quick to attend to ensure their order was brought to them.

Kitty settled back on the tapestry covered armchair and gazed around her with interest, appreciating the fine Turkish carpets on the polished wooden floor. The shelves nearby were stacked with a good selection of books and there were some puzzles for the amusement of guests.

Alice too settled in her seat. The room was quiet with relatively few people around, which seemed to reassure her.

The waiter returned swiftly with a gilt trolley containing an elegant white china tea set and side plates and a matching silver-coloured tiered stand with a selection of dainty sandwiches and pastries.

'This looks delicious, thank you.' Kitty was quite ready for something to eat. Lunch had been a hurried affair as she had been trying to ensure everything was in place before leaving the Dolphin. With her grandmother still keeping to her salon she had been responsible for ensuring the hotel would run smoothly in her absence.

'Shall I pour, miss?' Alice already had her hand to the teapot.

'Yes, please.' She encouraged Alice to fill her plate and had just made her own selection when she became aware of a familiar male figure making his way towards them.

'Miss Underhay, this is a most pleasurable surprise.' The man doffed his hat.

'Inspector Greville, how nice. You remember, Miss Miller, of course?' Inspector Greville had been involved in all the previous cases that she and Matt had been involved with.

'Indeed.' He smiled at Alice.

'Please, come and join us, or is this a business affair?' Kitty indicated an empty seat and said a mental farewell to the remaining pastries. The inspector was very fond of his stomach, despite his wife's admonishments.

'Pleasure, Miss Underhay, I assure you.' The police inspector settled himself comfortably on the empty seat as Kitty signalled the waiter for more tea and an extra cup. Something about his response made Kitty suspect that this was not strictly true, but she knew he would be unlikely to say more.

CHAPTER FOUR

'Will you be attending the hoteliers' dinner dance tonight?' Kitty asked as the waiter replaced their pot of tea and added an extra cup for the inspector.

The inspector's normally morose moustache twitched upwards. 'I have the honour of being asked to represent the chief constable at tonight's event. I expect you are representing the Dolphin Hotel?' He accepted a cup of tea from Alice and took a sip.

'Yes, my grandmother was to attend as she has been a member of the association for many years. However, she is unwell at present, so I have been deputised in her place. Captain Bryant is escorting me.' She offered the plate of pastries and sandwiches to the inspector.

'Thank you, most kind.' Inspector Greville accepted the offer of the sandwiches with alacrity. 'I'm sorry to hear Mrs Treadwell is unwell. Nothing serious, I hope?'

Kitty set the almost empty stand back on the table. 'Just a nasty cold, but she felt it best to rest. Will you be attending alone tonight? Or will Mrs Greville be accompanying you?' Kitty would like to meet Mrs Greville. She had built a mental image of the inspector's wife over the time she had known him from the little things he had let slip about his home life. She was curious to see if that picture was correct.

Inspector Greville dabbed crumbs from his moustache with one of the delicate pink linen napkins. 'Alas, Mrs Greville's mother is unwell so she is unable to accompany me.'

'Oh dear, I hope she will be all right?' Kitty asked.

The inspector's moustache twitched. 'Mrs Greville's mother is something of a martyr to illness.'

'Oh my goodness, that is most unfortunate. Such a shame she'll miss the dinner, and the band are said to be rather good.' Kitty finished her cup of tea. 'Are you staying at the hotel tonight?' She wondered if he had come early to check in or if her first inkling was correct that he had other, police business at the hotel.

Inspector Greville's eyes twinkled. 'No, I had a little business to conduct with the hotel manager. This is a large gathering with a lot of high-profile people and there are obviously policing matters to discuss.'

'Oh, obviously,' Kitty agreed, knowing she had been rumbled on her fishing expedition.

'Thank you so much for the tea, Miss Underhay, Miss Miller.' The inspector cast a regretful glance at the now empty stand of cake and sandwiches.

'It was our pleasure, wasn't it, Alice?' Kitty smiled as he collected up his things ready to depart.

'I expect I shall see you later with Captain Bryant. I hope to have a chat with him at some point, a small matter of business.' He inclined his head towards her.

'We shall look forward to it, and, of course, I'll pass on your message,' Kitty replied as he took his leave of them.

'The inspector fair loves his food, doesn't he?' Alice began to tidy up the empty plates.

'He does indeed. Please don't worry about the plates, Alice. I shall order a dinner for you this evening from room service. I wouldn't want you to go hungry.' She smiled at her friend. 'I wish you could attend the ball with us.'

Alice immediately shook her head. 'Oh, I shouldn't want to do that, miss. I shall be quite happy listening to the wireless and reading my magazines in the room. It'll be nice to have a bit of peace and quiet.'

Kitty remembered that Alice was the eldest of eight children, and she suspected that time spent alone must be in short supply in her house. 'If you're sure, then I shall feel a little less guilty.'

Alice gazed happily about her. 'I'm having a lovely time, miss. I never thought as I should ever be in a place like this as a guest. I'm having a rare old time. It's like being in the pictures.'

Kitty knew Alice loved going to the cinema and bought all the latest magazines with news and gossip about the actors and actresses. 'Then I'm glad you agreed to come with me.'

Later, after she had bathed and Alice had helped her to dress in her new gown and shoes, Kitty surveyed her appearance in the full-length mirror in her suite.

'You look smashing, miss,' the maid said as she admired her handiwork.

'Thank you, Alice. I do hope we have been seated with some interesting guests. I attended once before with Grams and everyone on our table was at least one hundred years old. They spent the entire evening comparing their various intestinal problems.' She shuddered a little at the memory.

'I'm sure you'll have a lovely time, and you'll have Captain Bryant to talk to.' Alice fussed at a thread on her waistline. As she spoke, there was a knock at the door.

'That will be Matt, now.' Kitty picked up her silver evening bag as Alice opened the door.

Colour stole into her cheeks at the look of approbation Matt gave her. He wore his own evening dress well, with that slight rakish air she had come to know so well.

'Hello, ladies.' He winked at Alice. 'You look lovely, Kitty.'

'Thank you. You scrub up nicely yourself.'

Alice handed her a fine silvery evening shawl. 'Have a nice evening, miss, sir.'

Matt offered Kitty his arm as they made their way down the Italianate marble staircase towards the ballroom.

'I do hope we have more exciting company this evening than the last event I attended,' Kitty said. 'Still, at least Inspector Greville is coming tonight, as is Mrs Craven, although not together as far as I know. He joined Alice and I for tea earlier. The inspector mentioned he would like to see you about something.' She grinned at his raised eyebrow at her news and wondered what the inspector wished to see Matt about.

There was a floor plan pinned on to a board at the entrance to the ballroom. Tables had been set for dinner around the edge of the room. The crystal sparkling under the light from the ornate chandeliers. Fronded potted palms were dotted around the room and fresh autumnal shaded flowers were arranged as the centrepieces on the tables. The room was already filling up with people and the sound of chatter mingled with the melodic sounds of a pianist.

'Are we seated with convivial company?' Kitty enquired as she tried to peep at the plan over the shoulders of the couple in front of them.

'Maybe, we might end up with Mrs Craven,' Matt suggested. She gave him a sharp glance and saw the dimple in his cheek flash.

'She will be seated with the most important people. You and I will be lower in the pecking order.'

'Well, it seems we are seated with Councillor Everton and his party. I met him the other day at a presentation. He asked for my card.' Matt sounded thoughtful.

'His daughter, Daphne, works at Miss Veronique, she sold me this gown. She said she would be attending tonight. She didn't seem terribly lively,' Kitty said.

Matt placed his hand on her waist and steered her a little out of the crowd towards the elegant polished boat-shaped wooden bar. 'Perhaps a cocktail then, before we take our seats?'

Kitty grinned. 'Bellini?'

'Your wish is my command, Miss Underhay.' Matt somehow managed to attract the attention of the bartender, returning to her side a few minutes later carrying two cocktails.

'Grams always insists on sherry as a pre-dinner drink,' Kitty observed as she took a sip of her drink. 'I rather like a cocktail as a change. She mentioned that Councillor Everton was not the easiest person.'

The corner of Matt's mouth quirked upwards. 'I think that is putting it mildly. He mentioned he might wish to consult me over a problem but that he wanted to check some things out first. He struck me as a man of strong opinions. I confess, I was not especially keen to take him as a client so gave him my card and he said he would contact me.'

'He didn't mention what the issue might be?' Kitty asked.

'No. I told him I didn't take divorce cases and he laughed. Said he and the "little woman" had no issues on that front.'

Kitty raised her eyebrows. 'Grams said she thought he was quite domineering. His daughter certainly appeared to be under her father's thumb. He wouldn't allow her to get a new dress for tonight.'

'Then let us hope he doesn't wish to talk business during dinner,' Matt said.

There was a movement in the crowd as people began to take their places at the tables ready for dinner service to commence. Kitty drained her glass and placed it alongside Matt's at the end of the bar before following the queue of guests into the dining area.

Kitty thought she caught a glimpse of Mrs Craven in black sateen with a plume of feathers in her hair taking her place at a table with the mayor's party. The waiter took their names and escorted them to a circular table on the far side of the dance floor. The other occupants were already seated, the gentlemen stood as she approached the table and Kitty thanked the waiter as she slipped onto the chair that he proffered her.

Matt took his place at her right side, neatly handwritten place cards on stiff cream coloured card indicated their seats. The table centrepiece was comprised of orange chrysanthemum and white dahlias. Orange candles complemented the autumnal theme and threw flattering lights on the faces of her new companions.

'Captain Bryant, and, um, Miss Underhay.' A small round man with a ruddy face and a heavy gold watch guard on his expansive stomach shook Matt's hand and nodded to her. Kitty assumed he had to be Councillor Everton. His wife, Marigold, appeared to be an older version of Daphne, dressed in wispy mauve chiffon. Daphne, herself whispered a 'Hello' across the table. She was dressed in a rather ugly dark green gown, which did little to suit her pale features. Her companion, however, was a rather stylish handsome gentleman of about twenty-five who the councillor introduced as his nephew, Thomas King.

Two other couples were seated with them. One couple were a similar age to the Evertons. They introduced themselves as Mr Ivor Silitoe, a solicitor, and his wife, Gladys. They apparently knew the councillor well and it soon transpired they played bridge together regularly.

The remaining pair turned out to be hoteliers. Clive Hendricks and his widowed sister, Lavinia Braddock, who between them owned the Conway Country House Hotel at Cockington, a small village just a couple of miles from Torquay.

Matt's rather unfavourable first impressions of Councillor Everton from their first meeting were confirmed during the dinner. It seemed that Mr Silitoe was legal advisor to the council, especially in matters concerning land purchase and use. Something that Mr Hendricks appeared very keen to discuss with Councillor Everton.

The councillor, however, did not seem to be willing to discuss anything with Mr Hendricks.

'You'll need to put everything in writing to the committee.' Everton pushed his empty bowl of consommé away from him and poured himself a glass of wine, ignoring the bleating plea from his wife about not overdoing things. 'Send it in writing to Thomas there, he deals with all the paperwork.'

Hendricks' pallid oval face flushed an unbecoming shade of red at the rebuff. 'I have done so several times. The last proposal was refused yet again, as you well know. There were points that—'

'Well, there you are then. Modify it and reapply through the proper channels.' Everton glared at him as he cut off whatever else Hendricks planned to say.

Mrs Braddock looked uncomfortable at the exchange. Her brother shook off her hand when she placed it on his sleeve. Matt glanced at Kitty who was composedly nibbling at her bread roll and exchanging small talk with Thomas King. That particular gentleman was paying Kitty far too much attention in Matt's opinion. In fact, his frequent compliments and attentive manner were starting to set Matt's teeth on edge.

The soup dishes were collected and replaced with the fish course of fillet of sole.

'The chef here is quite excellent,' Mr Silitoe observed. Matt did not know the solicitor very well, despite having run across him several times before at various functions. He was a thin man with jet-black hair that Matt suspected might owe more to art than nature.

His wife was a plump, sensible-looking woman with auburn hair styled in the latest fashion with kiss curls framing her face.

'Very good menu,' Mr Everton agreed. 'And how are you finding the detective business, Captain Bryant? Torbay still keeping you busy?'

'Busy enough, thank you, sir.' Matt hoped that the man had changed his mind about offering him a case, although he was curious about what the councillor had been concerned about.

'A real gumshoe, eh, as the Americans say?' Thomas King shifted on his chair and Matt was conscious of a change in the atmosphere around the table.

'Captain Bryant has been involved in several high-profile cases here in the bay. That reminds me, do you have a spare card at hand? Marigold here has lost the other one.' He glared at his wife, who immediately shrank back on her seat. 'Need to speak to you about something if you are free next week. That business I mentioned the other day.'

'Of course, sir. Please give me a call at my office and we can arrange a meeting.' Matt drew out his silver card case and handed a card to Councillor Everton. He didn't see how he could refuse the man.

CHAPTER FIVE

The meal continued, with the fish course being followed by roast beef. It proved difficult to engage either Daphne or Marigold Everton in conversation and Mr Silitoe was engrossed in conversation with Councillor Everton. Matt could see the feathers in Mrs Craven's headdress bobbing above the crowds over at the mayor's table.

'Have you seen Inspector Greville at all yet?' he murmured to Kitty.

'No, I did rather wonder if he might end up on Mrs Craven's table, but I think you have a better view than me,' Kitty said.

Matt was conscious that Thomas King was paying close attention to their conversation even though he was feigning indifference. 'I believe Doctor Carter might be here tonight too. I thought I recognised his car when I arrived.'

Kitty laughed. 'I think half of Torquay are here this evening.' She rested her knife and fork down on the white porcelain dinner plate. 'Goodness, I feel full, and there is still the sweet course to go.'

'Perhaps you might favour me with a dance after the speeches. It would aid the digestion?' Thomas King suggested to Kitty, cutting across the conversation.

Kitty's cheeks pinked. 'Oh, I, erm.' She looked at Matt, her eyes wide in what he could see was a mute appeal for help.

'I'm sure you can spare Mr King one dance, darling.' He kept his tone light even though he could quite cheerfully have floored the man. 'If Miss Everton will do me the honour of returning the favour?' He felt rather sorry for the girl. She had been toying with her dinner all evening and was patently having a miserable time.

Daphne blushed and looked at her father for his consent before nodding and giving her flustered agreement.

'So nice for you young people to enjoy yourselves,' Mrs Silitoe said. 'I remember a time when we cut quite a figure on the dance floor, didn't we, Ivor?' She nudged her husband's elbow.

'What? Oh, erm, yes.' Mr Silitoe didn't look pleased at having what appeared to be a subdued but heated discussion with Mr Everton interrupted.

Speeches by the mayor and the chairman of the hoteliers' association followed the dessert course of meringue fruit nests. Coffee and petits fours were finally served, and the Imperial's band started to play, with the dignitaries taking to the floor first to lead the way.

Kitty was feeling quite cross with Matt but hid her annoyance beneath a smiling demeanour. It was a little slighting to her ego to be foisted off to Thomas King for the first dance but she tried to console herself that the night was still young. She accompanied Thomas onto the dance floor and watched with mounting irritation as Matt offered his hand to Daphne Everton.

Thomas danced well and was a personable enough man, but Kitty had been looking forward to dancing with Matt.

'Forgive my forwardness, but are you and Captain Bryant walking out together?' Thomas asked as they completed their first circuit of the dance floor.

Kitty was always unsure how to answer that kind of question. They had kissed a few times and Matt had certainly seemed to wish to take things further in that direction. However, there always seemed to be some obstacle in their way. She had hoped that this evening, dancing and having fun, might have clarified where she stood.

'We are good friends.' She resorted to her standard answer and wished the number would finish so she could reclaim her seat and maybe obtain another Bellini. Mr Everton seemed to have drunk most of the wine.

Thomas King appeared pleased with her reply and led her back to her chair when she pleaded a need to sit down at the end of the dance. Mr Silitoe returned to the table with Mrs Braddock, Mr Hendricks having danced with Mrs Silitoe. Exercise that appeared to have called a blush to that lady's cheeks.

Mr and Mrs Everton were still in their seats, Mr Everton being more intent on his coffee and postprandial cigar. Matt joined them a minute later with Daphne.

'Marigold, have you brought my sachet in your bag?' Mr Everton demanded.

'Oh dear, I did say about having too much rich food.' Marigold hunted around in a capacious black leather handbag until she found a small octagonal silver gilt box. 'Here you are, dear, take one of these. I'll pour you some water.' She opened the lid as she set the box on the tabletop in front of the councillor.

He plucked out a paper sachet from the top of the pile and snatched the tumbler of water impatiently from his wife. 'Don't dawdle, Marigold.'

Kitty watched as he tipped the contents of the sachet into the glass, swishing the contents around for a few seconds before downing it in one swift gulp.

'Nasty stuff.' He shuddered at the last mouthful and set the glass down.

'Harold is a martyr to his digestion.' Marigold started to fuss with the lid of the box.

As she spoke, Councillor Everton's face turned a darker shade of puce, his eyes bulged, and his breath came in great wheezy gasps.

'Oh dear, Harold, whatever's the matter? Have some more water.' Marigold rose from her seat to reach for the pitcher, but even as she moved, the councillor gave one final gasp and collapsed motionless onto the tabletop. His complexion a pale blue, flecks of foam at the corners of his mouth and a surprised look on his face.

For a split second, all chatter around the table ceased as everyone stared at the prone figure of Harold Everton. Marigold was frozen in place, jug of water in hand. Then Daphne started to scream, a thin penetrating wail.

Kitty blinked as Thomas King leapt from his seat to grab Daphne by her shoulders. 'For God's sake, shut up.'

Matt was already at Harold's side, feeling for a pulse in the man's neck even though Kitty could see it was useless.

'He had a weak heart. I warned him not to eat so much.' Marigold was shaking. Gladys Silitoe took the jug from her trembling hands and placed a plump conciliatory arm around her shoulders.

Matt moved his hand and looked at Kitty, his expression grave as he shook his head.

Daphne had stopped screaming, her face pale with wide frightened eyes. Mr Hendricks and his sister were huddled together on the far side of the table. Mr Silitoe was near his wife.

The maître d' and several of the other guests had been attracted by Daphne's screaming and Kitty was both relieved and unsurprised to see Inspector Greville and Doctor Carter making their way swiftly towards them.

Doctor Carter took Matt's place and conducted a rapid examination of the body, while the maître d' steered other guests away from the area. Daphne sobbed quietly in her seat with Thomas next to her. Mrs Silitoe had guided Marigold to a vacant seat at a nearby table and was seated next to her, with Mr Silitoe observing the proceedings. Matt muttered something quietly in the doctor's ear and Doctor Carter nodded and looked at Inspector Greville.

Marigold produced a lace-edged handkerchief and blew her nose.

'Mrs Everton?' Inspector Greville asked.

'Yes.' She looked up at the inspector as he introduced himself.

Across the table Kitty was aware that Mr Silitoe's posture had altered, and he had moved a little away from Marigold and closer to his wife.

'Harold had a bad heart and he would eat and drink too much.' Mrs Everton dabbed at the corners of her eyes.

'I rather think we should all move to one of the side rooms. I'm afraid I shall have to ask you all to accompany me.' Inspector Greville's tone was sombre, and Kitty shivered. There was something very wrong with all of this.

'Mrs Everton and Daphne have had a great shock,' Mr Silitoe started to protest.

'Doctor Carter will, I'm sure, confirm this on further testing, but I am afraid it appears that Mr Everton's death was not due to a heart attack.' The inspector began to encourage the group to move and follow the maître d'.

'Rubbish, my uncle had a bad heart. We all knew that,' Thomas King spoke out, frustration evident in his tone.

'I'm sorry, sir, but it appears that your uncle's death was due to poisoning. Most likely cyanide poisoning.'

There was an audible gasp from someone, and Daphne's sobs immediately resumed and increased in volume. Inspector Greville shepherded the group out of the ballroom away from the scene, while the waiters hastily partitioned off the area and the remains of Mr Everton with some large wicker screens.

'Do you think the poison was in the sachet?' Kitty said softly to Matt as they trailed behind at the back end of the group.

'It would seem that way. The question is, who put it there?' Matt gave her fingers a gentle squeeze as they were shown into a small side lounge, which was obviously the hotel's reading room.

The walls were lined with well-stocked bookcases and comfortable overstuffed wine leather covered armchairs were positioned around near small oak tables. The lamps were lit throwing off a soft, mellow light and the velvet drapes drawn against the night.

'If you would all make yourselves comfortable, I shall arrange for some coffee to be brought in. I need to go and make some telephone calls and will rejoin you shortly.' Inspector Greville withdrew, leaving behind a sombre group of people.

Daphne continued to cry noisily into her handkerchief despite Thomas' exhortations to control herself. Marigold merely looked bewildered, repeating over again, 'But he had a bad heart.'

'Marigold, my dear, you must realise this looks very serious. As your solicitor I advise you to be cautious with whatever you say.' Mr Silitoe looked at Matt as he gave his advice. Mrs Silitoe nodded, her lipsticked mouth pursed in agreement.

'I don't understand. He ate too much, and he had a bad heart,' Marigold said.

'Oh, for heaven's sake, Aunt Marigold, can you not see the implications?' Thomas asked angrily.

His aunt continued to stare at him blankly until he walked away, clearly unwilling to put into words what they were all thinking.

'Well, I don't know why we should be here, we didn't know Mr Everton,' Mrs Braddock said. Her face was pale beneath her rouge.

'Not in person,' her brother elaborated.

Kitty took a seat on one of the armchairs, while Matt perched on the arm next to her. She found his proximity comforting. Her initial shock at witnessing the terrible event had been slightly displaced by faint annoyance that she had not had the opportunity to dance with Matt and she really could have used another Bellini now more than ever.

One of the white-jacketed waiters arrived with a polished silver tray of coffee and brandy. He set it down carefully on the large round walnut burred library table that stood near the curtained window, then withdrew.

'Oh good, brandy. Here, Marigold, take a drink, my dear, and one for you, Daphne.' Mrs Silitoe roped Mrs Braddock into assisting her with dispensing coffee and brandy as required to everyone in the group.

'Where has that policeman gone? It's quite ridiculous, keeping us here,' Mr Hendricks muttered.

'Perhaps they've made a mistake and Daddy did have a heart attack,' Daphne ventured. A bright spot of colour showed on each cheek, the brandy she had consumed beginning to take effect.

No one answered her.

Kitty accepted a coffee and sat back in her seat. A chill ran through her and she gave an involuntary shiver, before pulling her thin evening shawl around her shoulders. Thomas King had lit a cigarette and paced about the carpet blowing plumes of smoke into the air.

'I take it there is no doubt of it being poison?' Kitty murmured to Matt.

'There was a distinct odour of bitter almonds.' Matt's voice, low and husky, tickled her ear. 'I assume the inspector has gone to secure the crime scene and to make arrangements with Doctor Carter to remove Councillor Everton's body.'

Kitty shuddered. 'Such a horrid thing to happen. I expect he will look at the paper containing that sachet and the box they were stored in. With the speed at which he became unwell I can only think that must have been the cause of his death.' She kept her voice as low as she could.

'It would certainly appear that way,' Matt agreed.

'I don't suppose the chemist could have made some kind of error when he dispensed the prescription?' Kitty asked. Her mind turning over all the possibilities for who may have accessed the gilt box where the sachets were stored.

Matt shook his head, glancing around the room to ensure no one was within earshot. 'Unlikely, although I'm sure the inspector will investigate that possibility. My bet is one of the household. Mrs Everton must be the chief suspect.'

Kitty placed her half-drunk cup of coffee down on the small table next to her chair. 'It was so horrid.' She shuddered at the recollection of the councillor's bulging eyes and the terrible choking, wheezing sounds he had made before crashing down, lifeless onto the table. She half wished that she was safe upstairs in the suite with Alice, listening to the wireless, sharing a box of chocolates and reading the film magazines.

Matt seemed to sense her feelings as he claimed her hand with his. 'Chin up, old thing, Inspector Greville will be back soon and once we've given a statement, I expect he will allow us to leave.' The gentle pressure of his fingers against hers warmed and reassured her.

The white painted door to the lounge opened and Inspector Greville reappeared, accompanied by a young, uniformed constable. The low buzz of chatter in the room ceased at his entry and all heads turned in his direction.

'Thank you for your patience, ladies and gentlemen. I am going to need to ask all of you some questions about the dinner this evening and about Mr Everton.' He glanced around the room, his gaze coming to rest on Marigold, who looked dazed and confused.

'Will it take long, Inspector? Only my sister and I didn't really know the man and we have a taxi booked to take us back to Cockington at midnight.' Mr Hendricks looked at his sister as if for confirmation. 'We have a business to run and our assistant manager will need relief.'

Inspector Greville's moustache twitched. 'I'm sure we shall do this as quickly as possible, Mr…?'

'Hendricks, Mr Hendricks of the Conway Country House Hotel.'

'Yes, thank you, Mr Hendricks. As I said before we do need to talk to everyone who was present at the time of Mr Everton's death.'

Daphne let out another wail at the mention of her father's demise.

'Daphne, my dear, do control yourself,' Mrs Silitoe remonstrated in a kindly fashion.

'Mrs Everton and her daughter have had a terrible shock, Inspector. May I suggest you speak to them first so they can return home? As Mrs Everton's solicitor I would be happy to support her during the interview,' Mr Silitoe said, stepping forward and placing a hand on Marigold's shoulder.

'Thank you, Mr Silitoe. I shall bear your offer in mind. Of course, you yourself are a witness.' The inspector's tone was firm.

'Yes, yes, of course.' Mr Silitoe gave an ingratiating smile.

The constable took up his position near the door.

'Perhaps, Miss Underhay, you could spare me a few minutes?' the inspector said.

Startled, Kitty glanced at Matt and collected her evening bag before following the inspector from the room to a small office on the other side of the hall.

'Please take a seat, Miss Underhay.' Inspector Greville indicated a worn wooden chair next to the small battered writing bureau.

Once she was seated, he took out his notebook and pencil before seating himself on a matching chair.

'Now, please, tell me everything you observed and heard during the course of the evening that may be relevant to Councillor Everton's murder.'

Kitty took a deep breath and told him everything she had noticed. Inspector Greville took copious notes, scribbling furiously in his notebook.

'Thank you, Miss Underhay, that is most useful.'

'Am I free to go?' Kitty asked. She had lost all track of the time. She wondered what had become of the other guests. Had the ball been halted?

'Of course. I must ask you to return to your suite. I expect Captain Bryant will be free to go shortly once the other members of the party have given their statements.' He smiled at her and she suspected he knew she would have liked to have been in on those other interviews.

'Thank you.' She collected her things and walked out into the hall. Inspector Greville followed her, and, as she reached the lobby and looked back, she saw Mrs Braddock entering the office with the inspector.

'Kitty!'

Her heart sank into the bottom of her new high-heeled shoes as Mrs Craven's imperious tones reached her.

'Kitty Underhay! A word!' Mrs Craven bustled towards her, the ostrich feathers in her jewelled headband bobbing with every step like some bizarre exotic bird.

'Mrs Craven.' Kitty halted and waited for the older lady to catch up with her.

As soon as she came close Mrs Craven took hold of her arm and steered her to a quiet corner.

'My dear, is it true? Councillor Everton has been poisoned?'

'Well—' Kitty got no further.

'Such a scandal. What is the world coming to when one isn't even safe within a respectable establishment like the Imperial? It wasn't the food, was it? The fish seemed perfectly good to me, but one never knows.'

'I'm not sure quite what happened. Inspector Greville is interviewing everyone. Matt is still with the rest of the party.' Kitty drew her shawl more closely around her shoulders.

'Oh well, let us hope that the inspector doesn't take it into his head to arrest the wrong person this time. I presume it is murder then, not an accident?' Mrs Craven's eyes gleamed with interest.

Kitty suppressed a sigh. A few weeks earlier, Matt had himself been under suspicion of murder and she had no wish to revisit that dark time. 'I couldn't say, the inspector will wait for Doctor Carter's report I suppose.'

Mrs Craven released her grip on Kitty's arm. 'It's the talk of the place, it will be all over Torquay by tomorrow. Poor Marigold, I expect she had taken all she could from that husband of hers. If ever a man could drive a woman to murder it would be Harold Everton.'

A group of people in evening attire called to Mrs Craven from near the entrance to the lobby.

'I really must go, my friends are taking me home. Whatever your grandmother will make of all this I don't know.' Mrs Craven drew herself up, making the black sateen of her gown crackle as it moved across her foundation garments.

'You surely are not going to telephone her now?' Kitty asked in some alarm. The hour must be quite late, and her grandmother needed to rest.

'Of course not, I shall visit her tomorrow morning. I daresay you may have more information for me by then.' Mrs Craven turned and hurried away towards her friends, her heels tapping on the marble flooring.

CHAPTER SIX

Kitty made her way through the lobby, which was busy with departing guests and up the marble staircase to her suite. She was glad to leave the crowd, abuzz with gossip, behind her.

Alice opened the door on her first knock. The maid was already in her night attire, her flame red hair in a loose plait.

'Oh, miss, I've been so worried. Our Betty came up and told me someone had been murdered, and on your table too.' Alice's eyes were wide as she turned down the music on the wireless.

She took Kitty's shawl and folded it neatly as Kitty dropped her evening purse down on the small occasional table next to the armchairs.

'Did Betty see what happened?' Kitty asked as she took a seat and unbuckled her shoes, stretching out her stocking clad toes with relief once she was free.

'No, miss, she was waiting on the top table with the mayor and Mrs Craven and all them. She said they didn't know anything had gone on at first because of the music from the band and that.' Alice collected up Kitty's shoes and wrapped them carefully in their pale cream dust cloth ready to put them back in the box.

'Then what happened?' Kitty asked.

'Well, Betty said as one of the floor managers came over and started ordering the staff to get the screens as a man had collapsed. Betty said she saw Doctor Carter and Inspector Greville go hurrying across the room and she knew as it was your table from the seating plan.' Alice pulled the shoebox out and packed up the shoes. 'They said as the wife was the one who done it. Standing over him with an evil look in her eyes. Cor, it's just like the pictures, in't it, miss?'

'It was certainly very dramatic,' Kitty agreed. She tried to expunge the puce-faced image of Councillor Everton from her memory.

'Betty said as they said he was frothing all around his mouth with his eyes a-popping out his head and his wife had poisoned him with something.' Alice was bright-eyed with curiosity.

'It does appear that he may have been poisoned by something, but it was not quite as Betty depicted it.' Kitty shivered.

Alice perched on the edge of the armchair opposite Kitty, her long plait falling forward over her shoulder on her dark-blue flannel dressing gown. 'You don't half manage to get mixed up in some things, miss.'

'I could have done without getting caught up in this one, Alice. This was supposed to be a fun evening out and a bit of a break.' She wondered what was happening downstairs. Matt would no doubt be observing their fellow guests and might be unearthing some more information.

'You look all in, Miss Kitty. Shall I call down for some cocoa or hot milk?' Alice asked.

'Yes, please, and for you too, Alice, you must be tired.' Kitty glanced at the fine gold evening wristwatch her grandmother had given her as one of her twenty-first birthday presents two years earlier.

It was getting towards midnight already. She wasn't sure where the time had gone. The dancing had started at around ten, so Harold Everton must have been killed at around ten fifteen.

Alice was busy on the telephone to room service. A comforting mug of milk or cocoa might settle her mind and help her to sleep. Kitty suppressed a yawn as Alice finished on the telephone and began to turn the bed down.

'I've asked for a hot bottle as well, miss.' Alice gave the crisp white sheets a final stroke.

'Thank you, you think of everything.' Kitty was grateful to her maid. Alice, despite her youth, was eminently practical and level-headed. She was also a comforting companion.

The girl continued to bustle about the suite, fetching out Kitty's night attire and tidying. After a few minutes, a knock came at the door.

A uniformed bellhop wheeled in a trolley containing a large jug and a set of cups along with a plate of biscuits. On the bottom of the trolley were the requested hot water bottles.

Alice had no sooner thanked the lad and dismissed him with a tip, provided by Kitty, than there was another tap at the door.

Kitty answered as Alice was engaged in installing the hot water bottles in their beds.

'I'm not too late, am I?' Matt was in the doorway, a fine trace of stubble already beginning to darken his chin.

'No, come in.' Kitty peeped around him into the corridor, anxious that no one should have seen him come to her room. The less gossip the better, even though she had Alice with her, she knew how people liked to talk. Satisfied that everywhere was quiet, she closed the door behind him.

'Alice and I were about to have a bedtime drink. There is an extra cup if you'd like to join us,' Kitty said.

Matt seated himself on the armchair recently vacated by the maid. He reached up and undid his bow tie, leaving it loose around his neck as he unfastened his collar stud. 'I thought I would call in and make sure you were all right. It's been quite a night.'

Kitty busied herself with pouring drinks from the jug, which to her delight contained cocoa. She passed one to Alice and one to Matt before draining the last of the contents into her own cup.

'Has the inspector completed his interviews?' She took the seat opposite Matt, while Alice retreated to the far side of the room.

Matt sighed. 'I believe so. He intends to send officers to the pharmacists' tomorrow and, of course, he has requested laboratory tests on the sachets from the box.'

Kitty took a sip of her cocoa. 'Is he inclined to believe Mrs Everton to be the culprit, do you think?'

Matt frowned. 'In many ways she must be the most likely person, but any member of the household could have had access to that medication. We know that Daphne and Thomas King both reside at the house.'

'It sounded as if the Silitoes were also frequent visitors,' Kitty suggested. 'Also, anyone at the table may have had access to the box. Mrs Everton had her bag hanging by the strap from the back of her chair.'

'The thing that puzzles me most is why commit the murder at the dinner? In a ballroom filled with almost two hundred people?' The crease on Matt's forehead deepened and he took a long draught from his cup.

'Do you think then that all the sachets had been tampered with? Or was it just that one, and it was sheer ill luck that he selected it this evening?' Kitty asked. She finished her drink and returned her cup to the trolley.

'I suppose we will find that information out when the inspector receives the test results.' Matt copied her actions. 'I'm sorry about this evening, Kitty. It was not at all what we had in mind.' His mouth twisted wryly.

'I'm sorry too. Are you staying at the hotel tonight or returning home?' she asked.

'Doctor Carter has kindly offered me a lift. He is downstairs with the inspector. I expect he will wish to leave shortly.' His smile matched Kitty's. They both knew all too well the doctor's love of speed. Matt would no doubt be in for an interesting and somewhat hair-raising ride home.

Matt rose from his seat and Kitty stood to join him.

'I'm sorry we didn't get to dance.' He gazed into her eyes and her pulse leapt.

'Me too.' Her voice was unexpectedly husky.

'We have a few minutes now.' His voice tickled her ear as he took her into his arms, and they started to move to the faint strains of music coming from the wireless.

'I'm not wearing my shoes.' She leaned her head on his chest, conscious of her smaller stature next to him. The crimson satin of her dress swirled as they moved together in the small space.

'Did I tell you how nice you looked this evening?' His hand was warm on the small of her back.

She looked up at him. 'I believe you may have said so, but I have no objection to hearing it again.'

The dimple flashed in his cheek. 'Thank you for the dance, but I'm afraid I must leave, or Doctor Carter will be gone.' He released her, leaving her feeling suddenly chilled again.

'Of course, shall I see you tomorrow?' Her gaze locked with his.

'I'll be at the Dolphin around lunchtime.' He lowered his head and his lips brushed hers.

Kitty swallowed. 'I'll see you tomorrow then.'

He opened the door ready to take his leave. 'Goodnight, Miss Underhay. Goodnight, Alice.' Then he was gone.

'Coo, that was romantic, miss,' Alice said, sighing happily as she crossed the room to turn off the wireless and to assist Kitty out of her evening gown.

To her surprise, Kitty slept much better than she had expected to. She and Alice took breakfast together in the bright and airy dining room of the Imperial before waiting in the lobby for Mr Potter to come and collect them.

'I don't know what Grams is going to think about all this.' Kitty pulled on her gloves as the young bellhop who seemed to admire Alice came to carry their bags to the waiting taxi.

'I know, miss,' Alice agreed, her cheeks turning fiery red as the young lad risked a cheeky wink at her.

Kitty pretended not to notice as she took her place in the back of the car. 'I expect the newspapers will be full of it today.'

Alice hopped onto the seat next to her and Mr Potter pulled carefully away from the hotel entrance.

'Do you think as they'll arrest Mrs Everton?' Alice asked.

'I don't know, Alice. I expect the inspector may need more evidence first, but things do not look good for her. She has to be the most likely suspect.'

It was a cold, wintry day and the sky was grey and heavy over the sea as they followed the coast road out of Torquay back towards Kingswear and the ferry. Once back at the Dolphin, Kitty dismissed Mr Potter and they went inside the hotel. One of the porters helped Alice to take the bags to Kitty's room, while Kitty herself checked at the reception desk for any messages.

'Nothing, miss. Your grandmother is expecting you though, she said to ask you to go up as soon as you returned.' Mary, the receptionist, checked the pigeonholes and smiled cheerfully at Kitty.

'Thank you, Mary.' Kitty hurried up the broad oak staircase to her grandmother's salon on the first floor.

She knocked on the door to the suite, entering at the sound of her grandmother's voice. To her relief Grams was dressed in her usual neat daywear, her grey hair perfectly styled and her pearl necklace in place. Although she still appeared pale and her nose and eyes were slightly pink, she seemed much recovered from her illness and was in her favourite armchair beside the fire.

'Kitty darling, are you all right? I have had so many telephone calls this morning from members of the association, and then

Millicent dropped by just an hour ago. Such shocking news, I can hardly believe it. For such a thing to happen in the Imperial of all places.' Grams shook her head in disbelief.

Kitty pulled off her black kid gloves, stowing them away in her matching handbag. 'I'm fine, truly. It was indeed very shocking, but Matt and Alice both took good care of me. More to the point, Grams darling, are you feeling better?'

'Oh yes, this was just one of those trifling colds. I'm much improved now.'

'Well, I'm glad to hear it.' Kitty took her knitted scarf from around her neck.

Her grandmother watched as she folded it neatly, adding it to her bag. 'Inspector Greville was present at the dinner I understand? That was very fortunate.'

'Yes, and Doctor Carter too.' Kitty slipped off her coat and removed her hat, smoothing her short blonde hair back into place.

'Millicent seemed to believe that Councillor Everton had been poisoned by his wife. She said it was the talk of the place,' her grandmother said.

Kitty hung up her coat and came to sit on the chair opposite, stretching out her chilly fingers to warm them with the heat from the crackling logs in the fireplace. 'It seems fairly certain that he was poisoned but it may not be quite clear-cut as to who the culprit might be. If the poison was in his medicine then any member of his household, or even those at the table, could fall under suspicion. It appears he was not a popular man.'

Grams snorted. 'That is an understatement, darling, virtually everyone who ever met him disliked him before too long. He had an unfortunate habit of rubbing people up the wrong way. Poor Marigold, it's a bad business.'

Her fingers were thawing nicely now so Kitty relaxed back on her chair. 'He struck me as quite a rude man. Daphne had already said he wouldn't allow her to spend her money on a new dress and his wife seemed completely overshadowed by him. His nephew was at the table too, a Thomas King. I got the impression he worked for his uncle.'

'I'm so sorry, my dear, I had hoped you and Matthew would have had a nice relaxing evening out. You get so little time to enjoy yourself, and this year has been so very hard on both of you.' Her grandmother shook her head. 'The last thing I expected was that you would become entangled with another murder.'

Kitty laughed. 'It wasn't exactly a plan on my part either. By the way, do you know the people who keep the Conway Country House Hotel near Cockington?'

'It was sold a few years ago now I believe. It's a big, rambling old place. A beautiful setting but the roof was bad. There were bats in the attic I think, and it needed a fortune spent on it. Why do you ask?' Her grandmother took a poker from the set of fire irons next to the hearth and gave the fire a stir. The logs crackled and hissed in protest sending a shower of sparks up the chimney.

'I just wondered if you knew them. They were at our table, a chap in his fifties, Mr Hendricks, and his sister, she apparently is a widowed lady, younger than him, a Mrs Braddock.' Kitty felt better now she had warmed up and she was aware her grandmother knew most of the other members of the association from when she had been on the board.

Her grandmother frowned. 'The hotel used to belong to Major Conway, hence the name, but the poor man lost his son during the war and then his wife had a stroke which left her a complete invalid so he sold up. I think I vaguely remember them. Is he a tall man, losing his hair? She is quite a plump worried-looking woman, leaves the talking to her brother?'

Kitty smiled at the description. 'Yes, that's them. They were at our table along with some friends of the Evertons, a Mr and Mrs

Silitoe. He's a solicitor and does some work for the council. They play bridge with the Evertons.'

She could see her grandmother thinking. 'No, darling, I don't think I know them, although I expect Millicent will if you were to ask her. She seemed very keen to find out if you had said anything about the murder. She was most disappointed when I told her you hadn't yet returned from Torquay.'

Kitty groaned. 'Oh no, I do hope she is not expecting me to play Watson to her Sherlock again. It was quite bad enough before when those poor girls were killed, and she insisted on being involved. I think she rather fancies herself as a detective.'

'I take it that you and Matthew will be taking on the case then?' Her grandmother raised a delicately pencilled eyebrow. 'Or will you be entrusting Inspector Greville to do his job?'

Kitty blushed. 'Matt is calling here at around lunchtime. There may not be a case to investigate, you know. The inspector may have made an arrest already.'

CHAPTER SEVEN

Matt found a parking space outside the Dolphin shortly before one o'clock. He stood his Sunbeam motorcycle at the kerb and glanced up at the half-timbered frontage of the hotel. He thought he caught a glimpse of Kitty in the bay window of her grandmother's salon and smiled to himself. No doubt she would be anxious to discuss the murder.

He had spent the morning making some discreet enquiries about their fellow diners. Doctor Carter had been quite forthcoming with his thoughts on the affair on the drive back to Churston the previous night.

'It'll turn out to be the wife. It usually is, you know, and poison is a woman's weapon,' had been the doctor's opinion.

Kitty was just coming down the stairs into the wood panelled lobby when he entered through the glass and brass door.

'I saw you pull up,' she explained. 'Would you like lunch here, or shall we go into the town?'

'You choose, you know how busy you are.' He didn't really mind where they went.

'It's so cold out there today, shall we eat here? The hotel is quiet and most of our guests are out for the day.' She smiled up at him and his heart gave a jump.

'Of course.' He removed his long, brown leather overcoat, knitted muffler and cloth cap, which Kitty promptly stowed away in her small office behind the reception desk. 'Is your grandmother better? Will she be joining us for lunch?' he asked as they set off along the hall towards the bright and airy dining room.

'She is much better, but resting in her room for today,' Kitty replied.

The head waiter led them to a table in the window offering a view of the embankment with the river and its traffic. Once they had been seated and their order for lamb cutlets had been placed, Kitty poured them both a glass of water.

'Now, tell me everything. I know that you will have been poking around this morning.' Kitty gazed expectantly at him, the winter light making her blue-grey eyes sparkle.

'I may have found out some more information. I wanted to try and discover what it was that Councillor Everton wished to discuss with me. He had clearly been thinking it over since we met at the awards evening and it must have been a delicate or personal matter, or he would have involved the police.' He paused as the waiter reappeared to place their lunch in front of them.

Kitty shook out her linen napkin and draped it across her lap. 'I concur with that deduction. Mr Everton did not strike me as the kind of man to refrain from bringing in the police if he considered there had been wrongdoing somewhere.'

'He said it was not a marital issue, so I suppose that takes Mrs Everton slightly out of the frame.' Matt's brow creased as he tried to recall the councillor's exact words about the nature of the problem.

Kitty picked up the silver serving spoons and started to serve potatoes and cabbage onto their plates from the white china tureen in the centre of the table. 'Hmm, so it could be another family member, Daphne or Thomas, or possibly even a close friend or colleague. Mr Everton and Mr Silitoe were having a very heated discussion at one point last night. I don't know if you noticed?'

Matt helped himself to gravy from the sauce boat. 'I was aware that they were having an intense debate, but I didn't overhear any of the content. Mr Silitoe advises the council on many of its legal matters. He is especially involved with matters arising from the purchasing of land and the granting of permissions for development.'

'Mr Hendricks was asking something about that, wasn't he? Mr Everton told him to submit it to Thomas, and not very nicely either. It sounded as if they had argued about something to do with plans and planning before.' She speared a piece of cabbage with her fork.

'That is another interesting thing,' Matt said. 'After I left you last night, I went to find Doctor Carter. He and Inspector Greville were looking at the seating plan for the dinner.'

'And?' Kitty asked.

'Mr Hendricks and Mrs Braddock should not have been at our table. They should have been seated at another table. An older couple, Mr and Mrs Charters of Tweenaway in Paignton, should have been seated with us.' Matt enjoyed the expression of surprise on Kitty's face.

'Then what happened?' she asked.

'Inspector Greville asked the restaurant manager and the best explanation is that someone, probably Hendricks, switched the place names.' Matt took a drink of water.

'He wanted to sit at Councillor Everton's table to ask him about the planning for his hotel,' Kitty guessed, her eyes wide.

'I'm sure that's the line of enquiry the inspector will take,' Matt agreed. 'But would he have known about the councillor's medication? Or had access to it? Someone at our table came prepared for murder.'

Kitty busied herself with her lamb cutlet. Matt could tell she was running through the possibilities in her mind.

'I suppose the inspector will have made the enquiries at the pharmacy? And checked the poisons register?' she asked.

'I expect so, and no doubt has conducted a search of the Everton household and Mr Everton's office at the council,' Matt added.

Kitty's brow knitted in concentration as she placed her cutlery down neatly on her empty plate. 'Do you think there was something wrong at the council? Do you think that might be the matter that he wished to discuss with you? His nephew works for him there and Mr Silitoe is his friend and does business with the council. Either one could be involved if there was a problem of some kind.'

'It is a possibility.' He placed his own knife and fork down on his plate and they sat in silence for a moment as the waiter collected the used crockery and took their order for apple crumble and custard.

Kitty sighed. 'I presume Marigold must remain the chief suspect however?'

The waiter returned with their desserts. Once he was out of earshot Matt resumed their conversation.

'I think she has to be. Doctor Carter said that it is almost always the wife in these cases as poison is a woman's weapon.' He helped himself to custard and waited for Kitty to take the bait.

'I seem to recall there have been plenty of notorious male poisoners,' she pointed out with some asperity. 'But she remains the most likely person. She had the means and, from what others have said of Mr Everton's character, the motive. It was clear from her demeanour and from the little Daphne said to me at Miss Veronique that the household was not a particularly happy one.'

'Then there is the charming and handsome nephew, Thomas King. I have made a few discreet enquiries about him but have heard nothing back as yet.' He waited to see Kitty's response to his description of Thomas King.

It had been a green-eyed imp of mischief that had prodded him into encouraging Kitty's acceptance of a dance with Councillor Everton's good-looking nephew. He had spent most of his own dance with Daphne regretting it and wanting to interrupt them whenever they had circled past.

'He works for his uncle as a clerk and joined the household this summer when his mother passed away. She was Mr Everton's sister. I learned that much during our excursion around the dance floor.' Kitty peeped at him from under her lashes as she finished off the last spoon of her dessert.

Matt's pulse jumped as he caught her gaze. 'Was that all you learned?' he asked.

The corners of her mouth lifted in a smile. 'I learned that he is very flirtatious and that he has difficulty in keeping his hands to himself.'

He was about to suggest they go to the lounge for coffee when a rapping on the leaded windowpane outside startled them both.

Mrs Craven, swathed in fox fur and with a neat navy hat on top of her iron-grey curls, had tapped on the glass with the bone handle of her umbrella. She nodded in the direction of the hotel entrance and Matt surmised that she wished to meet them in the lobby.

'Oh dear, I was afraid of this,' Kitty murmured as they signalled their assent and rose from the table.

'Afraid of what?' Matt asked.

'I rather fear that Mrs Craven has developed a taste for detective work. I was button-holed in the lobby of the Imperial last night.'

Stunned by Kitty's answer, he was temporarily lost for words as he followed her to the lobby.

Mrs Craven was already waiting for them. Kitty requested a tray of coffee from the receptionist and unlocked the door to her small office so that they might talk privately.

'So very fortuitous seeing you both in the window.' Mrs Craven swept past Kitty and selected a seat, her mouth pursing with disapproval at the untidy sheaf of papers on Kitty's desk.

Matt waited until Kitty had assumed her usual position behind her desk before perching himself on the only remaining seat. He was curious to discover what Mrs Craven was so anxious to talk to them about.

'It's nice to see you, Mrs Craven. To what do we owe the pleasure of this visit?' he asked.

The older woman drew off her ivory kid gloves and loosened her furs. 'The murder, of course. Kitty, I saw your dear grandmother this morning and she said you had not yet returned from Torquay. I had a few errands to run in town and I stopped for lunch with a friend. I just happened to be passing when I saw you both at the window.' She paused as the tray of coffee arrived.

Kitty poured the coffee from a tall white china pot into matching modern cups. 'Please help yourself to cream and sugar, Mrs Craven. We don't know if Inspector Greville has made an arrest as yet.' Her gaze met Matt's and he struggled to keep from grinning as she passed him a cup.

'Hmm, my faith in that man was sorely tested when he arrested you, Matthew. How can we be certain that he will arrest the right person this time?' Mrs Craven added cream to her coffee and stirred her drink, chinking the spoon against the cup.

'The inspector is a good man. He is very thorough.' Matt hid his smile behind his cup and earned himself a glare from Kitty.

Mrs Craven gave a disparaging sniff. 'When I was leaving the restaurant earlier, I happened to see Daphne Everton.' She looked at Kitty and Matt as if expecting a reaction to this item of news.

'I'm sorry, I don't see—' Kitty started to say.

Mrs Craven cut her off. 'Daphne Everton was out and about as if she hadn't a care in the world. Not at all like a young woman who had just lost someone to murder. She wasn't even dressed in black, and she wasn't alone.' She nodded her head meaningfully.

'Do you know who was accompanying her?' Matt asked, his curiosity piqued.

'A young man and very familiar they seemed to be too.' Mrs Craven frowned disapprovingly.

'Are you sure it wasn't her cousin, Thomas King?' Kitty asked.

Mrs Craven drew herself up. 'It certainly was not Mr King. I've met him before when he delivered some documents to one of my committees. No, I hadn't seen this particular young man before but Daphne's conduct and demeanour was quite shocking. Laughing and joking as if she hadn't a care in the world and her father's body not yet cold. Well, that's very suspicious, don't you think?'

'Have you informed Inspector Greville?' Matt asked.

'Not yet. I intend to, obviously, as soon as I return home. However, as I was passing and saw you both I thought we should get our heads together first.'

Matt saw Kitty biting her lip. 'Well, thank you for thinking of us but I'm sure the inspector will have the case well in hand without our assistance.' He noticed Kitty's expression change to one of horror at the 'our' in his assurance.

Fortunately, Mrs Craven appeared oblivious to Kitty's dismay. 'I expect poor Marigold Everton will be his chief suspect. That woman has suffered for years with her husband's penny-pinching and bullying. It's a sad business.'

'Do you know Mr and Mrs Silitoe at all?' Kitty asked.

Mrs Craven frowned. 'The solicitor? Yes, of course. He was seated with you last night I understand. Dyes his hair, of course, although I don't know why. His wife is pleasant enough, she belongs to several clubs, flower arrangers and suchlike.'

Matt gave a gentle cough. 'Mr Silitoe does some work for the council so I'm told?'

'Oh yes, he works with the planning committee and a few other committees. He advises them on legal matters.' Mrs Craven set down her cup and saucer. 'Well, I must be off. You'll keep me informed, of course, of anything you hear.' She tugged on her gloves and rearranged her furs ready to depart.

'Of course,' Matt agreed, pretending he didn't see Kitty's horrified expression. 'Allow me to see you out.' He held the door open for her and saw her to the front door of the hotel.

He stood at the entrance for a moment watching her walking away along the embankment, her umbrella tapping on the paving stones. The cool air blowing from the river stung his face, clearing his head after the enclosed mugginess of Kitty's office.

Mist had already begun to rise from the water, blurring and softening the far bank and the view of Kingswear. A train hooted in the distance; the sound somehow dulled by the wintry weather. There were few people abroad and the ferries were quiet.

Mrs Craven had a point. After all Daphne Everton's weeping and wailing after her father's demise, it was not the kind of weather he would expect to discover her abroad disporting herself with a suitor.

Kitty gathered up the coffee cups and returned them to the tray. Matt had been gone for a few minutes and she wondered what he could be up to. Hopefully he would be dissuading Mrs Craven from playing detective.

She would dearly love to know what the police might have found during their search of the Everton household. The source of the poison must provide a large clue as to who the culprit might be.

Daphne Everton did not appear to be mourning her father's death. Marigold had seemed to be in shock last night, and Matt was right, why would she choose to murder him at the hoteliers' ball? If he had died at home then the death might have been attributed to natural causes.

A sense of restlessness pervaded her spirits. She hated being inactive. The door to her office cracked open and Matt reappeared.

'I take it our guest has gone?' Kitty said.

'Yes, she was headed towards the taxi rank, I expect she is gone to rouse Mr Potter from his newspaper and pipe.' Matt smiled at her. 'You look rather glum, what's wrong?' He took Mrs Craven's recently vacated seat. 'Don't tell me you aren't looking forward to Mrs C's assistance? I'm sure Inspector Greville will be equally delighted.'

Kitty leaned back in her chair, her hands automatically moving to tidy the papers that had annoyed Mrs Craven. 'I don't know. What happened last night feels so unreal, and, if what Mrs Craven reported is correct, then Daphne's behaviour seems quite strange and out of character.'

'Especially if her mother may be facing the noose.'

Kitty shuddered. 'Let us hope that Mr Everton's death turns out to be the result of some ghastly error rather than wilful intent.'

He gave her a sharp look. 'You don't believe that though, surely?'

'No, but I can hope.' A shiver danced its way along her spine, and she rubbed the tops of her arms to dispel the goosebumps that had suddenly arisen there.

'Are you feeling all right, Kitty?' Matt's expression was concerned.

'Perfectly, thank you.' Her heart had leapt at the tenderness she thought she saw in his eyes. Embarrassment at her feelings made her sound a little chippy and she cringed inwardly.

He inclined away from her and she immediately regretted sounding so sharp. 'What happens now? Do we investigate Councillor Everton's death, or do we await Inspector Greville's findings?'

He considered her question. 'For myself, I would like to discover what Mr Everton was so keen to discuss with me. It may have a connection to his death, or it may not, but I think it must be worth following up.'

Kitty nodded. 'I agree.' She noticed he had made no mention of what he thought she might do to assist.

'I think I may drop by the council chambers on Monday and see what I can learn there.' Matt rose from his seat and collected his outdoor things from the coat stand.

'I shall pay a condolence call on Mrs Everton and Daphne tomorrow. It seems only right, and I might discover something while I'm there,' Kitty said.

He shrugged his way into his coat and wrapped his muffler around his throat. 'Just have a care, Kitty. The woman may be a murderess.' He placed his cap securely on his head.

'Of course. I shall be discreet; it's merely a condolence visit,' she assured him as she stood to see him out of her office. He hadn't offered to go with her.

His expression was sombre as he prepared to leave. 'No more near misses, old girl.'

She swallowed. 'Scout's honour.'

He dipped his head and his lips brushed hers stealing her breath. 'I'll telephone you.'

She watched him stride away calling his farewell to Mary at reception. Then a few minutes later she heard the guttural note of the Sunbeam as he started her up ready to drive back to Churston.

His departure left her feeling low and she cursed herself mentally for lacking the courage to raise the status of their friendship with him. They had been through so many ups and downs since their first meeting. From a cautious friendship to something much closer and then their awful argument.

They hadn't spoken for weeks over the summer when Matt's somewhat old-fashioned and traditional views of a woman's role had surfaced and clashed with Kitty's pride and stubbornness at being a modern, independent woman. She thought he had moved towards her way of thinking, but then something like this happened and she was suddenly not so certain.

It had taken the threat of the hangman with Matt being wrongly suspected of murder to restore their friendship. Since then they had been friends once again. But friends didn't kiss and flirt in the way she and Matt did. Or did they? Kitty had relatively little experience to go on in that arena.

Then there were the shadows of the past that cast a long, dark pall over their future. The death of Matt's wife and baby, killed in a Zeppelin raid while Matt had been on active service, had left a scar on his psyche that she wasn't sure could be healed. His parents had hinted at this and that there were still secrets about his marriage that he hadn't shared with her.

Kitty sighed and stared at the tidy heap of work awaiting her on her desk. She was in no mood to tackle it now; she was far too unsettled and restless. Making up her mind, she left her office, locking the door behind her. She would go and investigate Jack Dawkins' box again instead.

CHAPTER EIGHT

Her mind made up; Kitty hurried up the flights of stairs to her room. The wintery afternoon light was already fading, and the corridor was dark and gloomy. No guests were ever given rooms on this floor. The space was used to house temporary staff and for storage. For most of the time, such as now, she had the floor to herself giving her the peace and privacy she longed for after her usual hectic days of dealing with guests.

She switched on the lamp in her room to give her better light to examine the contents of the cigar box once more. She had already removed the photograph of her mother and framed it in a small silver frame where it now stood on her dressing table next to the rosary beads, which had been its companion for so many years.

Kitty settled herself on the floral-patterned fireside chair and carefully lifted the lid from the cigar box. The interior smelled of tobacco and old paper, a mix that reminded her of the reading room at the public library. Strangely, it was one of the few places she had a clear memory of visiting as a small child with her mother when they had lived in London before coming to Dartmouth.

The unexpected recollection brought a lump to her throat and she was forced to pause for a moment before beginning to sort through the contents. Once she had recovered, she started to examine the small heap of papers. She had only given them a cursory examination before, half hoping something obvious would leap out at her from the faded press cuttings.

This time she took care to carefully examine and read each piece, studying both the front and back of the articles. Some were identical to the ones she and her grandmother already had themselves, carefully cut and curated into a large manilla envelope. That envelope also contained the results from the private detection agencies her grandmother had employed, letters from the public and readings by psychics who had claimed to be able to offer assistance.

She set those clippings aside and focused on any that were different. A few were from Exeter newspapers but didn't seem to offer any new information, so she added those to the set-aside pile.

There were a few random cuttings, some relating to recipes or household hints. She studied them carefully but concluded that Jack must have kept them thinking they were useful rather than for any other motive.

There were only three remaining articles. Kitty fidgeted and stretched; her back had begun to ache from sitting in one position. She held the cuttings closer to the lamp so she could read the print more clearly. The first article was about the Glass Bottle public house. Jack appeared to have written the date in pencil on the margin of the cutting. It was dated a few days after her mother's disappearance in 1916.

The article referred to the police having raided the pub and had made a number of arrests. The landlord, Ezekiel Hammet, was accused of serving alcohol after hours and a number of stolen goods had been found on the upstairs of the premises.

This appeared to confirm Jack Dawkins' assertion that the Glass Bottle was not a place with a good reputation. She assumed that Ezekiel Hammet must be the man that Father Lamb had said was the parent of the missing current landlord of the same name.

The next clipping was of a similar age. It referred to incidents of unrest and damage to properties and businesses in Exeter. Again,

Jack had felt it important enough to mark the date in the margin and to add it to his collection.

The final cutting was, in Kitty's view, the most interesting one. She had dismissed it on her first two sweeps through the box. It was a short piece referring to the proposal to reopen a section of the medieval underground water passages that were underneath the streets in the centre of the city. This clipping was only a few months old and indicated that guided tours of the old water courses were proposed.

She frowned as she studied the article. Jack Dawkins had not been known to have any particular interest in either history or architecture. Father Lamb would have mentioned it, she was sure. She held the paper closer to the light and realised that Jack had made another of his pencil annotations in the margin. This time it wasn't a date, instead, in faint, miniscule shaky lettering it said: Elowed? Cathedral cellars passage, bottle.

Her heart thumped against the wall of her chest and she suddenly felt quite sick. Was Jack implying what she thought he was implying? That somewhere near the cathedral the clue to what had happened to her mother lay in that long-forgotten buried watercourse?

Kitty returned the cuttings to the cigar box, setting the one about the passages to one side before she placed it in her Chinese style lacquered jewel box. Jack must have thought there was something about the tunnels that might provide an answer to what had happened in 1916, and it was somehow connected with the Glass Bottle and its clientele.

The mysterious note on the cuttings occupied her thoughts all through dinner with her grandmother, rendering her unusually silent as she puzzled over the information and its implications. It would have been nice to discuss it all with Matt, but she still felt nettled about their conversations in her office.

'Kitty, darling, are you feeling well? You have been very dull during dinner. I do hope you aren't getting my cold,' her grandmother said.

'I'm sorry. I think I'm rather tired from all the excitement.' She smiled reassuringly as she set down her dessertspoon. She had no intention of mentioning her discoveries of the afternoon until she had done some more research.

'So long as you are not coming down with something. Perhaps an early night would be in order.'

Kitty rose from her seat at the dining table and kissed her Grams' cheek. 'A good idea. I'll just go and check on the staff, then I think I'll go and finish Mrs Sayers latest book.'

Her grandmother snorted. 'After experiencing a real murder, I wouldn't have thought you would find reading about fictional ones terribly relaxing.'

Kitty laughed as she headed for the door to her grandmother's suite. 'Goodnight, Grams, I'll see you tomorrow.'

At the reception desk, Mary had her hand on the receiver of the telephone as Kitty walked down the stairs into the lobby.

'Oh, Miss Kitty, I was just about to telephone you. There's a lady waiting to see you.' She inclined her head towards the end of the lobby.

Kitty followed her gaze. A tall, thin woman in a shabby black coat and shapeless matching hat stood near the leaflet rack.

'Who is it?' Kitty asked.

'Mrs Miller, Alice's mother.' Mary looked anxious.

'Is there something wrong with Alice? She was well when she left here at lunchtime?' Kitty's stomach clenched with anxiety. Surely the girl wasn't sick or been in an accident.

'No, I don't think so, miss. She said as it were a business matter,' Mary said.

Kitty was perplexed. She straightened the skirt of her dark blue velvet evening gown and went to meet Alice's mother.

'Mrs Miller, this is an unexpected pleasure. How may I help you?'

Mrs Miller was an older version of Alice. They shared the same eyes and Mrs Miller's hair, what could be seen under her hat, must once have been the same fiery shade as her daughter's but was now faded to a duller hue.

'Begging your pardon, Miss Underhay, I hope I'm not keeping you from something important.' Mrs Miller appeared somewhat overawed by Kitty's appearance in full evening dress.

'Not at all. I've finished dinner and was just checking on the staff in the ballroom. There is a singer there this evening. Is something wrong? Is Alice unwell?' Kitty was at a loss as to what could have brought her to the Dolphin unless something had happened to Alice and her mother was loathe to say anything to Mary.

'No, our Alice is perfectly all right, thank you, miss. In fact, she doesn't know as I've come to speak to you. It's a bit delicate like.' The older woman fidgeted and glanced about the deserted lobby.

Kitty's brows raised. 'Perhaps we would be better in my office.' She led the way to her office at the back of the reception desk and unlocked the door, standing back for Mrs Miller to enter ahead of her.

'Do take a seat, Mrs Miller, and tell me what has brought you here.'

Once the woman was seated, Kitty took her chair and waited to hear what she had to say.

The older woman's cheeks reddened. 'It's about our Alice, Miss Underhay. Now, please don't take anything I say amiss, I mean we're very grateful to you for all the notice you've took of her. Making her your lady's maid and all. And I know as you treat her well. But her father and I are a bit worried.'

'Worried?' Kitty was still mystified.

'I mean it couldn't be helped what went on at Enderley Hall, Miss Underhay, but then there was the business at the Pavilion theatre and now there's been a murder at the Imperial Hotel as well. People are beginning to talk and we're a respectable family.'

'Yes, of course,' Kitty soothed. She could see Mrs Miller had a point.

'Now, I knows our Alice wasn't involved in this last bit of business but she was seen having tea with a police inspector in the public rooms at the Imperial. Well, we've never been a family to be involved with the police. I bring my lot up to be law-abiding.' Mrs Miller sat more upright in her seat. 'People are saying our Alice has ideas above her station and all these murders isn't nice for a young girl to be caught up in.'

'Mrs Miller, I really am terribly sorry. It's all my fault. Alice was acting as my chaperone. I wanted to take tea but it's not nice to do so alone so I persuaded Alice to accompany me. We were representing the Dolphin and one has to be so careful, I'm sure you understand. The inspector was in the hotel as a fellow guest, not on police business, and it would have caused more tongues to wag if he had taken tea with me without a third person present. Imagine if Mrs Greville, his wife, had heard of it. She may have misunderstood entirely. When poor Councillor Everton was killed Alice was safely in our suite.' Kitty could guess who was behind Mrs Miller's anxiety.

'Well, I suppose that's all right then.' Mrs Miller still sounded doubtful.

'Alice is a very valued member of my staff and my friend. She is a very bright girl and I'm sure will go far. I do understand your concerns, Mrs Miller. I know you only want the best for your daughter, as any mother would.' Kitty paused, wondering if she'd overdone it, but Mrs Miller appeared to have softened a little.

'Sometimes, others who are not so bright, or indeed as well-brought up as Alice, may become jealous if they see her getting on in life. Alice is a credit to you, Mrs Miller.'

Alice's mother was virtually preening at Kitty's praise. 'She's a good girl. Always been very obliging and good-natured, unlike some in the family.'

Kitty bit back a smile. 'Yes, I believe I've met her cousin, Betty, on a few occasions.'

Alice's mother sniffed. 'My sister Aggie's girl. A fast article she is and so sharp she'll cut herself one of these times.'

'Well, I do hope our talk has reassured you, Mrs Miller. I would never allow Alice to be in any danger and I promise I shall be very mindful of the issues you've raised in future.' Kitty stood and Mrs Miller followed suit.

'Thank you for seeing me, Miss Underhay. You'll not say anything to our Alice, I hope. You know what girls can be like.'

Kitty showed the woman to the door. 'No, of course not. It was lovely to meet you.'

She locked her office once more and headed for the ballroom marvelling at the mischief that the jealous Betty had attempted to make. For she had no doubt that it was she who had told Alice's mother about their tea with Inspector Greville and had deliberately stirred up lurid tales about the murder itself.

Kitty woke the following morning still possessed with the same restless spirit that had troubled her the previous evening. The weather had cleared overnight into a bright, crisp November morning. She decided her best time to call upon Mrs Everton and her daughter would be during the afternoon.

How then to fill her morning? She needed to talk to Father Lamb to discover what he knew of the old water conduit passages that lay beneath Exeter's streets. However, Sunday was his busiest day so her telephone call would be better made in the week.

Her grandmother had announced that, as she was feeling much better, she was meeting with her friends and they were dining at

Mrs Craven's for lunch. Kitty considered telephoning Matt to see if he were free to accompany her to the Evertons but decided that since he hadn't offered then he must have other plans for the day. Plans that she was not party to.

The winter sun sparkling on the river made up her mind. She would wrap up and go for a walk towards the castle. The fresh air would at least clear her head and help her to walk off some of her energy.

Accordingly, she donned her winter coat, a charming dark blue hat with a cheerful red trim and a thick blue and red plaid patterned scarf and set off. The cold air stung her face, but she soon warmed up as she began the ascent around Warfleet Bay towards Dartmouth Castle.

The streets were a jumble of terraced cottages all facing toward the river. The workers' houses were set on such steep slopes, linked by narrow flights of steps from the road, that Kitty had always felt the occupants must be part goat in order to tackle the daily climb.

She paused partway to look out across the bay. Since the old works had virtually halted the area had lost its industrial heritage and was rapidly returning to its fishing roots.

'Miss Kitty!'

She turned to see who had hailed her and saw Mickey, the hotel maintenance man, and his wife, Gertie, coming towards her from the direction of the castle. Mickey had known her since she had been a small child and had first returned to live at the Dolphin. He and his wife had lost both their sons during the war.

'Good morning,' Kitty greeted them with a smile. They had both been very good to her and she had spent many happy hours traipsing around the hotel after Mickey, getting under his feet when she had been young. Now, he acted both as her maintenance man and also as security for the hotel.

'Out taking the air, miss?' he asked as he and Gertie drew near.

'It seemed such a nice dry day that I thought I should get out for a while.' It suddenly occurred to Kitty that Gertie was from

Exeter originally. She had given Matt directions to Jack Dawkins' emporium, so she may know something about the passages.

'We were just at St Petrocs,' Gertie said. She was a tiny woman, even smaller than Kitty, with a large bun of grey hair securely pinned beneath her black felt hat.

Kitty knew Mickey's family had a long connection with the church there so forbore to make a comment as she guessed their visit might well have something to do with the loss of their sons.

'I was about to turn around and head back,' Kitty said. 'It's not so bad walking in the sunshine but there is a cold wind.'

'Can we invite you to call in and have a cup of tea with us, Miss Kitty?' Mickey asked.

She knew their cottage was nearby as she had visited many times before when she was younger. 'That sounds delightful.'

Gertie's face broke into a beaming smile at her acceptance of the invitation and Kitty felt a little guilty that she hadn't visited more often in recent times.

The cottage was a small whitewashed building in a row of similar houses. The red bricks of the step were freshly scrubbed, and the window frames and door painted a bright blue. A large black and white cat was in the window washing a front paw with an air of disdain as they approached.

Mickey unlocked the front door and Kitty followed them straight into the front parlour of the house. A blaze crackled in the hearth and the room smelled of furniture polish with a hint of tobacco smoke.

'I'll go and see to the kettle. Mickey, take Miss Kitty's things,' Gertie instructed as she shooed the cat from its perch on the sill. The room was cosy after the chilly outdoor air and, after surrendering her coat, scarf and gloves to Mickey's keeping, Kitty was soon installed on a wooden framed seat beside the fire.

The small room was crammed with furniture. A dark oak what-not was piled high with china figurines of shepherds and shepherdesses and photographs in gilt frames. A large aspidistra in a blue china pot filled the one corner of the room and pristine white linen antimacassars covered the backs of the armchairs.

The cat stalked past Kitty with its tail held high and vanished in the direction of the kitchen. Gertie emerged, clad in a dark-pink floral print day dress, carrying a tea tray that Mickey took from her and set on a small occasional table.

'There now, Miss Kitty. Cup of tea?' Gertie sat opposite Kitty on the other armchair while Mickey took his place on the two-seater sofa.

'Thank you, this is very kind of you.' Kitty watched Gertie pour the tea from the brown Betty teapot into the brightly-painted teacups.

She declined the offer of sugar and helped herself to milk and settled in to enjoy her visit.

The first ten or fifteen minutes were spent in catching up on news and a shocked discussion of Councillor Everton's murder. Mickey then turned the conversation towards Father Lamb and his visit to the Dolphin.

'Are you any further forward, Miss Kitty, with learning what become of your poor mother?' Gertie asked, her brown eyes warm with concern.

'Father Lamb has been very kind and he has passed on some information from the late Mr Dawkins which might be of use. I wonder, do either of you know anything about the passages which run under the city? There was a cutting in Mr Dawkins' papers saying they were very old and quite extensive.' Kitty took a sip of her tea, which was much stronger than she was used to and she wished she had taken up the offer of sugar.

The cat reappeared and installed itself next to Gertie's feet as she considered Kitty's question.

'Yes, there is a whole load of tunnels under the streets. Some are down quite a ways. They used to carry water years ago and there was some street fountains in places. I remember my granny telling me about them. They've been redundant a good long while now though, leastways for the transporting of water.'

'But some people may have used them to transport or to store other items?' Kitty asked.

'I couldn't say for sure. Not so much the main tunnels but there is access into them from a few places around the city where folk may have added their own ways in,' Gertie said.

Kitty's heart rate quickened. 'Through cellars, perhaps?'

Gertie exchanged a glance with her husband. 'Perhaps. It was a good way to get around and not be seen or to hide that which folk didn't want finding.'

Kitty set down her cup and saucer. 'I see. Like a keg of brandy or some suchlike?'

Mickey grinned at her. 'I'd say as that might be right, Miss Kitty.'

'There is talk of guided tours being held of some of the older passages near the cathedral for archaeological students and members of the public,' Kitty said.

Gertie laughed. 'They might have a shock if they're planning on walking through them parts. It's said they're haunted by the ghost of a monk. Don't want to see 'ee gliding towards them by the light of a candle.'

CHAPTER NINE

Matt had seen the unspoken questions in Kitty's eyes when he had left her the previous day. He was fairly certain they were reflected in his own conscience. He knew she must be wondering why he hadn't offered to accompany her to Councillor Everton's house. He had his own reasons why he couldn't, not today.

He had set off early to make the long ride back towards London. By the time he reached his destination, even with a stop midway for a welcome mug of tea at a roadside café, his fingers were frozen around the handles despite his thick leather gauntlets.

The weather in Devon had been bright and fresh but the nearer he had drawn to the capital the murkier it had become. The sun had vanished behind a growing blanket of thick grey cloud and he could almost taste soot on his tongue.

He steered the Sunbeam to a halt at the kerb and turned off the engine. The street was pleasant enough with neat respectable pairs of red-brick villas on the one side with names like Desiree and Mon Repos.

Matt dismounted with a groan and stretched his back. The old war wounds in his shoulder ached from where he had been crouched forward as he drove. His gait was stiff as he walked around his motorbike stretching his legs and trying to regain the feeling in his feet.

At the rear of his bike, carefully packaged at the back of the saddle, was a small parcel. Matt untied the string holding it in place and mentally braced himself for the task ahead. He had not visited this place many times. For a long while he had been unable to visit at all, but today was an important day and he hoped by visiting he might even find answers to some of the questions that were besetting him.

A low red-brick wall surrounded the churchyard while the church itself hunkered down beneath its black slate roof as if trying to bury itself in the green grass of the graveyard. The wrought-iron gate at the entrance squeaked in protest as Matt lifted the latch and pushed it open. Yew trees stood either side of the path, silent, dark sentinels as Matt made his way along the narrow path between the gravestones.

The path led away from the older part of the churchyard where the grey of the stones had been weathered and softened with yellow lichen to the new part further away from the church.

Matt swallowed as he took the turn along the second row of graves, having a care to walk softly on the path along the turf. In the distance he could hear the odd rumble of a car or clopping of hooves.

The place he sought was at the end of the row, where the trees bowed their branches, now almost bare of leaves, dripping silent rain-wet tears over the stones. He found the stone he was looking for. Edith and Betty, together forever under the marble slab that marked their final resting place.

He sucked in a breath and dropped onto one knee, tugging off his motorbike gauntlets so he could unfasten the parcel he had carried so carefully along the path. Two white roses, one full blown, the other in bud.

He placed them on top of the slab. 'Happy birthday, Edith. I didn't forget.'

Straightening up, he folded the packaging and stowed it inside his leather greatcoat before replacing his gloves.

'You would like her; I know you would. I've kept my word, Edie, but I have to tell Kitty about us, she has to know the truth. It's time I moved on, my love.'

He waited for a moment, even though he didn't expect a reply, before turning away ready to face the long ride back to Devon.

Kitty was in a better frame of mind when she returned to the Dolphin after visiting Mickey and Gertie. She had a light lunch in the main dining room and checked up on all her staff before returning to her room to change ready for her visit to the Evertons.

Mr Potter had assured her he knew Councillor Everton's address as he had taken him there once or twice in the past.

'A big square white villa, Miss Kitty, near Torre Station, called One Pine on account of there being a dratted big pine tree at the bottom of the drive.'

The bright clear sky of the morning had started to cloud over after lunch and by the time they had crossed the river and were heading for Torquay it seemed that the weather was about to turn.

'Would you like me to collect you later, Miss Kitty?' Mr Potter held open the rear door of the car for her to get out.

'I'm not certain how long I shall be. I'll probably take the train back, thank you.' She gave him his usual generous tip and started up the sloping gravel driveway to the house. The grounds looked, as many gardens did in November, a little unkempt. Leaves were heaped under a rather scruffy looking shrubbery and the exterior of the villa looked as if a lick of paint was in order.

The black paint on the front door was peeling and the step looked as if the maid had not done her job. Kitty put her gloved hand to the black cast iron bell pull and gave it a tug. An unmelodic clanging sounded within the recesses of the house.

She was about to try it again when the door was finally opened by a slightly slovenly looking girl in an untidy grey uniform.

'Is Mrs Everton or Miss Everton at home? Kitty Underhay.' She gave the girl one of her cards.

'Please to come inside and wait, miss. I'll see if Missus is receiving.' The girl took the card and disappeared, leaving Kitty to find her own way into what could have been a pleasant hall.

She heard the faint murmur of voices in the distance. The parquet floor could have done with a polish and the vase of flowers on the hallstand needed the water changing. The air smelt of stale cooking and damp.

The maid returned and relieved her of her outdoor clothing. 'If you'll follow me, miss.'

Kitty duly did as instructed and followed the girl into a large drawing room at the rear of the house. A small fire burned in the marble hearth and the air in the room was chilly. Kitty began to regret not retaining her coat. The room looked neglected, a thin layer of dust covered the tabletops and magazines were scattered on the floor. Marigold was seated on a dark green leather button-backed sofa. Her eyes were red-rimmed, and she looked as if she hadn't brushed her hair.

'Miss Underhay, it's very good of you to call.' Marigold sat up a little straighter. 'Bennett, please bring some tea.'

The maid sighed and left as if making tea for her mistress was too onerous a task.

Kitty took a seat opposite Marigold. 'I felt obliged to come and see if you and Daphne are all right. It was such a terrible thing to happen.' She hoped it didn't sound too thin an excuse for her to call.

Marigold produced a lace-edged handkerchief from the pocket of her black mourning dress and dabbed at her nose. 'Oh, Miss Underhay, you have no idea. It's been awful, simply awful. The police have been all over the house, in every nook and cranny. Where were the medicines kept? All of that kind of thing. I mean they were always in a box in the dining room, anyone could see them. The servants wanted to give notice as they didn't wish to remain in a household where the police were involved. I only have

Cook and Bennett left, and I've had to promise them higher wages to get them to stay.'

Kitty couldn't help feeling sorry for the woman. 'But at least you have Daphne, and your nephew, Thomas, with you.'

Her comment, intended to reassure, started another torrent of complaint. She had thought Marigold might not wish to talk to her, but it seemed the woman was glad to secure a listening ear.

'Daphne is out flying her kite with her young man. Never a thought for me and what I'm going through. She soon got over the shock of Harold dying the way he did. He was her stepfather, you know. We married when she was only a baby after my first husband passed away, and Harold adopted her as his own.'

This was news to Kitty and she wondered if this information was widely known. 'Oh, my dear, I'm so sorry. I hadn't realised you had been widowed before.'

Marigold blew her nose. 'Stephen, my first husband drowned in a boating accident. We were so young; it was a terrible time. Harold was like a knight in shining armour. I was alone with Daphne, and Stephen, poor soul, had left us in something of a financial fix. Harold took care of everything. He had his faults, but one thing about Harold, if he gave his word, he kept to it.'

'How fortunate you were to meet him at such a terrible time,' Kitty said. She wondered where and when exactly the accident had occurred.

'Oh yes, Gladys Silitoe introduced us. She was Gladys Day then, of course. Poor Harold.'

Bennett reappeared with a tea tray and set it down on the coffee table before walking back out without giving her mistress the opportunity to ask her to do anything more.

'Shall I pour?' Kitty offered, picking up the small china teapot.

'Thank you, Miss Underhay. Bennett is such a disobliging creature and bone idle but better than nothing at the moment.' Marigold sniffed.

'It can be so difficult with staff.' Kitty passed one of the old-fashioned delicate floral cups to Marigold.

'Harold insisted we ran the house with minimal staff. He felt that Daphne and I should play our part and, of course, he was very careful with money.' She took a sip from her cup.

Kitty stayed silent for a moment. She imagined that to mean that Harold had not been very generous with the staff wages, so it was no wonder they had little loyalty. 'I didn't realise that Daphne was courting,' she said.

Marigold's face brightened. 'Oh yes, a young man working at a garage near Miss Veronique. Harold disapproved. He hoped for someone with better prospects. Now, of course, there is nothing to stop her, she is of age.'

'He and Daphne must be serious then?' Kitty hoped she hadn't pushed her questioning too far, but Marigold seemed to be finding it a release to talk.

'Yes, she speaks of becoming engaged to Benjamin, and soon. Harold has left her a small legacy in his will and one to Thomas. Harold and I were never blessed with children together and he always took a keen interest in Thomas. I think he would have liked a son, but it wasn't to be. Although they hadn't been getting along very well together these last few weeks, petty disagreements. Harold would argue with his own shadow. The house is mine and the rest of the estate, so at least I have no worries there.'

'That must be a great relief,' Kitty agreed.

'Ivor Silitoe was Harold's solicitor, you know. The dear man called to put my mind at ease over the financial side of things.'

'That was very kind of him,' Kitty said and took another sip of her tea. Not that she really wanted a drink of tea. She was feeling rather awash with it today, but it seemed to be lubricating Marigold's tongue.

'What do you think could have happened to Harold? I know what people must be thinking. The whispering behind my back and the sly glances.' Marigold had set down her cup and was twisting her handkerchief between her fingers. 'But I can't help thinking that the pharmacist must have made some kind of error or that the police must be mistaken.'

'It was all so sudden and so shocking,' Kitty said. 'Mr Everton had not been unwell or anxious of late?' she asked.

Marigold frowned. 'He did seem to have something on his mind. He was very short with Thomas. They had a few arguments, to do with work, I believe. Then, of course, he was displeased with Daphne. He didn't really like her working for Miss Veronique. He tried to get her dismissed, but Miss Veronique agreed to pay Daphne's wages to Harold to invest on her behalf, so he permitted her to keep working.'

Kitty blinked, shocked that such an arrangement could have been made or have been satisfactory given that Daphne was of age and Mr Everton was it seemed her stepfather.

'Did Daphne not mind this?' She could not envisage that any modern, independent young lady would like such an arrangement, even though she knew it was common for most people living at home to have to turn up board money. No wonder Daphne had seemed depressed when she had been refused a new dress for the hoteliers' ball.

'Well, it would give her some security for the future Harold said. A little nest egg for when she married or turned thirty.' Marigold appeared to think the arrangement perfectly normal.

In the distance Kitty thought she heard the front door slam. A moment later the door to the drawing room opened and Daphne appeared. Dressed in a pale pink knitted twinset and tweed skirt with her hair styled and some cosmetics she looked a very different girl from the pale and insipid creature Kitty had first encountered.

'Oh, Miss Underhay, I hadn't realised you were visiting.' She stopped short at the sight of Kitty.

'I was in Torquay and called to see if you and your mother were all right after what happened on Friday evening,' Kitty said. 'It was so dreadful, and you were terribly distressed.' She did her best to appear sympathetic and concerned.

Daphne gave her a tight smile. 'It was awful, just awful. I think it was the shock more than anything and then the police. It seems so unreal. Poison, who would want to poison Father?' She shuddered.

'I can imagine how you feel, it does seem extraordinary,' Kitty said sympathetically. 'Your mother was saying how the police had disturbed the household.'

Daphne perched herself on the arm of the sofa. 'It was quite dreadful. They poked about everywhere, even in the old shed where the gardener keeps his tools. They took something away from there. God knows what. I mean apart from old Hodgetts no one ever goes anywhere near the place. Too many spiders, ugh.'

Kitty gave a mock shudder. 'I can imagine. Your mother was saying that at least there was some good news. You are to be married I understand?' She turned a bright, innocent face to Daphne.

The girl coloured, her gaze flickering to her mother. 'Yes, Benjamin and I hope to be married before Christmas. Well, as soon as decently possible, really. I know it will seem sudden, so soon after Father's death but, well, life goes on, doesn't it? And I'm not exactly young.' Her voice held a note of defiance.

'Happiness should be taken where we can get it. Something so awful as your poor father's death throws things into perspective, doesn't it?' Kitty remarked in an agreeable tone.

The girl's thin shoulders relaxed. 'Thank you, Miss Underhay. By the way, Mother, I shan't be here for dinner. Benjamin is taking me to meet his people.'

Marigold immediately looked deflated. 'Oh, but my dear, Cook will be most put out and you know the difficulty I'm having with her and Bennett.'

Daphne shrugged and got to her feet. 'I don't know why you are bothered about them, Mother. Let them go. Bennett is slovenly and as for Cook, half the things she produces are not even edible.'

Colour mounted in ugly crimson patches on Marigold's cheeks.

'Anyway, it was nice to see you again, Miss Underhay. I expect you'll be at the inquest later this week? Inspector Greville said the coroner would contact everyone who was at the table.' Daphne looked at Kitty.

'Then I expect I shall receive a letter.' She had forgotten that she might be required at the inquest. Her head was buzzing with all the information Daphne and Marigold had provided.

She turned to Marigold. 'I have probably been here much too long disturbing you, Mrs Everton. My grandmother will wonder where I've got to. Thank you so much for the tea and I do hope everything is resolved soon for you both.'

Daphne went to find Bennett to get Kitty's things and a few minutes later Kitty escaped into the now damp November air.

CHAPTER TEN

Kitty shivered and adjusted her scarf a little more closely around her throat as she set off down the drive towards the road. The weather had continued to close in, and it had begun to turn foggy. Her mind ran quickly over all the information she had unearthed. It had certainly been worthwhile and although Daphne had seemed surprised at her visit, Mrs Everton had appeared unsuspicious.

She reached the bottom of the driveway and immediately regretted that she hadn't asked Mr Potter to call back for her. What had seemed like a good idea to walk to the station and take the train to Kingswear now seemed ill-conceived.

As she started to walk at a brisk pace along the footpath the toot of a car horn caught her attention. She halted as a dark green Alvis car pulled to a stop beside her.

'Miss Underhay, may I give you a lift somewhere?' Thomas King leaned across from the driver's seat and smiled at her. His dark good looks enhanced by his motoring flat cap and cream silk muffler.

'Mr King, how very kind.' Kitty opened the door and jumped into the car beside him. 'I'm heading back to Dartmouth. Would you be able to take me to Kingswear?'

'Your wish is my command.' He grinned at her and, putting the car into gear, he pulled away.

'This is a very splendid car.' Kitty looked admiringly about her and wondered to herself how a young man working as his uncle's clerk could afford such a nice vehicle. If Mr Everton had paid his servants badly, she doubted he would be much more generous towards his office staff even if they were family.

'Thank you. When my mother passed away I received a small inheritance. I've always enjoyed motor vehicles.'

Kitty blushed and hoped he hadn't read her mind. 'I just paid a call to your aunt and cousin. I was concerned that they must still be very distressed after the events of Friday night.' She peeped at him as he confidently negotiated the car past the Grand Hotel and up the hill.

'It's a ghastly business. The police are playing their cards very close to their chests. I expect we're all under suspicion. Aunt Marigold especially, although she wouldn't harm a fly and she seems quite devastated by old Uncle Harold's demise. As for Daphne, well she's all loved-up with her fellow now she's over the initial shock of it all.' A frown furrowed Thomas' brow slightly marring his handsome features.

'Were you and your uncle close? You worked for him, you said?' Kitty asked in a nonchalant tone.

Thomas gave a slight shrug as he started the descent towards Kingswear. The mist was closing in quickly now around the car and the headlamps cut a yellowy-white pathway through the mist. 'I don't know if close is the right word. We got along all right. Uncle Harold was not the easiest of men to work for as you probably guessed. He had an unfortunate knack of annoying people. Like that chap Hendricks. He'd blocked his plans several times at the planning committee and as you saw was always dashed rude to the man. Uncle Harold had cut him short a few times I think when Hendricks had telephoned about his application.'

Another car swept around the corner a little too closely to them for comfort to Kitty's way of thinking and she wished Thomas would slow his speed a little. He had rather too much in common with Doctor Carter in his love of speed.

'I can imagine there were times when you must have found it difficult.' She did her best to appear innocently sympathetic when Thomas gave her a sharp glance.

He sighed. 'We would have words from time to time, but Uncle was good to me in his own way. He offered me a home and employment when Mother died.'

Kitty digested this information. 'Your aunt said he'd left a bequest for you too in his will.'

Thomas laughed. 'Dear Aunt Marigold, trust her to have checked up on the will. Yes, I believe he may have done. Mr Silitoe said he would give a formal reading of the will after the funeral, but Uncle did once say he intended leaving me five thousand pounds. I think Daphne gets a similar amount and Aunt Marigold gets the rest.'

Kitty's eyebrows raised. 'That is most generous.' It certainly provided all the members of the Everton household with a motive.

The car headlights were barely penetrating the mist now as they passed the start of the creek and headed towards the station and the ferry in Kingswear. Thomas pulled the car to a stop near the hotel at the waters margin.

'Thank you so much for bringing me back. I really am most grateful.' She placed her hand on the car door ready to take her leave.

'Not at all, Miss Underhay. The pleasure is all mine. I wonder if you would like to have tea with me sometime soon, when things are a bit more sorted?' His dark blue eyes held a serious intent.

Kitty was momentarily flustered. 'I, um, that would be nice, thank you.' She scrambled out of the car mentally cursing herself. Why had she agreed to have tea with Thomas? She had no intention of doing so, for all she knew he could be Harold Everton's murderer.

Matt almost didn't bother to answer the knock at his front door. It was late in the afternoon and he was tired from his long ride. The hot bath he'd taken on his return had warmed him a little and the aspirin he'd swallowed had begun to dull the ache in his shoulder.

It was with some reluctance then that he prised himself out of his comfortable Modernist black leather and chrome armchair and went to answer the door. The last time he had answered a summons at an unusual hour had led to his detention in a police cell with a murder charge hanging over his head. It was a strong sense of déjà vu when he discovered that Inspector Greville was on his doorstep.

'Inspector Greville, this is an unexpected pleasure on a Sunday afternoon. No problems I hope?' Anxiety flared for an instant at the sight of the police inspector, but he was relieved to see he appeared to be alone without any accompanying constables.

'No, Captain Bryant, this is more in the nature of a social call. I hope that is all right with you?' Greville asked.

Matt recovered his manners. 'Certainly, a pleasure to see you, come inside. The fog has come down and it's quite cold out there.' He stood aside to allow the inspector entry to the small hallway. His housekeeper would no doubt frown in the morning at the boot prints all over the red tiled floor.

After taking the policeman's coat and hat, stowing them on the bentwood coat stand at the foot of the stairwell, he led him through to the sitting room where a fire burned cosily in the hearth of the square stone fireplace and the wireless played softly in the background.

Inspector Greville stood before the fire, warming his hands appreciatively against the heat. 'I half expected to find your lady friend, Miss Underhay, here,' he remarked. 'I saw her less than an hour ago in Torquay accepting a lift from Thomas King. I recognised his green Alvis.'

'Kitty said she intended to pay a condolence visit to the Everton house. She was concerned about Mrs Everton and Daphne. Whisky, Inspector?' He offered the policeman a crystal balloon goblet.

'Thank you, Captain Bryant, that is most civil of you.'

Matt poured the whisky from the cut-glass decanter into a couple of glasses and passed one to the inspector who had now taken an armchair opposite his own seat. He wasn't sure how he felt about hearing that Kitty had been seen in company with Thomas King.

'What can I do for you, Inspector?' Matt was quite certain that the visit was not entirely social.

Inspector Greville swirled the amber liquid in his glass around slowly, the light from the fire and the small side table lamps on either side of the fireplace making the cuts in the crystal of the glass glitter. 'Councillor Everton was poisoned. Potassium cyanide as we thought, administered in one of those sachets from his medicine box. Only one of the sachets, the one he opened, contained the poison, so it would seem ill luck on Mr Everton's part that the evening he selected that particular sachet was the one where he was out in company with a ballroom full of people.'

'I take it, sir, that you have interviewed the dispensing pharmacist?' Matt asked.

Greville nodded, his moustache drooping raggedly in the soft light. 'Yes, there is no error on his part. The medication is checked by himself and an assistant during the dispensing. If the fault had been with the chemist then all the sachets would have been contaminated.'

Matt sipped his whisky appreciating the warming glow in his chest. The ride had taken more out of him than he had thought, and the inspector was presenting him with quite a puzzle. 'Who had access to Mr Everton's medication?' he asked.

The inspector sighed. 'Anyone and everyone it seems. Mrs Everton said the box containing the sachets was out on the side table in the dining room of the house and she would simply pop it into her handbag whenever they dined out.'

'Forgive me, Inspector, but did the search of the house discover any potassium cyanide?' Matt could see the inspector's problem. It would not be easy to make a case against a particular individual without more evidence.

'There was some in the gardener's shed.' The inspector took another sip of his drink. 'The servants are all fairly new at the house. Mr Everton was not a generous employer and staff moved on very quickly.'

Matt could see where this was heading. 'So, it is unlikely that any of them would have had a motive for murdering their employer?'

'Exactly.'

'Who benefitted from his death?' Matt asked. Money was often a motive for most crimes. The councillor had been renowned for his caution with fiscal matters and he wouldn't be at all surprised if there was a good sum in his bank account.

Inspector Greville groaned. 'All of them. Mrs Everton gets the house and a sizeable bank balance. Mr King gets five thousand pounds and Miss Everton seven thousand pounds. His friend, Mr Silitoe, also receives a thousand pounds.'

'So, how do you feel I can be of assistance to you?' Matt cut to the chase. Interesting as this information was, it didn't answer why the inspector was at his house.

'You mentioned in your interview at the hotel that Councillor Everton had indicated that he wished to consult you about something. You have had no further ideas what this could have been about?'

Matt shook his head. 'None. I know it wasn't a marital problem but beyond that I haven't anything certain. I planned to visit the council offices tomorrow to see what I could learn there.'

'You believe it may be a business matter?'

'It seems likely to me, which could imply motive for both Mr Silitoe and Mr King. Mr Silitoe had access to the house too and was involved with Mr Everton as both a friend and as a business colleague. There was a heated discussion during dinner before Mr Everton died. He must be considered a possible suspect,' Matt said thoughtfully.

'Our minds are working along the same lines. I would, of course, be interested in any information that Miss Underhay has discovered. She does seem to have a knack for nosing out secrets.' The inspector finished his drink.

'I will pass that on to her, although I am sure she will call you with anything she learns.' Matt was quite certain that Kitty had been ferreting around during her visit to the Everton household. He was a little disappointed that she hadn't telephoned him already to tell him of her discoveries. Unless, of course, she was too preoccupied entertaining Thomas King. The idea annoyed him deeply and not just because the man was the suspect in a murder investigation.

'Well, thank you, Captain Bryant. Please pass on my regards to Miss Underhay.' The inspector rose somewhat reluctantly to his feet, placing his empty whisky glass down on the table. 'I had better be off. I have to collect Mrs Greville from her mother's and the weather is not pleasant.'

Matt showed the inspector back into the hall and passed him his outdoor clothing.

'Good evening and thank you for the drink.' Greville tipped the brim of his hat slightly and departed into the cold and misty evening. Matt shivered as the distant eerie wail of the foghorn sounded in the distance. It was not a night to be abroad.

He returned to the cosy comfort of his lounge and refilled his whisky glass. He toyed with the idea of telephoning Kitty. He told himself it was because he wanted to discover what she had learned at the Everton house. In his heart, however, he knew it was because the inspector had remarked upon her being seen in company with Thomas King.

*

Kitty woke the following morning and decided that if Matt didn't telephone her or call to see her then she would have to bite the bullet and make the first move. She wanted to discuss all the information she had unearthed during her visit to One Pine, but decided that if she waited then he could share whatever he learned during his visit to the council offices.

In the meantime, she had other fish to fry. She rose early and had a couple of hours catching up with the hotel paperwork before taking breakfast with her grandmother. That should give her some time later on to place a telephone call to Father Lamb.

'You seem very perky this morning, Kitty dear.' Grams peered at her across the breakfast table. The older woman's health appeared back to normal and she was dressed in her usual smart twinset with her pearls at her throat.

'Oh, just getting ahead with my work.' Kitty smiled at her and added more jam to her toast.

'Hmm, nothing to do with a young man in a smart car dropping you off at Kingswear yesterday teatime?' Her grandmother arched an enquiring eyebrow.

Kitty blushed and laughed. 'Grams! Do you have spies watching my every move?'

Her grandmother had the grace to look a little abashed. 'You know you cannot do anything around here without the world knowing your business. You were seen, my dear, by one of the staff and now their tongues are wagging at both ends spreading gossip.'

Kitty chewed and swallowed her last morsel of toast. 'Well it was Thomas King, Councillor Everton's nephew. The weather was dreadful, as you know, so he was merely giving me a lift back after my visit to his aunt and cousin. Nothing more.'

'My dear, it's not me that you need to assure. I think there is another gentleman who might wish to hear from you.'

Kitty's face burned fiery red. 'Grams! I am an independent modern woman. I shouldn't have to explain myself to anyone, and especially not Matthew Bryant.' She took her napkin from her lap and placed it down on the table with some emphasis.

'Of course not, darling.'

Kitty saw a smug smile hovering at the corners of her grandmother's lips and, shaking her head, she left her grandmother to finish her breakfast.

Why did everyone persist in assuming that she and Matt were together? As if she were some sort of possession, belonging to him? Her heels clicked angrily on the marble of the lobby floor and she scowled at poor Mary when the girl offered her the post.

She let herself into her office and sat down in her chair. She would not telephone Matt. If he wanted to know what she had learned and why she had been in Thomas King's car then he could come and ask her. She wasn't going to explain herself to him or anybody else for that matter.

Kitty's temper cooled quite quickly, and she had the grace to feel a little ashamed of her hot-headedness. After apologising to her receptionist, she completed the remainder of her paperwork before placing her call to Father Lamb.

'Miss Underhay, how delightful to hear from you. How are you and your grandmother faring?' The elderly priest's voice was warm and soothing.

'We're both well, thank you, Father.' She asked after his own health and they passed a few moments exchanging pleasantries about their health and the inclement weather.

'I've been looking at the contents of Jack Dawkins' box and there was a recent newspaper cutting that seemed to have some special significance. It was to do with the old water passages that run under the streets in the city. Do you know anything about them, Father?'

There was a moment's pause and Kitty could imagine the priest thinking about her question.

'I have a young Anglican friend, a member of the lay staff at the cathedral, who is very interested in the medieval history of the city and how it relates to the cathedral. He is one of the party advising the group who wish to reopen them to scholars and other interested people. Would it help you if I ask him if he would be able to meet you?'

Kitty's spirits rose. 'Oh, that would be super. I'm not certain how the passages might relate to my mother's disappearance, but Jack has indicated there might be a connection.'

'I shall telephone him after lunch and let you know his response. Is any day a good day for you, my dear?'

Kitty told the priest when she could be free and hoped Mr Everton's inquest didn't fall at an inconvenient time. She ended the call and sat back in her chair suddenly feeling hopeful that she might find out a little more about the mystery of what had happened to her mother all those years ago.

CHAPTER ELEVEN

The town hall in Torquay was an imposing building. Built in the renaissance style out of local stone with a 200-hundred-foot-high clock tower it dominated the landscape and housed a large function room, the council chambers and various offices occupied by the councillors and their staff.

Matt had telephoned ahead, now that he had secured Inspector Greville's blessing to poke around, and had arranged to meet a Mr Schofield, who he was assured had known Councillor Everton well and would be happy to assist him.

Mr Schofield was waiting to meet him inside the large reception area, which was filled with marble statuary and portraits of the great and good of Torquay.

'Captain Bryant? Pleased to meet you, shall we adjourn to Councillor Everton's office?' Mr Schofield produced a key from the bunch hanging from his waist. He was a small, sprightly man in about his early sixties.

He moved quickly with a kind of scuttling gait that reminded Matt of a clockwork mouse. He led the way along a wide wood panelled corridor on the ground floor. They passed numerous closed doors and more portraits and statuary before the man halted at a particular door.

'Here we are, sir. The police have already been in and looked through everything. The inspector said as it was all right for you to examine the place. Mr Everton spoke highly of you after meeting you at the awards the other week.' Mr Schofield stood to one side to allow Matt to enter.

'That was most kind of him. Thank you.' Matt looked about him, curious to see what the office might reveal about Harold Everton's personality.

The room was a comfortable size, somewhat bigger than his own office in town and much grander than Kitty's small back office. A large window with square panes gave a view of the street and flooded the office with light even on a dull, wintry day such as this one. The room was handsomely furnished with an imposing polished wood desk, a bureau, filing cabinet and wine-red leather covered chairs. A portrait hung on the wood panelled wall and caught Matt's attention.

'Councillor Everton's father, sir, painted when he was deputy mayor,' Mr Schofield offered, noting Matt's interest.

A half-open door was set in the wall at the side of the desk revealing another, much smaller office filled with cabinets and furnished in a simpler style with a smaller, plainer desk.

'That's Mr King's office. Mr Everton's nephew. He's not here today,' Mr Schofield said.

'You knew Mr Everton well, I understand?' Matt looked at the small pile of papers in the metal tray on top of the late councillor's desk.

'Since he was a young man. He used to visit his father and help him, much like Mr King. His father was a lovely man. Very jolly and generous to a fault.' Mr Schofield sighed; his eyes misty as if lost in the past.

'And Mr Everton, what was he like?' Matt asked.

The older man frowned and scratched the side of his nose in a thoughtful fashion. 'He wasn't the easiest of men. Very to the point, he was, but honest to the core and a man of principle. If he said he were doing something, then that's what he did come hell or high water.'

Matt moved into Thomas' office. 'Did he and his nephew get on well together?' He leafed through some of the documents stacked in the trays on the desk.

'Pretty well, most of the time, sir.'

Matt glanced up. 'And of late?'

Mr Schofield's brow furrowed. 'There had been a few words, but it was strange, sir, there had been a kind of atmosphere recently. Mr Everton changed his habits.'

'Oh?' Matt waited for the man to explain.

'Well, young Thomas would usually come in some half an hour before Mr Everton. He'd pull up in that flashy green car of his, then he'd fetch the post from the pigeonhole and go and open it ready for when Mr Everton would arrive.'

'And this changed?' Matt asked.

'Last few weeks, Mr Everton insisted on fetching the post himself and he would do the opening and pass it to young Thomas.' Mr Schofield shrugged as if unable to explain any further.

'Did Mr King object to this change?' It struck Matt as curious. Had Everton been expecting a letter that he didn't want his nephew to see? Or was there something else? Perhaps he suspected Thomas of not giving him all the post, hiding something perhaps?

'He wasn't none too happy. I heard them rowing. My office is just the other side there. I do work for a lot of the committees. I heard Mr King mention something about trust and then he banged the door and went a storming off. His face was still as red as a turkey cock when he passed by my window a minute later and roared off in his car.'

Matt noticed the paperwork at the top of the pile was from Mr Hendricks. 'Did Mr Everton mention anything to you about why he had changed his routine?'

Mr Schofield shook his head. 'Not directly. I met him the one morning and said to him, "You're here early, sir?" and he said he had some things he had to attend to. He said he wanted to go over some papers.'

Matt sighed. 'You've no idea which papers he was referring to, I suppose?' He couldn't shake the niggling feeling that this had something to do with the matter Everton had wished to discuss.

'Planning applications, sir. He asked for the old files going back over the last few months. He mentioned there were aspects of the applications that he wished to check.' Mr Schofield gave another shrug. 'They had all gone through the committee and had legal advice from Mr Silitoe.'

'Did Mr Silitoe visit Mr Everton in his office often?' Matt was curious. Why did Everton want to revisit old applications?

'Only to advise on any legal matters ahead of the committee meetings. There had been a lot of land grabbing you see, sir, people buying up old properties from landlords and then knocking down the workers' places to put up holiday villas and hotels and the like, especially if there was a sea view or access to a beach. It was all willy-nilly and getting out of hand so they had to control it a bit or there would have been all sorts of eyesores put up.' Mr Schofield tutted in disapproval.

Matt sat down on Thomas King's chair and swivelled a little back and forth as he thought over Mr Schofield's information. 'So Councillor Everton chaired the committee and Mr Silitoe provided legal advice. Who else is on the committee to hear the plans?'

'Councillor Wainwright, the lady councillor, she's more interested in children's matters and the libraries, and Councillor Perkins, he would agree with anything so long as the meeting finished in time for him to get to the nearest public house.' Mr Schofield gave a disparaging sniff.

'I see.' Matt was beginning to see much more clearly. It sounded as if Councillor Everton and Mr Silitoe would have been responsible for steering most of the committee's decisions with information provided by Thomas King via the applications.

Mr Schofield glanced at his wristwatch and Matt realised the man must be anxious to be back about his business.

'I'm sorry, Mr Schofield, I really do appreciate your help. Mr Everton had indicated that he wished to consult me about something just before he died, and I wondered if it could have been about some business matter.'

The older man scratched his head. 'I don't know, sir. I can't think of anything other than what I've told you. Mr Everton wasn't the kind of man that made confidences. Everything was pretty much black and white with him.'

Matt sighed and took a last glance around the offices before getting to his feet. 'One last thing, Mr Schofield, forgive me, but I'm unfamiliar with planning laws and by-laws, is there a fee payable in these matters?'

The older man's shoulders stiffened, and Matt guessed he had touched on something. 'There is the standard fee, payable to the council. They check for working and erosion risks and suchlike. The plans are checked by the architect's office and the intentions published in the newspaper, especially if it is a big scheme or one put forward by the council itself. No other money is exchanged. Councillor Everton was scrupulously honest. You can ask anyone.'

Matt was quick to mollify the man's feelings. 'Forgive me, I wasn't insinuating anything. I really wasn't certain how the procedures worked. I, and I suspect the police too, will consider if someone might hold a grudge against Councillor Everton, if for instance their applications were refused. They might become desperate, especially if they were unable to sway the councillor.'

He could see Mr Schofield turning this possibility over in his mind. 'There were a few schemes that got denied. The Conway Country House Hotel one got knocked back a few times. Then some got through that were a bit surprising over Babbacombe and St Mary Church way.'

'Well, thank you very much, Mr Schofield, you have been most helpful.' Matt had a lot to think about. It would be interesting to compare notes with Kitty before handing over their information to Inspector Greville.

'My pleasure, Captain Bryant, sir. I hope they catch whoever did it. Councillor Everton could be a difficult man, but he didn't deserve that.' Mr Schofield followed him out of the office, turning to lock the door once more when they were in the corridor.

Matt made his way out of the building after bidding farewell to the elderly clerk. He turned his collar up against the cold and pulled on his thick cloth motorist's cap before sitting astride the Sunbeam. He took a quick look at the time on the town hall clock whilst pulling on his gauntlets.

It was almost twelve. He wondered if Kitty would be free for lunch.

Kitty was in reception when she heard the familiar rumble of a motorcycle outside the Dolphin. Her pulse quickened, but she forced herself to concentrate as she finished going over the forth-coming bookings with Mary.

Sure enough a few moments later the door to the hotel reception area opened and Matt's tall, lean figure appeared clad in his leather greatcoat and motorcycling gear. A swirl of cold air rushed inside with his entrance making Mary shiver as Kitty closed the ledger.

'Good afternoon, ladies.' He leaned both arms on the reception desk and winked at Mary making her giggle.

Kitty frowned. 'Good afternoon. Please don't lean all over the desk, you make the place look untidy.' She had fully intended to be cross with him for not contacting her.

He straightened up and grinned at Mary, who had to turn away to hide her own smile. Matt's smile widened. 'Yes, Miss Underhay. Are you free for lunch at all today?'

'You seem very pleased with yourself,' Kitty remarked.

'I have information that you may care to hear. I can be persuaded to part with it if you'd like to brave the cold and venture to Bayards Cove tea room?' He gave her his most beguiling look and Kitty's resolve to be stern crumbled. She had toyed briefly with the idea of keeping him waiting but her curiosity to learn what he had discovered had got the better of her.

'I'll get my things, but this had better be good,' she warned as she ventured back inside her office reappearing with her coat, hat, gloves, scarf and bag. 'Mary, I shall be gone for about an hour if Mrs Treadwell wishes to know where I am.'

'Very well, Miss Kitty.' Mary assumed her usual professional demeanour.

Matt assisted her on with her coat as she issued more instructions to Mary about the rota and expected bookings. Finally, Kitty adjusted her hat and pulled on her gloves.

'Very well, let's go. I can't be away for too long. I have a lot to do today.' She gave Matt a severe look. She was still a trifle annoyed that he had disappeared for the whole of the previous day without a word and then had popped up expecting her to drop everything in order to find out what he'd uncovered. She was even more annoyed with herself that she was going along with his plan.

CHAPTER TWELVE

She set a brisk pace as they tramped along towards Bayards Cove and the small, cosy tea room situated in one of the whitewashed cottages. The cold air stung her face and the grey clouds over the river looked pregnant with snow or sleet.

Matt, instead of his usual long, loping strides overtaking her, dawdled along behind her as if her annoyance amused him in some way. By the time they reached the door to the tea rooms Kitty was feeling distinctly put out.

'After you, Miss Underhay.' Matt put his hand to the tea room door, his face creasing in a slight grimace at the movement.

Kitty's mild irritation with him vanished as she caught a glimpse of his expression. 'Matt, are you all right? Is the cold aggravating your shoulder?'

'It's quite all right, Kitty, please don't fuss, old girl.' He followed her inside the welcoming warmth of the tea room.

The tea room was popular in summer with walkers and holidaymakers, but at this time of year it attracted an older clientele who appreciated the log fire in the wide brick hearth and the small highly-polished brass jugs that adorned the tables with the dried flower arrangements.

The café was quiet as the cold weather and time of year seemed to have deterred many customers from making the expedition for lunch. Kitty, however, recognised two of the elderly ladies taking luncheon in the window seats as friends of her grandmother.

She forced herself to smile and acknowledge them, groaning inwardly at the knowledge that she was about to become the subject of further gossip.

'Friends of yours?' Matt asked once they had hung their outdoor clothes on a coat hook and had been seated at one of the small dark oak tables.

'Two of the "gals" in Grams inner circle of friends,' Kitty explained as she opened her menu.

Matt glanced across the room to the two well-dressed ladies who were busy talking with their heads close together. He flashed them a smile when they looked his way and they quickly resumed their conversation.

'Now what's left of my reputation is probably completely shot.' Kitty frowned at the menu.

'Oh?' Matt smirked at her and she glared at him.

'I've had Alice's mother tell me off for taking Alice to tea with a policeman. Then, not to mention yesterday, it seems everyone wishes to know my business,' Kitty huffed.

Matt's eyebrows rose. 'Oh, you mean your outing with the dashing Thomas King in his Alvis?'

Kitty stared at him, her mouth open in surprise. 'For heaven's sake, can't a girl do anything in this town without the whole of Torbay knowing what she is about? Which gossip gave you that juicy titbit?'

His grin widened. 'Inspector Greville happened to spy you outside Councillor Everton's house accepting a lift from Mr King.'

'Really, and he was "just passing" I suppose? I find it astonishing how on a gloomy and foggy November evening so many people managed to see me in Thomas King's car.' Indignation made her tone sharp.

'Apparently he noticed you as he was on his way to take Mrs Greville to visit her mother,' Matt said soothingly.

The conversation was interrupted by the elderly waitress who came to take their order. Once they had decided on cottage pie and a pot of tea Kitty resumed her interrogation.

'When did Inspector Greville pass on this information?' she asked.

'When he called at my house yesterday evening, just after I'd got home from London.' Matt smiled at the waitress as she deposited their tea on the table in front of them.

'I didn't realise you were going to London yesterday?' Kitty asked. Had he been to see his parents? Surely, he would have told her if he'd been thinking of paying them a visit.

Matt placed the tea strainer on top of Kitty's florally decorated china cup and poured her tea. 'It was a personal matter.' A shadow crossed his face.

'No wonder your shoulder is painful today if you rode the Sunbeam there and back. It was such horrid weather,' Kitty remarked, longing to know what the personal matter was all about.

'A hot bath and some aspirin soon sorted it out. Inspector Greville arrived just before supper.' Matt set the teapot back on the table just as the waitress returned with their food.

Kitty waited until the woman had moved away before resuming the conversation. She knew he was attempting to divert her away from his London journey and a lecture on not aggravating the wound in his shoulder that he had acquired during the Great War.

'What brought the inspector to your door?' she asked.

Matt told her everything the inspector had said while they tucked into the deliciously hot plate of cottage pie. She raised her brows when he passed on the inspector's compliment about her being good at unearthing information.

'I suppose I had better tell you what I learned during my visit to One Pine and my now notorious car journey with Mr King,' she said and told him all that she had discovered.

'I can see Inspector Greville's dilemma as everyone stands to benefit from Councillor Everton's death. They all had opportunity. Very tricky. I wonder if he knows about Mrs Everton being widowed before?' Matt mused as he placed his cutlery down on his empty plate.

Kitty sighed. 'It would be nice to know the full story behind that. Marigold said her first husband drowned in an accident. Daphne is certainly not spending time grieving for her stepfather.'

'What were your impressions of Thomas King?' He took a sip of his tea while he waited for her reply.

'He has an expensive car and a taste for expensive clothes and shoes. His watch is a very nice one too. He told me he'd had a small legacy when his mother died but it makes you wonder about things. A clerk's wages would hardly cover the money that no doubt his uncle would have expected him to pay for his keep.'

The frown on Matt's brow deepened as he told her of Mr Schofield's reaction when he had raised the subject of money during the morning's visit to the council offices.

'You think that perhaps Thomas and Mr Silitoe might be at the bottom of some irregularity?' Kitty asked.

'I can't see how Mr King could do it alone. Mr Silitoe would have to be involved if that were the case. It would explain Mr Everton's hesitation in coming to see me if some kind of fraud was occurring, and he thought they might be implicated.' Matt ceased speaking as the waitress came to collect their plates.

After they had ordered jam sponge and custard for dessert Kitty returned to the conversation. 'We need to share this information with Inspector Greville.'

'I suggest we telephone him on our return to the Dolphin.' Her spirits lifted at the warmth of his tone.

'I haven't told you of my other discovery.' Kitty smiled her thanks to the waitress as she delivered their desserts.

Matt's spoon was poised above the thick slice of jam sponge islanded in the sea of yellow custard. 'More discoveries?'

'Jack Dawkins' box. I finally had the opportunity to examine the contents more thoroughly.' Kitty enjoyed seeing the look of enquiry on his face.

'Any clues relating to your mother's disappearance?' Matt waited for the steam to disperse from his spoon before popping it into his mouth.

'There was one cutting in particular. At first I couldn't see what relevance it could have as it was a fairly recent article, but then I noticed Mr Dawkins had made some pencilled notes along the margin.' She could see that she had Matt's full attention.

She told him about the possible opening of the medieval water passages beneath Exeter's streets to scholars and interested members of the public. 'Father Lamb has promised to introduce me to a member of the group who are behind the scheme.'

'Interesting, and you say that Mickey's wife said she had heard that the passages may have been used by people for other, more nefarious purposes? How do you think this might link into your mother's disappearance?' Matt asked.

Kitty sighed. 'I'm not entirely sure but clearly Jack Dawkins thought the article was significant and I can't help but think this is somehow linked to the Glass Bottle public house.'

'I agree. It's strange that the landlord, Hammet, has now suddenly disappeared.' Matt placed his spoon down in his empty dish.

'Very strange. I would like to know if there is a map of the passages and if they pass anywhere near the Glass Bottle.' Kitty followed Matt's lead and placed her spoon down in her dish. She felt extremely full.

'You are thinking that public houses have cellars?' Matt said.

Kitty grinned. 'Exactly, although after your foray into the smugglers' tunnels behind the Dolphin in the spring I do not expect you to accompany me into the passages.' She knew his experiences in the trenches had left him with a dread of confined spaces. Hence his ownership of the Sunbeam rather than the enclosed environments of a motor car.

'When do you intend to meet Father Lamb and his colleague?' Matt asked.

'He is telephoning me to confirm a meeting, but probably Friday. It depends, of course, when the inquest for Councillor Everton is called.' Kitty wasn't looking forward to the inquest.

It was quite upsetting to think that Marigold, Daphne or Thomas might have murdered Harold Everton. Unless, of course, it was Mr Silitoe, or even by some stretch Mr Hendricks. Still, someone had done it. They had cold-bloodedly taken one of Mr Everton's sachets, removed the contents and replaced them with deadly potassium cyanide before resealing it and returning it to the box.

They were about to request the bill before leaving the tea room when the door reopened and Mrs Craven, swathed in fur, descended upon them.

'Captain Bryant, and Kitty.' She waved to her friends who were still seated at the window table and bore down on Kitty and Matt. 'Well? How goes our case? Have they arrested Marigold Everton yet?'

Kitty exchanged a look with Matt.

'Mrs Craven, I'm afraid we were just about to leave. I don't think there have been any developments as yet. I expect we may know more after the inquest,' Matt said.

'I don't suppose there will be any surprises there. Murder by person or persons unknown unless the inspector pulls his finger out. I had hoped that you might have made some progress.' Mrs Craven's expression clouded.

'I dare say the police are making vigorous efforts to determine who the murderer might be,' Kitty said.

Mrs Craven pooh-poohed this sentiment. 'I don't believe the police know what vigorous means. I've said as much to the chief constable on a number of occasions, not that he ever appears to do anything. I still think the way Daphne Everton is behaving is highly suspicious. Then there's that nephew of the councillor's, Thomas King. I hear you have been seen out motoring with that particular gentleman, Kitty. I'd advise you to be careful about keeping company with Mr King, you know how some people love to talk.'

Stung by the implications of Mrs Craven's statement, Kitty's temper flared. 'Thomas merely gave me a lift back to Kingswear as the weather was so dire yesterday. I had been to see Marigold and Daphne to pay my condolences.'

Mrs Craven looked triumphant. 'So, I was right about their suspicious behaviour. I don't know how you would get on, Kitty, without my assistance.'

'Mrs Craven, how well do you know Marigold Everton?' Matt asked.

The lady adjusted her furs as she considered the question. 'Oh, I've known her for a long time, ever since she and Harold Everton married. He was older than Marigold by about ten years.'

'Then you knew she had been married before?' Kitty asked.

'Yes, her first husband died in a boating accident, terrible tragedy, it was in all the papers at the time. He couldn't swim, you see. Daphne was a babe in arms.' Mrs Craven paused, her eyes brightening. 'Do you think she has done it before? Murdered a husband? There were some rumours at the time about Stephen's accident. I believe she had a nice little payout from the insurance company, but then it turned out that he'd left quite a few debts. Harold Everton bailed her out. She was a pretty little thing, you know, in her youth. Still would be if she made something of herself. One of those helpless sorts that men like rescuing.'

'I see, well, thank you, Mrs Craven, that has been most illuminating,' Matt said. 'I believe your friends are waiting for you.' He nodded his head in the direction of the two ladies who were looking their way.

'Yes, I'd better get on. You will keep me fully informed?' Mrs Craven arched her brow sternly at Matt.

'Of course,' he agreed.

'That woman is insufferable,' Kitty muttered as Matt helped her on with her coat. She saw his lips twitch upwards as he adjusted his cap.

'She is a good source of information.' He raised his hand and gave Mrs Craven and her companions a cheery wave as he steered an indignant Kitty out of the tea room.

While they had been dining the weather had deteriorated and soft, slushy, wet flakes were falling onto the cobbles that formed part of the path.

'Take my arm, Kitty. It's become very slippery underfoot,' Matt suggested as her shoes slithered on the path.

She was glad to avail herself of his support as their direction left the shelter provided by the buildings and they were forced to cross the more exposed space. An icy breeze tugged at the brim of her hat and Kitty was glad the warm felt was a snug fit. Otherwise it would no doubt have been blown away into the river, and she was quite fond of this particular hat.

By the time they reached the Dolphin they were both quite soaked and the snow had begun to settle on their shoulders in a soft white layer. Kitty noticed Matt wince once more as he opened the door to the hotel.

'Come into the office and dry out. Perhaps this will lift a little before you head back across the river.' She wiped her feet on the mat inside the entrance.

'I've got your post here, Miss Kitty.' Mary passed her a small bundle of mail as she went to unlock her office door.

Matt followed her into the office, and they divested themselves of their wet outdoor clothes. Kitty carefully pulled her beloved hat into shape before setting it to dry out on a shelf near the ornate metal radiator.

Matt took a seat in the chair opposite Kitty's desk as she poured him a tumbler of water from the jug next to the decanter set she kept on the small side trolley.

'Here, I've aspirin in my desk drawer.' She found the brown bottle of tablets and placed them in front of him. She was careful not to express any sympathy, for she knew that it would be unwanted. Matt disliked showing any signs of weakness and especially hated anyone feeling pity for his past injuries.

She took her own seat and started to open her letters with the small brass paperknife she kept in a tray on top of her desk.

'This one is about the inquest. It seems I am requested to attend on Wednesday morning at ten o'clock.' Kitty reached for her desk diary and checked her commitments.

'I expect there is an identical letter awaiting me,' Matt said. She noticed he had taken the aspirin.

'We had better telephone Inspector Greville and make him aware of our findings. We may have information that he is unaware of which could help his investigation.' Kitty stowed the tablets back in the drawer of her desk.

Matt grimaced as he adjusted his position to reach for the black candlestick-style telephone. 'I'll call him now. We might even learn something more from his side of things.'

Kitty finished opening her post while she listened in on the conversation as Matt relayed their findings to the inspector. She wished she could hear the inspector's responses. Instead she had to be content for a moment with interpreting Matt's monosyllabic responses and raised eyebrows as he talked.

'Well, that was interesting.' Matt replaced the receiver.

'Is the inspector any further forward? Does he anticipate an arrest?' Kitty asked.

Matt eased back into his seat. 'The inspector has been looking at Thomas King's financial affairs and it seems as if he regularly pays a healthy sum each month into his bank by cash.'

Kitty was intrigued. 'Do we know the source of the money?'

Matt shook his head. 'Inspector Greville is making a few more enquiries before he questions Mr King.'

'I suppose he may be involved in something illegal, but it may not have anything to do with his uncle's murder.' Kitty was thoughtful. It was still suspicious, however.

'True, but it may provide a motive. The inspector has also said he will look into the circumstances around the death of Mrs Everton's first husband. He sounded interested in the information that Mrs Craven gave us.'

'Then she will be pleased that she has been useful,' Kitty remarked.

Matt grinned. 'Mrs C loves to be of use.' He rose from his seat and reached for his coat. 'I must head off. The weather is not good.'

Kitty watched as he wrapped his scarf around his neck and tucked it inside his coat before picking up his cap.

'Do please be careful riding back.' She wished he wouldn't go. She knew he still had discomfort in his shoulder and although the journey was not a long one, the weather would render the drive treacherous.

He stood for a moment, turning his cap in his hands as if considering what to say to her.

'I shall be careful,' he promised.

His lips brushed hers, still cold from their walk back from the café.

'Kitty, I know you want to ask what I was doing on Sunday, and I promise I shall tell you, but not right now.'

She gazed at him in surprise but knew him well enough now to give him the space he was requesting from her even though she longed to know where he had been.

'Very well.' She offered him a small smile. She would be content for now. He had given his word and he always kept his promises.

CHAPTER THIRTEEN

The journey back to Churston proved to be as difficult as Matt had anticipated. He was glad of his thick gauntlets and the protection from his coat as he took the ferry across the Dart. Snow was falling now in a flurry of fine flakes and visibility was poor as he disembarked at Kingswear.

He was relieved to see a thin plume of smoke coming from his chimney when he arrived back at his home. His housekeeper had been busy when he had left in the morning and she had obviously banked the fire before leaving for her own home on the far side of the common near the windmill.

The small hall was warm and welcoming, smelling of the beeswax polish Mrs Smith had used on the side table. He placed his cap and scarf to dry and stowed his gauntlets and coat. His new housekeeper was much more amenable than the woman he had employed previously. Mrs Milden had proved untrustworthy and Kitty had helped him to recruit a replacement, a relative of one of the kitchen staff at the Dolphin.

His post was neatly stacked on the hall table next to a small crystal vase of autumnal flowers and greenery. The top letter looked remarkably like the one Kitty had received about the inquest. The rest appeared to be circulars.

The sitting room was clean and cosy, and he sank down thankfully on the armchair nearest to the fire. Despite the aspirin Kitty had forced upon him his shoulder still ached. The journey to Edith's grave had taken more out of him than he had anticipated.

When he had proposed lunch with Kitty at the tea room he had hoped once they had exchanged information on the murder that they would have had time to talk of other more personal matters. There were things he needed to tell her if they were to move forward in their friendship, and Thomas King's attentions towards her had stirred his emotions more strongly than he could have ever imagined.

Kitty attempted to apply herself to her work once Matt had departed. She was concerned that his shoulder appeared to be bothering him so much. She dealt with some of the correspondence and then leaned back in her chair, twiddling her fountain pen between her fingers. What had he been doing on Sunday in London and where exactly had he been?

She was jolted from her reverie by the insistent ringing of the telephone.

'Dolphin Hotel, Miss Kitty Underhay speaking, how may I help you?' She answered the telephone herself rather than waiting for Mary to take the call.

'Oh, Miss Underhay, this is Lavinia Braddock, we met the other evening at the Imperial, you know when poor Councillor Everton…' The voice tailed off as if unsure how to proceed.

'Yes, I remember. You were with your brother, Mr Hendricks,' Kitty said. Her curiosity was piqued by the unexpected contact. This was an opportunity to discover the full extent of the siblings' relationship with the councillor.

'I wondered if you had received a letter requesting you to attend the inquest for poor Councillor Everton?' Lavinia asked.

'Yes, it arrived this afternoon. I presume we shall all have one asking us to go,' Kitty said.

'Oh dear, I've never been to such a thing before.' Lavinia sounded quite flustered.

Kitty had only attended one previously, a number of years ago when she had accompanied her grandmother after a member of staff had died unexpectedly.

'Inspector Greville will give a statement and I imagine we shall only be required to confirm our statements are correct and answer any queries the coroner may have.' Kitty tried to remember the procedure.

'I must confess the whole affair has made me feel quite ill. I wondered, Miss Underhay, if you might possibly be free at all tomorrow afternoon to visit and have tea with me? My brother, you know what men are like, thinks I am worrying unnecessarily but one can't help it. I feel so terribly alone here.' There was a faint quaver in her voice.

'Of course, that sounds delightful. A little female solidarity would no doubt help us both,' Kitty said. She wondered what exactly was bothering Lavinia Braddock and why she had decided that Kitty should be her sounding board. It would give her the opportunity to find out more about Lavinia and her brother and their connection with Harold Everton.

'Thank you so much, would three thirty suit you?' Lavinia said.

Kitty glanced at her diary and agreed the time. Tomorrow afternoon's visit to the Conway Country House Hotel promised to be very interesting. She replaced the receiver and wondered what Matt would make of her invitation.

The following morning arrived as a crisp dry day. The clouds and sleet of yesterday replaced by a thin clear blue sky. The remains of the snow lingered only in a few shady corners, piled up like spilled icing sugar that someone had swept up and forgotten to disperse.

Kitty telephoned Matt, ostensibly to tell him of her unexpected tea date with Lavinia Braddock and that Father Lamb had confirmed the meeting in Exeter on Friday. However, she really wished to judge from his tone if he was recovered from his mystery errand of Sunday, which had taken so much out of him.

'I agree, Mrs Braddock's excuse to invite you to tea certainly sounds rather thin. It will be very interesting to find out what it is she really wants,' Matt said.

'At least the weather has improved. I would not have fancied the journey to Cockington if it had still been icy. The lanes there are quite narrow and more fit for horse and carts than Mr Potter's beloved taxi.'

Matt's deep throaty chuckle tickled her ear. 'Very true. I'm looking forward to our expedition to Exeter too. I wonder if Mr Dawkins' newspaper clipping will prove useful.'

Kitty sighed. 'I know it could be another wild goose chase but at least I shall have tried.' She knew all too well that this latest clue offered a slim prospect of finding the answer to where her mother had gone on a fine June day in 1916 after leaving her aunt's home at Enderley Hall.

'The inquest is to be held at the town hall in Torquay, no doubt it will attract a large attendance. There was a report again yesterday in the newspaper.'

'Perhaps that was the trigger for Mrs Braddock's invitation,' Kitty suggested.

She ended the call having agreed to meet Matt before the inquest to tell him how she fared with Lavinia and her brother and so that they might go in together.

Mr Potter's taxi arrived to take her to Cockington shortly after two thirty but Kitty was somewhat surprised to discover Robert, Mr Potter's son, in the driver's seat.

'Robert, this is a change, is your father well?' she enquired as she hopped into the back seat.

'Yes, Miss Kitty. He has gone with Mother into Exeter in the Daisybelle so has entrusted me with the motor car.' Robert gave her a shy smile. He was a pleasant, sturdily built young man only a little older than Kitty.

Kitty arranged the thick red tartan travelling rug around her legs to keep out the draughts and settled in for the journey. After her grandmother's remarks about the condition of the Conway Country House Hotel Kitty had opted to wear her thick tweed two-piece with a pink cashmere sweater under her topcoat. She had no desire to be frozen to death just to gain information.

'You are very honoured that your father has entrusted you with the car, Robert.' Kitty leaned forward so she could converse more easily.

Robert's earlobes pinked under the edge of his cap. 'Aye, miss. We're partners though now since I got the Daisybelle.'

Kitty smiled. 'I think it's perfectly splendid, it's very entrepreneurial.' Talking to Robert brought something back to her mind that she had been considering for a little while. 'Tell me, Robert, is it easy to learn how to drive a motor car?'

Robert scratched the side of his head, slightly dislodging his cap. 'I don't know, Miss Kitty. I reckon so if you've the right turn of mind.'

She waited for a few minutes as they disembarked from the ferry and Robert set the taxi in motion to drive out through Kingswear.

'Do you think that I could learn?' Kitty asked. She had been toying with the idea for a while, having seen some particularly dashing roadsters. It would be rather pleasant to have the power to go wherever she wished without having to take a bus, train or taxi.

Robert's gaze met hers briefly in the mirror before his flicked away again back onto the road.

'I don't see why not, Miss Kitty. Would you be after having your own car?' Robert asked.

'My father has given me some money in my bank account. I should very much like to do something useful with it and, as you know, Captain Bryant is very attached to his motorcycle and I have no desire to be hauled around in a sidecar.' Not that he has ever suggested that he get a sidecar, Kitty thought.

'You would need somewhere to keep it, miss, a garage some-place near the hotel,' Robert mused, appearing to take her idea seriously.

Kitty had seen a notice advertising some garages to rent only a short walk away. 'I think I might be able to find a place to rent. How does one learn though? I would require a teacher.'

They were heading now towards the outskirts of Torquay ready to take the turn away from the coast towards the small village of Cockington.

'I reckon if'n you had a car, Miss Kitty, you would just need someone who could drive who would be willing to sit alongside you and show you the ropes. You would need to get a licence as well from the town hall,' Robert said.

Kitty settled back in her seat and considered the idea. They were in a maze of narrow lanes now bordered at times with drystone walls topped with scrubby growth that in summer would be green and full of life, but which was now mostly bare of leaves.

'Would you be willing to teach me?' She leaned forward again.

'Me, miss?' Robert seemed quite startled by the suggestion.

'I would pay you, of course, for your time.' It seemed to her that Robert would be an excellent tutor. He drove well, had a great deal of experience and always struck her as a very patient person. She had a feeling that anyone teaching her to drive might require patience.

'Well, I've never taught no one before, Miss Kitty,' Robert said as he steered the taxi onto the start of the long gravel drive leading to the Conway Country House Hotel.

'But if I did purchase a car, would you be willing to give it a try?' Kitty persisted. The idea of herself behind the wheel of a natty little red roadster definitely appealed to her imagination.

'I expect I could try,' Robert conceded as he pulled the taxi to a stop outside the hotel.

Kitty beamed. 'Thank you, Robert. It will probably be in the New Year.'

'That would be fine, Miss Kitty.'

She looked out of the taxi window at the façade of the Conway Country House Hotel. Clearly it had once been a rather grand house with a fine stone portico in the classical style above the front door. It was a square Georgian building, the whitewash flaking now on the exterior and a depressed looking climbing plant, devoid of its leaves, struggling to retain its hold at the side of the building.

Kitty climbed out of the car and requested that Robert return to collect her at four thirty. She had no intention of making her visit to Lavinia a long one. She brushed a little piece of fluff from her skirt and approached the front door.

She had barely reached the step when she heard the sounds of an argument emanating from the interior. Much to her chagrin, she was unable to hear what was being said but could make out a female voice arguing with a male one.

Undeterred she pushed open the dark blue painted door and ventured inside. The lobby was square with some dispirited palms in pots languishing in the corners next to the white plaster columns. The chequerboard pattern tiled floor could, in Kitty's opinion, have done with a mop.

An equally languid receptionist was slouching over the mahogany desk opposite the entrance. Kitty noticed that she was not in uniform and had the same general air of neglect as the building. She eyed Kitty, clearly noting her lack of luggage.

'Can I help you, miss?'

'I have an appointment to see Mrs Braddock, Kitty Underhay.'

'One moment and I'll tell her you're here.'

She expected the girl to pick up the telephone to summon her mistress but instead the girl slipped out from behind the desk and off through a side door leaving Kitty alone in the lobby.

Kitty couldn't resist running a kid gloved finger across the surface of the desk and barely managed to suppress a tut at the amount of dust on her glove.

'Gracious, I am turning into my grandmother,' Kitty murmured, noticing the untidy display of leaflets in a rack on the far wall.

The sound of the side door reopening returned her attention to the desk as the receptionist reappeared.

'I'm to take you through to the lounge, miss.' The girl led the way to a glass-panelled door and waited for Kitty to follow her. They continued on along a parquet-floored hallway with cream painted walls until they reached a room at the back of the hotel.

The whole place was very quiet and still and Kitty wondered who she could have heard quarrelling on her arrival. The receptionist must have heard the racket and was seemingly unperturbed, indicating perhaps that it was not an unusual event. The girl showed her into the lounge and indicated a seat near the French doors after relieving her of her outdoor things.

The room was dated with floral chintz covered armchairs and china knick-knacks on the various side tables. The Turkish carpet in the centre of the room looked as if it required a good beating but at least there was a fire in the hearth and the room was not cold.

Kitty had been there for a few minutes when Lavinia Braddock appeared, dressed in a dusty pink floral day dress and a navy knitted jacket, her dark curls carefully styled.

'My dear Miss Underhay, I am so sorry to have kept you. I have ordered the tea and Euphemia should bring it for us in a minute. It is so good of you to come. I was afraid that if the bad weather had continued you might have had to cancel.' Lavinia took the armchair opposite Kitty.

'The pleasure is mine. I rarely have cause to travel in this direction and one forgets how pretty it is around here,' Kitty said politely.

A skinny young girl entered the room in an ill-fitting black uniform with white apron. She carefully steered a small wooden trolley laden with the tea things.

'Leave the trolley there, Euphemia, I shall serve tea.' Lavinia intercepted the girl and shooed her away.

Kitty's brows rose a little and she wondered how Alice would take to being dismissed in such a fashion. Lavinia placed a tiered china cake stand on the table containing what appeared to be small triangular sandwiches of some kind of meat paste or cheese. There were a few jam tarts and a couple of fingers of Victoria sponge.

Lavinia placed an old-fashioned china cup with a country rose design before Kitty and set out the small matching side plates.

'I had intended us to have scones with cream and jam, but our supplier let us down this morning. The weather you know.' Lavinia poured them both a cup of tea from the flowery teapot.

'It can be so difficult in this business at times,' Kitty sympathised and privately wondered if they had not been paying the supplier, hence the shortage of foodstuffs.

Lavinia smiled gratefully at her. 'I knew you would understand. It can be very trying. This place was in such bad shape when we acquired it and the difficulties with the improvement plans have not been helpful.'

Kitty helped herself to a jam tart deciding they were the most attractive of the fare on offer. 'I seem to recall your brother mentioning something to Councillor Everton about your plans when we were at the Imperial. The councillor was chair of the planning committee I think.' Lavinia had given her a good opening to try for some information.

Lavinia spooned sugar into her cup and gave her tea a good stir. 'Yes, he was. Well, this planning business has dragged on for ages. The problem is that the Mallocks, who owned much of the area, sold their estate this year and the land and its environs, which includes us, must be preserved. There is some sort of Trust being formed and the council are involved.'

'Oh dear, that must be very aggravating for you with all the bureaucracy.' Kitty was careful to keep her tone sympathetic.

'Without the improvements it will be very difficult for us to continue in business here.' Lavinia's plump, pleasant face fell. 'We had been led to believe that if we approached the right people then we might find a… well, a solution.' She lowered her voice and glanced around the empty lounge as if she suspected someone might be lurking in the shadows. 'I realise that you must have been surprised by my invitation to tea, but this inquest, well, there are matters playing on my mind. My brother feels that I am being foolish.' She paused for breath.

'If I can help you in any way, I'm happy to do so,' Kitty assured her. She was intrigued by what Lavinia appeared to wish to confide.

The older woman gave a weak smile. 'I thought that perhaps with your gentleman friend being a private investigator that you might have some insight on certain matters.'

Kitty took a bite of the jam tart and decided that she had been wise to avoid the other food on offer if the leaden pastry and unpleasant jam were anything to go by. 'You are concerned that you may have some information that might be pertinent to Councillor Everton's murder, but it may be unrelated, in which case there would be no need to be worried about it?' She decided to be more direct.

Lavinia's shoulders drooped. 'Exactly. You see, we heard that… well, a person might pay for, um, advice, that would smooth the path of certain plans to get them through the committee.'

Kitty looked at Lavinia. 'I understand. Who were you to speak to in order to obtain this advice?'

'Thomas King facilitated the matters, but he indicated that he was acting on behalf of others. We naturally assumed it must be Councillor Everton, since he headed the planning committee and his opinion had great sway.' Lavinia's hands fluttered helplessly in her lap. 'But the plans kept being rejected. My brother kept trying to speak directly to Councillor Everton but could never get an appointment. My brother tried telephoning him but got nowhere. Mr King said that he would try to arrange matters. Then, when we finally spoke to Councillor Everton that night at the Imperial, it was evident that he either was unaware or was not prepared to assist us.'

Kitty began to see the picture quite clearly. She and Matt had been correct in their supposition of corruption. 'Have you parted with much money for this, um, advice?'

'Two hundred pounds.' Lavinia looked as if she were about to cry.

'That is why you exchanged the place cards at the dinner, so you could share the table with Councillor Everton?' Kitty asked.

Crimson spots flared on Lavinia's cheeks. 'Oh, Miss Underhay, we thought that if we could just talk to Thomas King and his uncle that we might find a way forward. Councillor Everton wouldn't see my brother. Now I don't know what to do. My brother says we have done nothing wrong, but I wish I could be as certain.' She turned beseeching eyes on Kitty. 'Should we tell the inspector? Will we be in trouble? Any scandal will be the nail in the coffin of this business, and we have sunk everything into this hotel.'

Kitty discarded the remains of the jam tart and wiped her fingers on one of the pale pink linen napkins. 'I assume that the inspector has asked how you came to be seated at the table?'

'Yes, my brother told him that the Imperial made a mistake but if the coroner calls us and we are under oath… Oh, Miss Underhay, I haven't been able to sleep with the worry of it all.'

Kitty could see Lavinia's dilemma. Payment for advice sounded as if it were an attempt to bribe a public official. She wasn't certain if that was an offence in legal terms, but she was fairly sure it would be heavily frowned upon. Councillor Everton had certainly not been a party to the scheme, everything they had learned about his character indicated that he had been unaware of anything amiss until recently when he had started to look back over past decisions and had asked to consult Matt.

She was conscious of Lavinia waiting for her response. 'My advice would be to make a clean breast of things to the inspector. This could be pertinent to Councillor Everton's murder.'

Lavinia let out a little moan of dismay and pressed her napkin to her lips. 'They might think that my brother and I conspired to kill Mr Everton. My brother is not an easy man, he has a temper, and someone may get the wrong idea. Then there is the matter of the money.'

'It seems to me that Mr King and whoever he might be working with has more cause to be afraid than you or your brother. Perhaps some gentle pressure from the police may even get some of your money back.' Kitty wasn't entirely sure of this, but it was a possibility. 'It is better that you tell the inspector all of this now, yourselves, rather than have him discover it from some other means. If he finds out from someone else then he is bound to think the worst.'

Lavinia appeared to concede defeat. 'I shall speak to my brother again. We have had some terrible arguments on the matter.'

Kitty was curious. 'How did the two of you come into business together? Have you had other hotels before this one?'

'My husband and I had a small guest house in Southend-on-Sea. We were never blessed with children and Bert was older than me. He became ill and when he passed away, I struggled. He'd always managed the business side of things. He dealt with the suppliers and the finances.' She dabbed at the corners of her eyes with her napkin. 'My brother has never married. He worked at a number of places; a chemist, a tailor, he could never settle. I had a small sum of money saved and we decided that it would be nice to make a fresh start and invest together.'

Kitty nodded. 'I see.' Both brother and sister seemed to be quite naïve in the ways of business and it was easy for her to see how they had run into trouble. She wondered why Mr Hendricks had held so many jobs. The mention of a chemist was definitely interesting.

'Thank you for coming to see me. You must think me very foolish.' Lavinia managed a sad smile.

'It can be very difficult running a business such as this. There are so many things to consider. Inspector Greville is a very fair man, I am sure he will be glad to hear from you before the hearing tomorrow.' Kitty glanced at her watch. Robert Potter should be arriving at any time to collect her and take her home to the Dolphin.

As if on cue the door to the lounge opened and the young maid reappeared. 'Begging your pardon, miss, but your taxi is here.'

'Thank you, if you could bring my things I'll be right out.' Kitty smiled at the girl.

'I expect we shall meet again tomorrow at the inquest.' Lavinia rose and brushed crumbs from her lap.

'Yes, I shall look out for you.' Kitty accepted her coat from the maid and donned her scarf and hat.

Lavinia walked with her to the waiting taxi, shivering as the cold wind blew across the front of the hotel. Kitty noticed in the gathering darkness that a bulb had failed in the portico casting eerie shadows across the frontage.

'Thank you for tea.' She climbed into the taxi.

Lavinia waved her off as the car started away down the long gravel drive and Kitty sank back against the leather seats with a sigh of relief.

CHAPTER FOURTEEN

Matt had arranged to meet Kitty outside the town hall in a small side street. He had judged that there would be a great deal of interest in the inquest. Not just from newspapermen, but also locals due to Councillor Everton's long years of public service. Usually the inquest would have been held in a local hostelry or at the police station, but the county coroner had felt a larger room would be more appropriate in this case.

Mr Potter's taxi pulled up near where he was waiting, and Kitty hopped out of the back. She had dressed in her warm black coat and matching hat, clearly judging that a sombre note was called for. Her fair hair and skin were pale next to the dark colour as she hurried over to meet him.

'I'm not late, am I? The ferries were busy this morning due to the early hour and then Torquay itself seems to be full of people and a lot of them were headed in this direction.'

Matt smiled at her, his spirits lifting as usual whenever he was in her company. 'Mr Schofield has kindly said he will let us in through a side door so we can avoid running the gamut of people entering through the front of the town hall.'

'That is most kind of him. I need to tell you what I found out yesterday while I was at Cockington.' She fell into step beside him and quickly told him of Lavinia's conversation.

He let out a low whistle of surprise. 'It seems that Mr King is indeed up to something, but who is his partner? He hasn't the ability to sway a committee decision alone.'

'Ivor Silitoe would be my guess, but he might prove very slippery,' Kitty said as they halted before a small nondescript door set in the side of the building.

Matt gave a tap on the door and heard the chink of keys on the far side. The door opened a crack and Mr Schofield peeped out. On seeing Matt, he opened the door wider and ushered them inside, relocking the door behind them.

'This is very good of you, Mr Schofield,' Matt said.

'It's greatly appreciated. There seems to be quite a large crowd pressing for admission in the reception area. I saw it from the taxi when I arrived,' Kitty said.

'My pleasure, miss.' The elderly man favoured her with a small bow.

They followed him along the corridor that Matt remembered from the previous day, stopping shortly partway along for Mr Schofield to open another door. 'These are the staff stairs. If you go up one flight it will bring you out right by the chamber where the inquest is to be held.'

Matt thanked the man and followed Kitty as she hurried up the stairs. Ahead of them he could hear the hustle and bustle of people and murmur of voices. A harassed-looking uniformed constable was at the entrance to the chamber overseeing the admission and seating of the public.

Matt guided Kitty through the small crowd and gave their names to the constable.

'Make your way to the front, sir, right-hand side, the seats are labelled,' the man said.

Matt nodded his thanks and he and Kitty made their way into the chamber. At the front of the room was a small dais set out with a table and a few chairs. A decanter of water and some glasses were in position and Matt assumed the coroner and his clerks would be seated there when the inquest began. The jury would be seated at tables that had been similarly placed to the side of the dais where they could have a good view of the witness stand and the coroner.

The rest of the seating was in rows with, presumably, witnesses and the police seated at the front. It was a large room and many of the seats were already being filled. A galleried landing ran around the chamber and there was a buzz of chatter from there too. Glancing up, he could see the pressmen appeared to have that as their favoured spot, judging by the number of cameras he could see.

'Heavens, it's like a circus,' Kitty muttered as she was jostled by a couple pushing past her to secure their seats.

Eventually they reached the front and found their seats some three rows back from the dais. Lavinia Braddock and her brother were already seated. Lavinia gave Kitty a tight smile, while her brother stared stonily ahead. Daphne Everton arrived, attired in a navy suit and matching hat on the arm of a gentleman that Matt presumed was her young man.

She too smiled at Kitty as she took her seat. They were swiftly followed by Mr and Mrs Silitoe, who were flanking Marigold Everton. Marigold was dressed in black and heavily veiled, she leaned on Mr Silitoe as if afraid of falling. Mrs Silitoe, in a neat dark grey suit, walked a little apart from them, her gaze fixed on the platform ahead. Thomas King arrived shortly after in an expensively cut dark navy suit and sat restless and fidgety in a seat next to the aisle.

Matt glanced at his watch. The hubbub in the hall had risen with each new arrival and he was conscious of the interested stares of the public at their small group. Doctor Carter and Inspector Greville were among the last to arrive. The doctor's cheery demeanour somehow reassuring amidst the melee.

A side door opened near the dais and the county coroner and his clerks took their seats. The jury, looking very conscious of their responsibilities, were also seated. Their entrance immediately hushing the crowd as they waited expectantly for the inquest to commence.

The inquest opened and began along the lines that Matt expected. Inspector Greville gave an outline of the events and provided the statements he had gathered during the interviews with everyone who had been at their table. He confirmed that the household, their staff, and any visitors could have accessed the box containing the medication at any time. He was careful not to ascribe any possible motives for the poisoning to any particular person. He did confirm the financial benefits from Mr Everton's will for Marigold, Daphne and Thomas King.

They were then each called in turn and sworn in to confirm the statements they had given the inspector during their interview at the Imperial and to answer any questions from the coroner. Kitty was calm and collected, her head held high as she spoke. Daphne appeared nervous but also composed.

Marigold was tremulous under her veil as she confirmed that the medication was stored on the sideboard in the dining room and topped up each week with the sachets from the medicine cabinet in the upstairs bathroom. The press in the gallery were restless as they strained to get a good look at Marigold's veiled figure.

Mrs Braddock and Mr Hendricks were called and confirmed what they had witnessed. No mention was made of the seat swap or the planning dispute and Matt detected Inspector Greville's hand in this omission.

Finally, Thomas King was called. He cut a handsome figure as he was sworn in to confirm the evidence he had given and to state that although he and his uncle argued from time to time they were generally on good terms. Their working relationship was amicable, and he had no particular dispute or grudge against his uncle.

Doctor Carter was called and produced a gasp and ripple around the room of excitement when he affirmed that Mr Everton's death was due to potassium cyanide poisoning ingested shortly before death. He also confirmed that Mr Everton's own physician had been correct in his diagnosis of long-standing heart disease.

In response to the coroner's questions the silver gilt box was produced and the wrapper from the sachet. This was passed for the jury to examine along with an original sachet so they could discern that it had been altered.

Mr Protheroe was the next person to be called and sworn in. Matt had noticed the rather nervous young man in the shiny suit seated at the far end of the row and had wondered who he might be.

It transpired that he was the dispensing chemist who had made up the medicine.

'And there is no possibility of an error whereby potassium cyanide could accidentally contaminate the medication?' The coroner peered at Mr Protheroe over the top of his spectacles.

'Absolutely none, sir. Poisons are kept locked away and there is a rigorous procedure for their dispensation. Mr Everton's medications were quite straightforward. A digoxin preparation for his heart and his sachets for indigestion.' Mr Protheroe sounded clear and confident as he answered an additional question as to the content of the sachets.

Matt glanced along the row and saw that Marigold Everton had Mr Silitoe's arm in a tight grip. Mrs Silitoe's mouth was pursed, her expression impassive. Daphne's young man had hold of her hand. Thomas King's posture was tense, like a man about to take flight.

Inspector Greville was recalled to the stand.

'Having established that there are several people who had the opportunity to tamper with the medication, is it possible that Mr Everton may have acted this way himself?' the coroner asked, glancing down at a slip of paper on the table before him.

Matt suspected this question was from the jury to exclude the possibility of suicide.

'Mr Everton was in good spirits. He had no financial concerns and it would be extremely unlikely that a gentleman of his standing would choose to take an action to end his own life in such a public and horrific manner. My investigations thus far all indicate that the poison was administered by a third party. He would have had no call to tamper with his own medication in such a fashion.'

His statement sent another faint buzz of conversation around the room and jostling amongst the members of the press in the gallery.

The inspector was stood down once more and the coroner summed up for the jury on possible findings before dismissing them to a side room to debate. They were gone barely five minutes before returning.

'What are your findings?' The coroner looked to the elderly man who had been elected as chairman of the jury.

'Murder by person or persons unknown.'

A ripple ran around the room at having this confirmed. The coroner rapped a gavel to restore order before directing the findings be recorded by the clerk and thanking the jury. He then addressed Inspector Greville.

'I am sure the police will continue their investigations into this matter to ensure justice is served.'

In the ensuing hubbub as the public began to disperse Matt placed his hand on Kitty's sleeve. 'We would do better to return to the side door. The press will have a free for all at the front of the building.'

Kitty nodded her agreement. Matt noticed that Thomas King had been the first out of his seat to escape into the crowd. He hadn't stayed to support his aunt or cousin. Daphne Everton's young man now had his arm around her waist, while Marigold continued to be supported by Mr Silitoe. Mrs Silitoe had fallen in with Mrs Braddock and her brother.

Kitty followed Matt out of the hall past the constable and together they made their way along the corridor to the door they had used earlier. Matt was unsurprised to discover Inspector Greville and Doctor Carter had also had the same route in mind.

'After you, Miss Underhay,' the doctor declared gallantly, doffing his hat as Kitty beamed at him.

They made their way as a small group down the staircase and shortly afterwards out into the side street.

'Shall we adjourn for a cup of tea?' Doctor Carter suggested. 'There is a small café just along here. It may be prudent to avoid the newspapermen and to allow the crowds to disperse.'

The affable doctor led the way and took them along a narrow side road to a small tucked away café of the type usually frequented by workmen. He appeared to be quite well known by the owner and swiftly procured their group a small table at the back of the room.

'I delivered the proprietor's son,' Doctor Carter explained as a plate of toasted and buttered teacakes appeared before them, along with cups of strong tea in thick plain white cups.

'This is most welcome, I'm sure.' Inspector Greville carefully proffered Kitty the plate of teacakes before diving into them himself.

'Did Mr Hendricks contact you with the information his sister shared with me about the payments to Thomas King?' Kitty asked.

Doctor Carter looked on with interest as Inspector Greville confirmed everything that Lavinia had told Kitty.

'The man is clearly naïve, but he knew full well that what they were doing was not above board. He has quite a reputation too with his temper.' Inspector Greville licked a blob of butter from his thumb.

'Hmm, there has been a lot in the newspapers about the plans to conserve the village atmosphere and the countryside. I believe there is some talk of building a public house near the green amongst other plans. The Conway Country House Hotel is further out of the village I think.' Doctor Carter sipped his tea.

'Yes, it looks rather run-down, I'm afraid.' Kitty patted her lips with the corner of her handkerchief.

'I need to have a talk with Mr King.' Inspector Greville frowned. 'If it turns out that he was swindling applicants and his uncle found out about it, then that would be a strong motive for murder.'

'He would have lost everything: his job, his home and I fear Mr Everton would have cast him off no matter how fond of him he might have been beforehand. That was the thing with Everton. He was not an easy man, but he was an honest one. I know several of my patients have told me the same thing. I suspect that was why he was elected as a councillor. His father had a good reputation too.' Doctor Carter replaced his cup down on the saucer.

'I presume the jury raised the possibility of it being suicide?' Matt asked.

Inspector Greville nodded. 'Yes, I saw the foreman pass the note to the coroner. It was as well to rule it out so there could be no claims of self-harm as a defence for the murderer when he is caught.'

Matt saw Kitty shiver slightly at the inspector's words. They finished their refreshments, the inspector and the doctor walking back together in the direction of the police station.

'I'll walk with you to the taxi rank. It's not far from here,' Matt offered.

Kitty smiled at him and slipped her arm through his. 'I suppose it would be better than my riding pillion on your Sunbeam. I shall be glad when I get my own motor car and learn to drive.'

Her statement stopped him in his tracks for a moment. 'I didn't know you were thinking of learning to drive?'

She gave a small shrug of her shoulders. 'It can be quite tiresome always having to take a taxi or bus whenever I want to go into town. I thought perhaps a small roadster. I have seen a darling one in red.'

'They are quite an expense, Kitty. You would need somewhere to keep it.' Matt wondered what had triggered this fancy.

'There is a large shed I could rent not far from the Dolphin. It was used by a boatbuilder but is now surplus to requirements. My father has, unbeknown to my grandmother, deposited a sum of money in my bank account. He says it is to make up for the years when he was out of my life. Grams would not be amused if she knew and, to be honest, I had to double-check how he had come by such a sum before my conscience would permit me to accept it.'

Matt had met Edgar Underhay briefly in the spring when he and Kitty had almost been killed recovering a missing ruby worth several thousand pounds. He knew her father led quite a shady lifestyle, so he didn't blame her for being careful about accepting money from him. Kitty's grandmother did not approve of Edgar at all and would no doubt have a great deal to say on the matter if she learned about it.

'You seem to have it all worked out,' he said lightly, a little hurt that she hadn't shared this desire for a motor car with him.

'Mr Potter's son, Robert, has said he will teach me if I acquire a car.' She glanced up at him from under the brim of her hat.

'Brave fellow.' He received a light blow on his arm from Kitty's fist for that remark.

'I think I shall make a good driver. You would not object to riding around with me, would you?'

Matt suppressed a groan. He could see that Kitty fancied herself zipping along behind the wheel of a sporty open-topped red roadster. 'I could always have a sidecar fitted to the Sunbeam.'

Kitty rolled her eyes. 'I don't think so.'

They had reached the taxi rank and she released his arm. 'I had better get back to the Dolphin. We have three bedrooms being refurbished and I wish to check on the workmen.'

'Tomorrow I'll call at the offices of some of the developers which Mr Schofield indicated might have dealt with Mr King.' Matt intended to try and gather some evidence to prove his theory correct about the source of some of Thomas King's money. It might also give him the answer to why Mr Everton had wished to consult him.

'Inspector Greville will also be investigating Thomas' affairs,' Kitty said.

'I wonder if the inspector will let us know what happens when he catches up with your friend Mr King?' Matt mused.

'Thomas King is not my friend. He merely gave me a ride home as the weather was so bad. If I'd had my own car it wouldn't have been necessary.' Kitty gave him a look making Matt chuckle out loud.

'Very well. If I hear anything, I'll telephone you. If not, I expect we shall meet on the train at Churston Station on Friday?' he said.

'Our trip to see Father Lamb and his friend. Yes, I'm looking forward to finding out if there could be anything in Mr Dawkins' clipping.' She looked up at him, her clear blue-grey gaze meeting his.

Matt was reminded immediately of his journey on Sunday and his need to explain everything to Kitty. Mindful of the watching gaze of the waiting taxi driver he kissed her briefly on the lips and opened the rear door of the car for her to get inside.

'I'll see you on Friday.' He closed the door.

CHAPTER FIFTEEN

The following morning dawned damp, dreary and cheerless. Kitty found herself feeling unaccountably irritable and out of sorts as she supervised the taking down and rehanging of the drapes in the ballroom.

Perched halfway up a rather rickety wooden stepladder, her mood was not improved by the unannounced arrival of Mrs Craven. Her grandmother's friend bustled into the room clad in her usual fox fur.

'Kitty!' She beckoned imperiously with a kid-gloved hand.

The stepladder swayed and Mrs Homer, the head housekeeper, had to tighten her grip to secure it. Kitty reluctantly made her way back down the ladder, making a mental note to ask Mickey to look at a damp patch she had noted near the window frame.

'I'm afraid Grams has gone into Torquay on a business trip,' Kitty said.

'I haven't come to visit your grandmother; I have come to see you. I have information.' She leaned in close to Kitty to impart this news in a hissed whisper and with a meaningful nod towards where Mrs Homer and one of the housemaids were folding the drapes.

Kitty suppressed a sigh. 'Shall we go into the residents' lounge. I believe it is nice and quiet in there just now.' She led the way along the corridor to the deserted residents' lounge.

Mrs Craven seated herself on the edge of one of the cosy armchairs and waited impatiently for Kitty to sit on the chair opposite her before leaning forwards in a conspiratorial manner.

'I have come here straight from my floral arrangement class,' she said, clearly waiting for Kitty to ask her a question.

'Who was there?' Kitty asked and hoped Mrs Craven would hurry and get to the point of her visit. She had a lot to get done if she were to go to Exeter tomorrow.

Mrs Craven looked triumphant. 'Gladys Silitoe. I made sure I got the place on the workbench next to her. We were at the back of the classroom so could speak quite freely without being overheard.'

Kitty was conscious of a throbbing developing in her left temple. This was clearly going to take some time. She hoped Matt was having better luck with his enquiries in Torquay. Even so, she was curious to discover what Mrs Craven had learned that had sent her scurrying to the Dolphin. 'What did she have to say?'

'Well, I asked her about the inquest, how it had all gone. There was a big report in yesterday evening's newspaper and on the front page of the daily papers this morning.'

Kitty nodded, she had seen and read the reports herself. The Dolphin ordered newspapers in for guests and placed copies of the most popular in the residents' lounge, so she was always abreast of the news.

'Marigold Everton telephoned their house this morning, all of a twitter, asking for Ivor Silitoe. Harold Everton's nephew, Thomas, has been taken to the police station for questioning by Inspector Greville. Well, that looks bad, doesn't it? Marigold was in quite a state about it. Between us, I rather think that Marigold is becoming quite a nuisance to the Silitoes. She is one of those helpless kinds of women, I fear, and Mrs Silitoe is not happy with her constant calls on her husband.' Mrs Craven nodded her head sagely as she imparted this latest titbit.

'Hmm, I noticed she was leaning on Mr Silitoe yesterday at the inquest and Mrs Silitoe did appear a little sour,' Kitty said, recalling Marigold's grip on Ivor Silitoe's arm while Thomas King gave evidence and when the pharmacist, Mr Protheroe, had dismissed any speculation of a dispensing error.

'But what about Thomas King? I said he was suspicious. I warned you about him. I rather think I have a talent for this sleuthing business.' Mrs Craven smiled smugly, and Kitty tried not to groan out loud.

'I didn't think Mrs Everton was overfond of her nephew. After all, he is related to Mr Everton, is he not? His sister's son? She didn't show any particular affection for him when I had tea with her and if he is the guilty party then you would think she might be relieved. The press attention was very focused on her yesterday. She was aware of how things looked for her.' Kitty frowned.

'I suppose she has to be seen to be supportive of him,' Mrs Craven mused. 'What was interesting though was Gladys Silitoe's reaction to Marigold Everton. She was spearing foliage into her block of oasis as if she would have liked to knife the woman when she was talking about her. Ever since Harold Everton died Marigold has been telephoning Mr Silitoe and he's been spending hours at One Pine "advising" her on various matters.'

'I wonder why it bothers her so much. Mr Silitoe and Mr Everton conducted a great deal of business together and he is handling Mr Everton's will. The two couples were friends and bridge partners by all accounts,' Kitty said.

'The friendship it seems was between Mr and Mrs Everton and Mr Silitoe. Gladys was not close to Marigold and only went to the house for the bridge parties. Gladys and Marigold are not particular friends.' Mrs Craven's delicately arched brows lifted, and she gave Kitty a meaningful look.

'You mean Marigold Everton and Ivor Silitoe may be conducting some kind of liaison?' Now this was an interesting supposition. It would certainly provide even more of a motive for Ivor Silitoe to wish Harold Everton dead, and one for Marigold.

'It seems that Gladys Silitoe believes so.' Mrs Craven beamed triumphantly.

'I wonder what Inspector Greville will discover from talking to Thomas King.' A delicate shiver ran along her spine. She had danced with the man and been driven by him in his car. He was implicated in some kind of financial misdeeds. Was he also a cold-blooded murderer?

'Well, I can't stay around here all day.' Mrs Craven rose and gathered her furs about her. 'I must get on; I'm meeting some of the gals for luncheon. You will pass on my information to Captain Bryant, won't you, Kitty? If Thomas King turns out to be innocent, unlikely I know, then this may be important.'

'Of course, Mrs Craven.' Kitty stood. Mrs Craven's words and a rumble in her stomach reminding her that it had been quite a while since breakfast.

'And don't forget to keep me informed,' Mrs Craven instructed as she drew on her gloves and prepared to sail out of the hotel.

Kitty forced a smile and agreed politely as she escorted the older woman to the lobby. By the time she had waved her off the throbbing in her temple was threatening to become a full-blown headache.

Thanks to Mr Schofield's co-operation Matt had made a note of the names on some of the planning applications that the elderly clerk had said had been unusually successful. He intended to pay a few calls and ask some questions. He had already telephoned the other councillors on the committee and had quickly established that they were unaware of anything amiss. If Councillor Everton had concerns, he had not shared them with his fellow committee members.

His first call was at the offices of Babbacombe Holdings, a development company situated in that area. They had recently received the go-ahead to purchase and demolish several older properties and to replace them with a modern low-rise block of apartments, all with sea views.

From his research the plans had been controversial as initially some of the property holders had not wished to sell to the company but somehow permissions had been given and any remaining objections from householders further from the beaches complaining of loss of their view or light had been overruled.

Matt had arranged to meet the managing director, a Mr Brown, to discuss the development.

He was shown into the office by a smart young lady with chestnut curls, a rather short skirt and a lot of red lipstick. Mr Brown was a plump, self-important looking man in a brown suit. His desk was large and imposing with a tray piled high with papers. Cigarette smoke curled in the air from the overflowing china ashtray on the desk, tingeing the air blue.

Matt sat and waited while Mr Brown finished dealing with the letter in front of him.

'Now then, how can I help you? A private investigator, eh?' Mr Brown squinted at him through the haze.

'I'm sure you will have seen, sir, something in the newspapers recently about the murder of Councillor Everton?' Matt looked at the man opposite him.

Mr Brown took out a silver cigarette case and offered one to Matt. 'Murdered at the Imperial. Poison, wasn't it?'

Matt declined the cigarette and Mr Brown closed the case with a sharp click, returning it to his jacket pocket before lighting up.

'Yes, sir. Before he was killed Mr Everton had indicated that he wished to engage me on a case. I'm visiting all the people he may have had some business with recently as part of that investigation.' Matt was careful not to be too specific.

Mr Brown relaxed in his chair and pulled on his cigarette. 'I never met the man. Dealt with all the planning paperwork with his assistant. What's his name? King.'

Matt produced a small notebook and made a show of scribbling a few words in it. 'I understand that there was some doubt originally if the plans submitted would be allowed under the council's corporate vision for the area?'

The other man's eyes narrowed. 'There's always some who want to stand in the way of progress.'

'Of course, sir. Did you require any special help or advice from a member of the councillor's staff to ensure the scheme went through?' He was careful with his choice of words. He wished to rattle the man but not unduly antagonise him or his errand would be in vain.

Brown's hand holding his cigarette stilled for a moment. 'Are you implying something wasn't above board?'

'Not at all, sir. It merely surprised people that the application met such little resistance at the committee. I know from speaking to some other applicants that they had the benefit of, shall we say, some extra advice from a member of Councillor Everton's staff.' Matt met Mr Brown's gaze and held it.

'Mr King was very helpful to us,' Brown conceded.

'That's what we've heard from other applicants. It would be perfectly natural for you to show your gratitude for such assistance in some way, would it not?' Matt mused. He held his breath, knowing he was on tricky territory.

The man shifted in his chair, making the leather squeak. 'It wouldn't be unknown for such a thing in business. A small thank you present perhaps.'

Matt smiled. 'Thank you, Mr Brown, you've been very helpful.'

The other man eyed him shrewdly. 'Does this have any bearing on the councillor's murder?'

'I'm not certain. The police are also looking into the matter, as you might expect,' Matt said.

A shadow passed over Brown's face. 'Our business arrangements were all conducted in good faith.'

'Then I'm sure you will have no difficulties in explaining them to the police should they call on you. Their interest lies in finding Councillor Everton's murderer.'

He left Mr Brown's offices and sat astride the Sunbeam. The interview had confirmed what Mrs Braddock had told Kitty. Thomas King had a profitable sideline smoothing the path for certain planning applications. However, he lacked the power to ensure their success alone.

His most likely partner in the scheme had to be Ivor Silitoe. The other councillors would be guided by Silitoe's legal advice on the matters arising. But how to make the connection? He was certain that Silitoe would have covered his tracks well and it would be a difficult matter to link the two.

The next two companies on his list garnered a similar response mixed in with suspicion and belligerence at the implication of wrong-doing and fraud. His final call was at the office of a private individual.

Mr Mason refused to see him, dispatching his secretary to pass on a not too polite refusal. The secretary was in the same mode as the other girls he'd encountered that morning. Kitty's age, short skirts, high heels and expertly made-up.

'I'm so sorry about Mr Mason,' the girl explained.

Matt smiled at her. He'd heard the explosion and bear-like growls of rage coming from Mr Mason's office when the girl had ventured in to ask if he would see him.

'Oh it's perfectly all right, Miss… erm…' He waited for the girl to supply her name.

'Poppy.'

'Miss Poppy, perhaps you could help me?' Matt asked, leaning casually on the corner of her desk.

She blinked at him with expertly outlined wide blue eyes. 'Well, I don't know.' She glanced over her shoulder at Mr Mason's office door.

'Just a couple of quick questions.' Matt smiled winningly at her. 'Do you recall a gentleman called Thomas King ever telephoning or visiting Mr Mason?'

The girl flushed and bit her lower lip. 'Yes, a few weeks ago. I placed the telephone call for Mr Mason and then a few days later Mr King called at the office. Proper good looking with a nice green car.'

'Was this around the time Mr Mason had submitted his plans for a marina development?' Matt asked.

The girl glanced nervously at Mason's closed door and lowered her voice. 'Yes, he sent me out on an errand just after Mr King arrived, which I thought was a bit odd. He doesn't usually like me to fetch things in office time. He usually gets me to call at the post office and places on my way home.'

'Thank you, Poppy.' Matt smiled at her and made a swift exit as noises from within Mason's office indicated he might be about to come out. He had no desire to cause the girl any trouble with her employer.

CHAPTER SIXTEEN

Kitty looked for Matt on the platform when the train pulled into Churston the following morning. She waved at him from the window of the carriage. His tall, rangy figure materialised out of the mixture of late autumnal mist and steam from the train's engine and her heart thumped as he approached.

He had called her after supper the day before and they had exchanged information and confirmed their arrangements for their trip. The opening of the carriage door let in a blast of cooler air as Matt entered and took his place opposite her for the rest of the journey to Exeter. They were fortunate to have the carriage to themselves as the train was quiet.

'Another chilly morning.' Matt rubbed his leather-gloved hands together.

'It was still very misty as I crossed the river and it looks as if it's lingering.' Kitty glanced out of the window once more as the train gave a slight jolt before starting forward with a sharp hiss of steam.

'I didn't get much out of Inspector Greville when I telephoned him after our conversation last night.' Matt stretched his long legs out into the gap between the seats taking advantage of the empty carriage.

'I didn't either when I passed on Mrs Craven's information. I checked the newspapers last night and the dailies this morning and didn't see anything about an arrest,' Kitty said.

'King claims the money is from gambling wins. Mr Silitoe had advised him to say as little as possible and the inspector decided to try and dig for more information on that gentleman before tackling him head on. He was interested in the information I got from following up the planning leads. The other councillors that I spoke to all said the decisions were always made on aesthetic and legal guidelines.' Matt paused as the train stopped at the next station and they waited to see if anyone else boarded in their carriage.

'What did he think of Mrs Craven's assertion that there might be some kind of liaison between Marigold Everton and Ivor Silitoe?' Kitty asked as the train moved on again without anyone having joined them.

Matt's brow creased. 'Everton asserted to me that he and Marigold were perfectly happy when I tried to discover what he wished to consult me about at the Chamber of Commerce event. Silitoe doesn't have a reputation as a lady's man either, although Marigold did appear to be leaning on him at the inquest. It's not impossible but it may simply be a combination of Mrs Craven's fertile conjecturing and Mrs Silitoe's annoyance at Marigold's intrusions into their family life.'

'That's true, and even if Silitoe or Marigold murdered Mr Everton, then Mr Silitoe is still a married man. Oh, I don't know, any more. Let's leave it with Inspector Greville for now and focus on what Father Lamb and his friend may have to tell us.' She strongly suspected that it was unlikely that this vague clue provided by the contents of Jack Dawkins' box would lead anywhere but at least she would have tried.

By the time the train pulled into Exeter St David's their carriage was full and they had little further opportunity to talk. Kitty could see that Matt was eager to disembark. The close proximity of the other passengers had obviously made him uncomfortable as the space had become more confined.

She shivered as they walked out of the station amidst the small group of people who had exited their train. The day was still foggy and there was little sign of the pallid winter sun being able to break through.

'What are you hoping to discover today, Kitty?' Matt asked as they set off through the city streets towards Father Lamb's home.

'There has to be a reason why Jack Dawkins thought there was a connection between my mother's disappearance and the article about the reopening of the tunnels. I strongly suspect that the Glass Bottle public house and the people who kept it were involved in some way or had some information. I am hoping this friend of Father Lamb's might hold the key to what links those things.' Kitty held on to Matt's arm as they hurried across a busy street picking their way between the carts and the motor vehicles that rumbled past.

'You said you thought the cellars might link in some way to the water passages?' Matt asked as he steered her through a throng of people gossiping together outside a shop.

'Mickey's wife said that when the passages were not used for transporting water any more, there were some people who were rumoured to have found a way in so they could exploit them as a way of getting around the city without notice. Mickey thinks this is also where the rumour that the tunnels are haunted by a monk came from. He thinks the smugglers started the story to deter nosy parkers.'

Matt laughed. 'It would make sense. It will be interesting to see what Father Lamb's friend thinks of your theory.'

They had left the main street and were walking towards the residential area near the cathedral. There was far less traffic and fewer people around them now. Their footsteps sounded eerily echoing in the misty street.

Kitty found her fingers tightening around the strong muscles of Matt's arm as they turned the corner towards Father Lamb's house. It would be all too easy to believe some medieval monk walked the streets on a day such as today.

She was glad when they finally reached their destination and the front door of the presbytery was opened by Father Lamb's beaming housekeeper, who was quick to usher them into the warmth of the hall and to relieve them of their hats and coats.

'My dear Miss Underhay and Captain Bryant, come in by the fire and get warm. Allow me to introduce my colleague. Mr Pace is one of the lay team at the cathedral and is happy to give you some information on the water passages. He has been very involved with the proposals to open the passages as the cathedral's representative.' Father Lamb smiled happily at them like a bespectacled and benevolent tortoise as he showed them towards the fireplace and a pleasant middle-aged gentleman in a tired tweed suit, greying hair and an earnest expression.

'I'm delighted to meet you both. Father Lamb has told me some of the story behind your request for more information.' Mr Pace shook hands with them both before they all settled onto the worn but comfortable chairs before the fire.

Once they had all been suitably refreshed with a very welcome cup of coffee and slice of apple cake, Mr Pace produced a sheaf of papers from the well-used brown leather document case that he had at his feet.

'Now, I thought you might like to see these first and then, afterwards, Father Lamb has permitted me to make use of his dining table to lay out my map of the passages.'

Kitty looked with interest at the first document. It was a small sketch plan and an outline of the proposal to reopen the passages to visitors.

'Now, the oldest of the passages was built during the thirteen hundreds to serve the cathedral. Over the centuries these were added to right on into the seventeen hundreds until they were no longer used and fell into disrepair. They are quite a feat of engineering and extend quite a considerable way beneath the city. Even under the defensive walls at some points.' Mr Pace frowned as he added. 'Some of the tunnels are no longer accessible as they were damaged when the railway was built.'

Matt studied the document. 'How large are these passages?'

'Oh, easily the width and height of a man, especially the older tunnels which are quite marvellously constructed out of brick. The later parts are not so well finished. They used to contain lead piping but of course that has all gone. You can walk through them with ease carrying a lantern if you are careful.' Mr Pace's eyes gleamed with enthusiasm.

'There is a committee dedicated to opening the passages up to interested parties. Archaeological students and the like. There is also interest from the public. Monies raised would help conserve them,' Father Lamb explained.

Matt glanced at Kitty. 'Miss Underhay has heard that some of Exeter's less upright citizens have made their own access into some of the tunnels in the past and used them as a way of avoiding the scrutiny of the law. Is this true do you know, sir?'

Mr Pace blinked. 'There are rumours, and with the extent of the passages I could not rule out such a possibility. There are several known access points and there may be some secret points too. There are tunnels leading from the quays back into the cellars of some of the houses in that part of the city, they could well be connected to a wider network.'

Kitty's heart thumped in her chest that her theory might be correct. If she had her geography right, then there could be a connection. 'May we see the larger map, Mr Pace? There is a particular location that I have in mind and I would like to see if the tunnels are known to run anywhere near that spot.'

'Of course, dear lady, come.' He led the way into Father Lamb's dining room. A pleasant old-fashioned space with cream plastered walls dominated by the dark oak dining set and vast Pembroke table on which were laid out two large maps. The air felt cooler as the fire had not been lit in that room. Kitty shivered.

Father Lamb switched on the electric light so that they might see better as they studied the plans. Mr Pace produced a pair of spectacles from inside the breast pocket of his jacket. He polished them with a white cotton handkerchief and perched them on the end of his nose, the lens gleaming in the light from the lamp.

'Now, Miss Underhay, which area of the city interests you?'

Kitty looked at Matt. 'Where is the Glass Bottle situated?'

Matt moved forward to stand beside her, his shoulder brushing against her arm as he came closer to study the documents more closely. 'I think if you follow the road from the quays, towards Lucky Lane, and go further around into the side streets.' He scrutinised the map for another few seconds before marking the spot with his finger.

Kitty could see the relationship between the river with the quay area where goods were loaded, unloaded and stored, back through the maze of narrow streets marked on the map to the site of the Glass Bottle not far from the Mermaid Yard.

Mr Pace's lean features became quite animated. 'Yes, if you consider the other map and we were to overlay the two you can see that it would be perfectly possible to hypothetically have a point of connection between the smugglers' tunnels and the water conduits in that area.'

Kitty stared at the map. What did it all mean? Was it possible for her mother's body to be hidden somewhere under the city? The coffee she had enjoyed just a short time ago swirled uncomfortably in her stomach and rapid heat replaced the chill she had first felt on entering the room.

'Kitty, have a seat.' Matt had his arm around her and was guiding her to sit on one of the dining chairs that he had pulled out from the table. Her legs wobbled as she sank down onto the wooden chair.

'Shall I fetch a glass of water?' Father Lamb peered at her, his kindly face wrinkled with concern.

'No, really, I'm quite all right.' She attempted a smile to reassure them all. If only she could access the Glass Bottle and get into the cellars to take a look for herself.

'If you have seen all that you need, my dear, then let us go back to the drawing room. It's a little chilly in here,' Father Lamb suggested. Mr Pace collected up his documents.

Matt assisted her to her feet, and they returned to the cosy warmth of the parlour. Kitty's mind was busy, perhaps she could enter the tunnels from the other end and find a way towards the Glass Bottle.

She picked up the leaflet again that had the prospectus for the proposed guided tours of the passages. 'How accessible are the passages, Mr Pace? Are all of them safe enough to explore? Obviously, I'm thinking of the ones leading towards the area we were just considering.'

Mr Pace scratched his head and removed his spectacles. 'I'm afraid that as you travel further from the cathedral and the city centre then the passages are narrower and less well maintained and built. Indeed, where they had to run pipework under the medieval defences such as the East Gate then one would have to virtually crawl. Those areas sadly must remain off-limits. There is also no electric light just yet.'

'I see. Thank you so much for all your help today, Mr Pace. You've been terribly kind.' She smiled at him and was privately amused to see the trace of a blush appear on his cheeks.

'Not at all, Miss Underhay, and if at any time you wish to join a group to see the passages for yourself, please let me know. You too, of course, Captain Bryant.' He nodded at Matt.

Kitty knew full well there was nothing Matt would like less than to enter those passages.

'Thank you, sir, you've been very helpful,' Matt said.

Mr Pace stowed his paperwork away carefully in his case and insisted that Kitty keep a copy of the prospectus before he made his farewells to return to his work at the cathedral.

'Is there any more news of the landlord of the Glass Bottle?' Matt asked Father Lamb as the housekeeper returned with a fresh pot of coffee and another plate of cake.

'The pub remains shuttered up and there is a great deal of muttering amongst the regulars. Hammett is known for taking off at times for a few days here and there, but this is the longest he has been gone. He has a half-brother, Denzil, who visits occasionally but the two don't get on and he hasn't been seen for some time now.' Father Lamb helped himself to a piece of cake and tucked in happily.

'He didn't tell anyone where he was going or for how long?' Kitty asked.

Father Lamb shook his head sending a small scattering of crumbs down the front of his black cassock. 'No, my dear, he is not a communicative man. Surly, and unpleasant even with those who know him well.'

'I wonder what will happen to the place if he doesn't return,' Matt mused.

'Oh, he will be back. He always comes back. Like a bad penny.' The priest shook his head again somewhat mournfully.

'Will you let us know, sir, if you hear anything?' Matt asked.

'Of course. I don't know if you will get anything from him or his brother. As I said he is an unpleasant fellow, but I can understand that you may wish to try.' Father Lamb noticed the crumbs and brushed them away.

Kitty and Matt declined the priest's invitation to stay for lunch and said their farewells before venturing back onto the city streets. The mist had not lifted much and now held a yellowish tinge where the winter sun was failing to break through.

'Would you like to go into the centre for some lunch?' Matt asked as they walked back through the side streets.

'I must confess I feel rather full of Father Lamb's excellent coffee and apple cake. Also, seeing those maps and realising that the answer to my mother's disappearance may be connected to them in some way made me feel rather queer.' It was true that the murky weather and the thoughts that kept pressing to the forefront of her mind were making her feel unusually unsettled.

She stopped suddenly and Matt turned to face her, a surprised look on his face. 'What's wrong, old girl?' He spoke lightly but she could see concern in his eyes.

'I need to go and see the Glass Bottle for myself, Matt.'

He nodded slowly. 'Very well. I don't think we should go on foot. The area is not good, and I feel we would attract unwanted attention.'

She fell back into step beside him. 'We can take a taxi and just ask the driver to stop for a moment so I can see it for myself.'

They had reached the main shopping area. Matt sighted a taxi dropping off a lady further along the high street and let out a piercing whistle to attract the attention of the driver.

Kitty quickened her steps as they hurried towards the waiting car.

'We will be returning to Dartmouth, but we wish to visit a public house called the Glass Bottle on our way. Do you know it?' Matt asked as they tumbled breathlessly into the rear seat.

The driver gave them a puzzled look from under the brim of his flat cap. 'I knows it all right but it isn't the nicest place, sir and t'es been closed now for a few weeks.'

'That's quite all right, we just wish to see it. There is a possibility that my employer may wish to invest in a property near that area.'

Kitty marvelled at Matt's quickness of thought.

'Well, good luck to him and all if he is thinking of investing around there. A regular rat's nest it is. I'll get you as close as I can.

T'es alleyways round there.' The driver set off along the street and Kitty settled back to watch her surroundings with interest.

She had visited Exeter several times but only to the shopping area and the cafés and tea rooms near the cathedral. They had turned away now and were in a small tangle of streets going in the direction of the river. The road surface was lumpy, shaking them about as the car rattled slowly along. The larger Georgian houses were replaced by cottages and terraces. The frontages were shabby and unkempt and there were few shops.

They passed a boarded-up frontage and she recognised the name above the boarding, faded now and peeling. Jacky Daw's Emporium. They travelled on further along another couple of streets, the road was more of a muddy, pitted track now. The driver pulled to a stop.

'There it be, sir. The Glass Bottle.'

Kitty peered out to see a squat whitewashed building on the corner of the street almost melting in the lingering fog. The whitewash was dirty and grey with soot. A battered, crudely painted sign was attached to the wall depicting a glass beer bottle and a tankard. The one window was shuttered over, and the front door firmly closed with a white notice pinned to it.

'Wait for just a moment.' Kitty opened the car door and wriggled out. She crossed the street to read the sign. Matt followed after her.

'Closed until further notice,' Matt read out loud.

Kitty looked up at the building noticing the decaying downspout with weeds still verdant in the gutter and the ragged curtains visible in the window on the first floor.

'We should go.' Matt touched her sleeve. She returned to the taxi where a couple of street urchins aged about eight or nine in dirty trousers and thin coats were loitering, watching them with unabashed curiosity.

'You boys, do you know anything about that place? There is a penny or two in it for you,' Kitty asked the lads.

The boys looked at each other as if deciding what to say. 'Pub is shut, miss. Been closed up a while now,' the bolder of the two boys answered.

'Do you know where the landlord might have gone?' Kitty asked.

The boys shook their heads. 'Might have done a flit, miss,' the other lad suggested.

'Thank you.' Kitty delved into her bag and found her purse, dropping coins into the boys outstretched and grubby hands. She also added the remains of a small bag of barley sugars that she had acquired.

'If you hear of the landlord returning or of anyone visiting the pub take a message to Father Lamb at the presbytery in Bear Street near the cathedral and he will reward you. Tell him Miss Underhay gave you the instruction.'

The boys grinned and nodded at her and disappeared as quickly as they had arrived.

Kitty took her place next to Matt and the driver restarted the car.

'Satisfied now?' Matt asked.

Kitty glanced at him. 'It helps me to see the place. I wish we knew what had gone on.' She kept her voice low.

'When you opened the door and took off, I was concerned you were going to try and break in.' Matt grinned at her.

Kitty smiled back and poked his arm. 'Why, Captain Bryant, what a thought. I'm a respectable woman.'

'Don't tell me the thought hadn't crossed your mind?' he teased her openly now.

'Maybe for a second or two,' she admitted. She had hoped to see some sign of life from within the building. Some clue to where the occupant had gone and some way into the cellars. The great wooden delivery hatch in the pavement below the shuttered window had however looked surprisingly sturdy and was well secured with bolts and a substantial padlock.

Everywhere had appeared deserted and forlorn. Even the peep she had taken through the tiny gap where the window shutter was broken had revealed nothing. The glass beneath the wood had been thick with grime and the interior too dark for her gaze to penetrate.

How was this place linked to her mother's disappearance all those years ago?

CHAPTER SEVENTEEN

Kitty was quiet on the journey back to Dartmouth and Matt knew her thoughts were dwelling on her mother's disappearance. The mist that had been present all day had deepened into fog as they drove down the hill past the entrance to the naval college and on into Dartmouth.

'Stop here.' Matt instructed the driver to halt near the Boat Float. Kitty looked at him in surprise.

'Let's go and have tea before we return to the Dolphin. We missed lunch and I think you need some time before you discuss today with your grandmother,' Matt said.

Kitty nodded and they disembarked into an eerily silent world. The sun had given up on its efforts to break through and had already started to sink in the sky. Matt placed his arm around Kitty's narrow waist.

They made their way through the deserted streets in the direction of The Butterwalk. Yellow light spilled out from the window of the small tea room, a welcome glow in the swirling mist.

Unsurprisingly, given such a day, the café was deserted, and the rosy-cheeked young waitress seemed astonished to see a customer. The room was warm, and the delicious aroma of pastries and baking hung in the air. Matt ordered a platter of sandwiches with scones, jam and clotted cream with a large pot of tea. Kitty looked pale and in need of sustenance.

'Terrible weather today, sir, miss. Can't scarcely see a hand in front of your face,' the girl remarked as she returned with their order.

'Has it been like this here all day?' Matt asked. He knew that the weather near the coast could vary a great deal from the weather inland.

'Yes, sir, came on worse after lunch,' the girl said as she deposited a loaded tiered platter cake stand onto the pale pink tablecloth.

Matt was relieved to see some colour returning to Kitty's face as she tucked into the cucumber sandwiches.

'I wish we knew what had happened to that landlord, Hammett, and his brother. Not that I expect they would be able to tell us much even if they were willing. I'd dearly like to get into the cellar of the pub and poke about though,' Kitty said as she selected a scone from the stand.

'The chances of either of those things happening are slim to remote.' Matt sounded a note of caution in case Kitty was getting one of her ideas. He could understand her frustration, she had patiently been following up leads for years and it was only in the last few months that she had achieved anything like a breakthrough.

Kitty ladled clotted cream onto her scone and added a generous blob of strawberry jam. 'I know, but still…' She gave a cheeky grin and bit into her scone with relish.

Matt found himself grinning back at her. He enjoyed being in Kitty's company. She had a zest for life that had been lacking from his own existence ever since he had been widowed. It was why he needed to choose the right moment to talk to her.

They finished their tea and he walked with her back towards the hotel. It was already much darker now and the lights along the embankment were a welcome guide.

Mary was still on duty behind the reception desk as they entered the warm, brightly lit lobby of the Dolphin.

'Miss Kitty, Captain Bryant, Mrs Treadwell asked if you would go straight up to her salon when you came in. Mrs Craven is there too.' The girl gave an apologetic smile as she added the last piece of information.

Kitty looked at Matt. 'This sounds ominous. Perhaps the inspector has made an arrest.'

Matt agreed with her as they hurried up the oak staircase. Kitty pulled her gloves off as she walked and rapped on the door to her grandmother's apartment with her bare knuckles.

Matt followed behind Kitty as she opened the door. Mrs Treadwell was seated in an armchair on one side of the fireplace and Mrs Craven was installed on the seat opposite her.

'Kitty, Matt, at last. The weather is so awful out there. Have you heard the news?' Kitty's grandmother asked as they divested themselves of their coats and hats and came to sit on the sofa near to the fire.

'What news, Grams?' Kitty asked as she stretched out a hand towards the blaze in the hearth.

Mrs Craven's eyes gleamed with triumph. 'Oh, it's dreadful. Such a tragedy. We only found out by accident.'

'What's happened?' Matt could see Mrs Craven was bursting with news.

The two elderly women exchanged glances, and Mrs Craven took up the tale again. 'I heard it from my maid who had it direct from Potts, the butcher. He had been out in his van to make some deliveries and he came across the accident. He said the car was completely wrecked; he said it looked as if it had spun off the road in all this fog, hit one of the drystone walls and finished up in the ditch. There was still steam coming up from the burst radiator, Mr Potts said, so it must have happened only a moment or two beforehand. Of course, he parked his van and hurried over to help but it was too late.'

Matt could guess what the answer would be but asked the question anyway. 'Whose car was it, Mrs Craven?'

'Thomas King's, of course, that green Alvis of his. He always did drive a little too quickly. Anyway, he was dead. Nothing to be done for him. It made Mr Potts feel quite ill. He jumped back in his van and drove to the nearest place that had a telephone to call the police.'

Matt looked at Kitty, she had gone quite pale again.

'How dreadful. Where did this occur?' Kitty asked.

'Out near Cockington. Mr Potts doesn't usually deliver out that way, but he has contracts with some of the hotels and businesses and was owed payment from some of them, so he had gone in person to get settlement on the accounts.' Mrs Craven pursed her lips disapprovingly that any business would run their affairs in such a manner.

'Do you happen to know if this was anywhere near the Conway Country House Hotel?' Matt asked.

Mrs Craven beamed at him in approval. 'Yes, that's right and where Mr Potts went to make his telephone call.'

Kitty shuddered. 'It's horrible, quite horrible.'

'I suppose it was an accident?' Matt asked. He took Kitty's slim fingers in his hand and gave them a reassuring squeeze. The unexpected news had clearly shocked her. As well it should have, Thomas King had been so youthful and full of life.

'It seems the most likely thing. The weather, as you know, is quite dreadful and it seems this Mr King was fond of speed. The lanes around Cockington are very narrow and there are many unexpected twists and turns.' Mrs Treadwell met his gaze. 'You are inclined to think it may have been foul play?'

Matt frowned. 'It seems a very unlucky coincidence when Mr King spent yesterday with the police answering questions about the murder of his uncle and now there has been this terrible accident. I'm not fond of coincidences.'

'I agree,' Kitty said. 'Mr King did drive quickly but he was very proud of his car and he wasn't careless.'

'Did Mr Potts say anything else about the accident? Anything he mentioned at all about the scene?' Matt asked.

Mrs Craven's brow creased as she tried to recall what had been said. 'He was in quite a state still when he returned to the shop. Mrs Potts had to give him a tot of brandy. He said that steam was pouring from the radiator and that the driver must have hit the wall with a fair old bang because the front wheel had come right off.'

'Hmm, that strikes me as curious. It's unusual to lose a wheel. Unless, of course, someone could have tampered with it.' Matt looked at Kitty.

'Would that be a difficult thing to do?' she asked. 'Would a person need to be strong or have special knowledge or tools?'

'I wouldn't have thought any special knowledge would be necessary and the nuts are easily loosened on most cars with an ordinary wrench. A woman could manage it as easily as a man, if that is what you are asking,' Matt said.

'Daphne's fiancé is a car mechanic,' Kitty said.

'This is all speculation any way. I'm sure Inspector Greville will investigate it all very thoroughly.' Matt gave Kitty's fingers another gentle squeeze.

'I'm thankful that if it was an accident that it didn't happen when you were in his car, Kitty. It could have occurred when he brought you home on Sunday.' Kitty's grandmother's face was creased with anxiety.

'I wonder what he was doing out at Cockington?' Kitty said. 'Do you think he might have been calling on Mr Hendricks and Mrs Braddock?'

'There is every possibility.' Matt had been thinking the same thing. He could have gone to visit them to warn them off from saying anything more to the police or to try and get more money from them. There were any number of plausible reasons for why Thomas King had been in Cockington in such dreadful weather.

'If you ask me, he could have driven off the road on purpose,' Mrs Craven stated. 'Overcome with guilt at murdering his uncle.

A man who had taken him in and given him a job and a home, treated him like a son by all accounts.'

'I suppose that is possible, but unlikely. Thomas King didn't strike me as a man likely to be filled with remorse even if he had killed his uncle,' Matt said.

'I agree. He was quite confident and not at all the kind of person to seem suicidal,' Kitty agreed.

Mrs Craven appeared slightly nettled at having her theory dismissed. 'I still think he was the murderer. I wonder what will happen now? I thought Mr King was almost certain to be arrested and charged.'

Matt wondered the same thing. He might have to drop by the police station and see if he could extract any information from Inspector Greville.

After Matt had left with Mrs Craven to share Mr Potter's taxi, Kitty slumped back on the sofa.

'Are you all right, darling?' Her grandmother's voice was warm with concern.

Kitty managed a weak smile. 'It has been a very strange day, Grams.' She told her grandmother what they had learned at Exeter and about her visit to see the Glass Bottle.

'Whatever could your mother have been doing there? I suppose she could have become lost after leaving Jack Dawkins' shop and stumbled into something.'

'I just wish I knew what Jack thought the connection was between the Glass Bottle and the passages and why he believed it had something to do with Mother's disappearance.' Kitty sighed. Her head ached from trying to work it all out.

Her grandmother gave a wry smile. 'Knowing your mother anything could have happened. She may have become lost or seen someone or something in trouble and intervened when she shouldn't.' Her grandmother sighed. 'I remember her when she was young coming home covered in scratches with an enormous black eye because she had tackled a man trying to drown a sackful of kittens in the river. Her dress was torn, and she was holding on to the kittens. We had such a job to find homes for them all.' Her grandmother's expression had softened at the memory and her eyes filled with tears.

'Oh, Grams.' Kitty slipped off the sofa and stood behind her, wrapping her arms around her neck in a loving embrace.

'Well now, it seems we can go no further with that for a while.' Her grandmother produced a lace-edged handkerchief and dabbed at her eyes.

Kitty slept badly that night. She woke in a cold sweat having dreamt that Thomas King had come to take her to tea, and they had set off in the green Alvis. It had been a bright sunny day but then a storm had started, and everything had become dark. She had turned to ask Thomas something and instead had seen the dead face of Councillor Everton looking at her with his protruding glassy sightless eyes and that blueish tinge to his skin.

Her room was still dark, so she sat up in bed and switched on her bedside lamp. A glance at her alarm clock told her it was only five o'clock in the morning. Her pulse was still racing as she propped herself up against her pillows and took a small sip from the glass of water she habitually kept next to her bed.

She wasn't sure if it had simply been the dream that had woken her or something else. Her skin was clammy with sweat and she shivered in the chilly air of her room. Everything seemed quiet and still in the corridor outside. She could hear the faint familiar sounds of the Dolphin at night.

Reassured that it had just been the dream she snuggled down beneath her blankets and eiderdown. She dozed fitfully and woke again before her alarm clock went off. Matt had said he intended to call at the police station later that morning to see what he could learn about Thomas King's accident. She wondered if it had been this that had been playing on her mind giving her bad dreams.

Kitty pulled on her thick red flannel dressing gown and stuffed her feet into her house slippers. She might as well get up and start her day, she had invoices to make out for departing guests and allocations to prepare for new arrivals. Catching murderers might be Matt's business but running the Dolphin was hers and it might stop her mind from reliving the dreadful events of the last week.

When the receptionist put a telephone call through to her office a little after ten Kitty expected it to be from Matt, updating her. Instead she got the breathy, tremulous tones of Lavinia Braddock.

'Miss Underhay, I hope you don't mind, I simply had to call. Have you heard the terrible news? About Thomas King?'

'Yes, Captain Bryant and I heard yesterday when we returned from Exeter. The weather was so awful yesterday with the fog. I suppose it must have been an accident?' Kitty was only slightly surprised to hear from Lavinia. She was interested to try and find out as much as she could however.

'I suppose it must have been, the roads would have been slippery, and you could hardly see in some places. So shocking. It's made me feel quite ill.'

Kitty thought she sounded unwell, her voice had a wavering note as if she were trying to hold back tears. 'I know how you feel. Two unexpected deaths in such a short space of time. The accident happened near your hotel too, didn't it? Had Mr King been to see you?' She longed to know if visiting Lavinia's hotel had been the purpose of Thomas' journey.

'Oh, Miss Underhay, Mr King had been to see my brother just before he died. I don't know what went on, Clive won't tell me. His temper flares up and he shouts at me. That police inspector just telephoned and said he wishes to speak to my brother and I'm horribly frightened. I keep thinking about the money and poor Councillor Everton's death.' Lavinia's voice broke in a small sob.

'You poor thing. I'm sure it's merely a formality to retrace Mr King's steps or something. Did he say where he had been before he came to see your brother?' Kitty asked. If Mr King's death was not an accident it would be interesting to know who could have had an opportunity to tamper with the car and how long it would have taken for that meddling to have had an effect. Could Mr Hendricks have tampered with the car?

'Yes, he had been at home with his aunt and Daphne. Her fiancé had been there too, they were discussing how soon after the funeral it would be considered decent to hold the wedding. He mentioned it when he arrived, he joked and said he had advised Daphne to elope.' Lavinia gave an audible sniff and Kitty could picture her holding the telephone receiver in one hand and her handkerchief in the other as she spoke.

'The weather was so bad, I doubt he was out for a pleasure drive, so he probably came straight to see your brother,' Kitty mused.

'Oh no, wait, he had to call in at Mr Silitoe's home on the way to take some paper's for Mrs Everton. Something to do with the probate for the will,' Lavinia said.

'I'm sure that will all be helpful to Inspector Greville to help determine what may have gone wrong. If it was something mechanical or if it was to do with Mr King's driving, for instance.' Kitty tried to sound knowledgeable and reassuring. It was vexing to realise that virtually any of them could have sabotaged the Alvis.

'Do you think so? My nerves feel so stretched with everything that's happened. I can hardly think straight,' Lavinia said.

'You were terribly kind to me, asking me to tea last week, please let me return the kindness. Why don't you come to the Dolphin tomorrow afternoon if you are free and take tea with me here? It would do you good to have a little break away from everything for an hour,' Kitty said. She did feel quite sorry for Lavinia. The woman sounded so miserable and in need of a little pleasure. It would also enable her to discover the outcome of Inspector Greville's visit to Lavinia's brother.

'That really is very kind of you. I would love that.' Lavinia immediately sounded more cheerful. They fixed the time and ended the call.

Kitty sat and frowned at the telephone after she had replaced the receiver back in its cradle. From what Lavinia had said pretty much anyone could have tampered with Thomas King's car if they had been so inclined. The Silitoes, Marigold, Daphne, Daphne's fiancé, Lavinia, or her brother. She couldn't rule any of them out.

CHAPTER EIGHTEEN

Matt decided to ride into Torquay straight after breakfast in the hope of catching Inspector Greville at the police station. The weather had improved a little with a bright, cold, blustery day blowing away the last remnants of yesterday's fog.

He parked the Sunbeam near the station and walked up the steps into the small reception area. One of the sergeants he knew quite well was behind the desk. The man seemed unsurprised to see him.

'Good morning, Captain Bryant, what can we do for you today, sir?'

'Is Inspector Greville in? I wondered if I might see him for a few minutes,' Matt asked.

The sergeant picked up the telephone receiver and dialled what Matt assumed was the extension number to the inspector's office.

'Captain Bryant is in reception, sir, wants to know if you can spare him a few minutes.'

Matt didn't catch the answer but gathered it must have been in the affirmative when the sergeant placed the receiver back on the cradle and opened the hatch to show him along the familiar whitewashed corridor to Inspector Greville's office. Further along were the stone steps leading down to the cells where he had been briefly incarcerated just a few weeks earlier. The memory sent a chill through his body.

The sergeant stopped by a door and rapped on the frosted-glass panel inset into the top half.

'Here you are, sir.' The sergeant opened the door on hearing Greville's response.

Matt entered into a fug of pale blue cigarette smoke. The inspector was barely visible behind a towering pile of brown manilla folders stacked in various trays on his desk.

'Captain Bryant, take a seat.' The inspector moved some of the paperwork mountain so he could see his visitor more clearly. 'I assume you have heard the news about Thomas King?'

'Yes, sir, a dreadful business. Can I ask if it was an accident?' Matt took a seat on the wooden chair opposite the inspector.

Greville frowned and his moustache appeared even more depressed than usual. 'It seems not. The weather, as you know, yesterday was perfectly foul with very poor visibility. Our friend, Mr King, was a gentleman who was quite fond of speed, but he was not an especially reckless driver. He had been visiting the Conway Country House Hotel and was on his way back to Torquay.' He paused and looked at Matt as if to make sure that he was following.

'Go on, sir,' Matt urged.

'The Alvis was new and well-maintained. Indeed, both his aunt and Daphne have confirmed that it was his pride and joy and he took a great deal of care of it. He left the hotel in the fog, his headlamps were on, there were only a few marks on the road. It seems unlikely that he swerved to miss something and there was no sign of excessive braking. The car left the road near a bend and hit one of the drystone walls that holds back a bank of earth. It then span around and ended up in the drainage ditch facing the opposite direction. The front wheel was completely detached from the car but there was no sign of shearing or metal failure. Mr King unfortunately took the full impact on the driver's side, broke his neck.'

'You believe that someone tampered with the front wheel of the car?' Matt asked. He couldn't help shuddering slightly at Greville's calm, matter-of-fact description of the accident.

The inspector sighed heavily. 'I have had mechanics looking at the car and it seems that is the case.'

'Do we know when it was done? Could he have driven far with the wheel nuts loosened or is it something that must have been done while he was visiting Mr Hendricks and Mrs Braddock?' Matt asked. He had some basic mechanical knowledge gained during his time in the Great War, but he suspected that the mechanics would be able to provide a far more definitive answer.

'It's hard to say. It's not far from Torquay to Cockington. Two miles or so depending on the route taken. The wheel could easily have been tampered with before he arrived at the hotel.' Inspector Greville's expression was grave.

'Do you feel Thomas King's death is linked to that of his uncle?' Matt asked. It would be natural to assume they were, but he was curious to hear the inspector's thoughts on the matter.

'I think so, yes. What I don't know is why. There is definitely something awry with the affairs of the planning committee. Councillor Everton, from everything we have been able to discover, was not a party to whatever his nephew had been up to. Mr King admitted having an argument with his uncle about his work but denied that his uncle had accused him of wrongdoing. He did say though that his uncle had instigated some recent changes in their routine. Mr Everton was collecting and opening his own post and contacting all new applicants personally.' The inspector looked at Matt.

'You think that the supply of payments for, ahem, advice, was about to be cut off?' Matt met the inspector's gaze.

'Councillor Everton had also mentioned a couple of times in front of witnesses that he wished to consult you about something.'

Matt nodded. 'Did Mr King admit to charging for his advice when you interviewed him?'

Inspector Greville snorted. 'Mr Silitoe had advised Mr King to say as little as possible. It was like getting blood from a stone. He claimed the sums of money deposited in cash in his account were from gambling wins on the horses. He was very fond of the horses and the dates did tally.'

'The committee members told me that all the decisions they made were based on legal advice given by Mr Silitoe and on aesthetics. The council has passed a series of by-laws to deter certain types of planning applications as they wish to present the area in a positive light for trippers and visitors. Hence the clearance of some of the slum areas. Mr King would have needed Mr Silitoe's advice or co-operation, surely, if he were not to have disgruntled customers wanting their fees returned if their applications failed,' Matt said.

'Mr Hendricks was not a satisfied customer according to your friend, Miss Underhay. Mrs Braddock has said they had paid over two hundred pounds in total to Mr King. I will be interested to find out from Mr Hendricks what Mr King had to say yesterday when he visited. I asked him a few questions and I've left him to stew for a while before I return. Mr Hendricks is a man who needs to be worked up a little if you are to get anything sensible from him.' The inspector drummed on the edge of his desk with a pencil.

'I have to say that it does not look good for Mr Silitoe. He has motive, means and opportunity.' Matt shifted restlessly in his seat. Was Ivor Silitoe a murderer?

'We have touched on a few matters with Mr Silitoe but he is either a good actor, or he was genuinely surprised at the suggestion that payments were taken for advice to the committee to favour certain applications.' The inspector ceased his drumming. 'There is no money trail leading to Mr Silitoe. We have checked his bank accounts and those of Councillor Everton and apart from one large payment paid in just a day or so after the councillor's death, there appears nothing amiss.'

'What next then, sir?' Matt asked.

'I'm going to talk to Mr Hendricks again today and then I think I need another interview with Mr Silitoe. A more formal one with a lot more questions. Always tricky when interviewing a member of the law profession so we've been very much gloves on up till now.' Inspector Greville was thoughtful but Matt detected a hint of steel in his tone.

Kitty told Matt of Lavinia Braddock's impending visit to the Dolphin when he telephoned from his Fore Street office to tell her the results of his interview with Inspector Greville.

'It will be very interesting to hear what she has to tell you after Greville has spoken to her brother.' Matt's voice tickled her ear down the receiver.

'Do you think the inspector will find enough evidence to arrest Ivor Silitoe?' Kitty asked. It didn't look good for the man, but she knew that at present there was no concrete evidence linking him to the murders. It was all supposition and conjecture. A good barrister would make mincemeat of the case.

'He needs a paper trail of evidence, money or something more substantial.' Matt's opinion reflected her own thoughts.

'It could still be Daphne or Marigold. If Thomas had discovered either of them were guilty then they may have seen him off,' Kitty said. 'Daphne's fiancé could well have helped her to tinker with the car.'

'True. She was under her father's thumb. He controlled her money and dictated who she could see. Plus, she benefits financially from the will.' Matt sounded thoughtful. 'No doubt Inspector Greville will have thought of this too.'

'Well, I shall see what I can learn tomorrow from Mrs Braddock.' Kitty replaced the receiver with a click.

She had scarcely had time to pick up her pen when there was a knock at the door of her office. She was pleasantly surprised when Alice entered. She hadn't seen the girl since Alice's mother had made her visit a week ago.

'Begging your pardon for interrupting you, Miss Kitty, but I wondered if I might have a word.' Alice's cheeks were pink and there was a faint tremor in her voice.

'Of course, sit down, Alice. Is something the matter?' Kitty was concerned, she was very fond of her young maid and had come to look upon her as a friend as well as an employee. She hoped the girl wasn't ill or about to resign.

Alice took a seat in front of the desk, pleating the corner of her starched white apron in her fingers. 'I found out as my mother paid you a call last Saturday, miss.'

Kitty sighed and set her fountain pen down carefully on her brass pen tray 'Yes, your mother did call to see me.'

The colour deepened in Alice's pale freckled cheeks. 'I want to apologise, miss. She had no right to come here and interfere.'

'She is your mother, Alice, and it was quite natural for her to be a little concerned that there have unfortunately been a number of murders this year and I seem to have been caught up in them.'

Alice opened her mouth to protest and Kitty held up her hand to prevent her from speaking out.

'Because I have been involved, I have also involved you. Your mother naturally wanted to be assured of your safety and your reputation. You are still a minor and under her care.'

'What it really was was our Betty astirring the pot, that were all. She's proper jealous.' Alice's chin tipped mutinously upwards. 'I enjoy our adventures, miss, I don't want to just spend my days in the linen closet afolding sheets for Mrs Homer and giving out towels and ascrubbing floors. Not that I don't like working here. It was lovely going to the Imperial Hotel and visiting your aunt and uncle's house at Enderley even with the murders. It was like being in a wonderful dream like I see people in the cinema.'

Kitty grinned. 'I like having you with me too, Alice. Please don't worry. My discussion with your mother was perfectly amicable. I see no reason why you shouldn't continue to accompany me as my maid and chaperone when the need arises.' Alice's words touched a chord with Kitty. She too wanted more from life than managing the Dolphin. Matt's entrance into her life had introduced an element of adventure that had been sorely lacking before. Even if she could do without people trying to kill her, as they had done in the past.

Alice beamed at her, the spark returning to her eyes. 'Oh good, miss. I was worried my mum had put a stopper on it.'

'No stopper,' Kitty said and picked up her pen once more as the young maid jumped up from her seat.

Alice flashed her another grin and disappeared back to her jobs before Mrs Homer, the housekeeper, could come looking for her.

Next morning Kitty arranged to have a table set up for tea with Lavinia in a quiet nook in the residents' lounge. There was a nice view of the river and they were unlikely to be disturbed. At this time of year, they only had a few long-term resident guests and some regular commercial visitors here to do business in the town.

The Dolphin always carried out refurbishments to various parts of the hotel during November and January, following a rota to ensure that the hotel always looked at its best for the main season. Kitty was currently making improvements to her own room as part of the refurbishments. Her grandmother had suggested turning the small room next to Kitty's bedroom into a sitting area and the idea had struck her as a good one. Thankfully the workmen were nearly finished.

Lavinia arrived punctually in the lobby. She had clearly dressed for the occasion in a smart emerald green two-piece under her black coat. A modish black hat with an emerald band complemented her outfit.

'Mrs Braddock, Lavinia, you look lovely.' Kitty greeted her warmly as one of the maids took Lavinia's outdoor things to the cloakroom. 'Come through to the lounge.'

She noticed that despite Lavinia's efforts with her clothes, the woman looked tired and careworn.

'This is quite lovely, Miss Underhay. No wonder the Dolphin is so well thought of.' Lavinia looked about her with interest all the way to the table that Kitty had requested be laid ready for them. Once they were seated the maid left to fetch the trolley and Kitty waited for Lavinia to settle into her seat.

The girl returned with the tea trolley and set out the stand before taking her leave. After she had gone and the pleasantries were out of the way, Kitty loaded up her plate with delicate prawn and cucumber sandwiches, savoury pastries and slivers of pork pie while she waited for her guest to raise the subject of the murders.

'Inspector Greville called again yesterday to speak to Clive. You remember I said he had telephoned?' Lavinia paused to take a sip of her tea.

'You said it was worrying you,' Kitty said in an encouraging tone. Lavinia clearly had concerns about her brother and Kitty wanted to know why.

'Oh, Miss Underhay, Kitty. You see, Mr King and Clive had a terrible quarrel when he visited. Clive tends to shout when he is angry, and I heard raised voices. Clive, well, he's been in bother before because of his temper. I don't know exactly what was said. My brother is old-fashioned and believes a man should handle any unpleasantness. I know he intended to have it out with him about the planning advice he had given us, and he wanted to try and get some of our money back.' Lavinia's lower lip wobbled, and she looked as if she was about to burst into tears.

'That doesn't seem unreasonable to me. After all that was a good deal of money and you have nothing to show for it,' Kitty soothed. She could see Lavinia and her brother's point. They had been defrauded of a lot of money. She was only surprised that Thomas King had agreed to discuss the matter. Clive Hendricks had good reason to be angry, but was he angry enough to tamper with the car? That was a cool, planned act, not something done in a rush of blood to the head.

Lavinia chewed and swallowed one of the bite-sized savoury pastries from her plate. 'Clive wouldn't tell me what went on, but when I heard the door slam, I knew it wasn't good. I was worried Clive might have lashed out and Mr King was a much younger, fitter man.'

'Did he say anything to you after Mr King left?' Kitty asked.

Lavinia brushed some crumbs from her lips with a napkin. 'He told me that King had laughed at him when Clive had said we should get our money back. He claimed it wasn't his fault, he just gave advice. There weren't any guarantees that the applications would be successful. I saw him come out of the office looking as cocky as you like in his fancy shoes and gold watch. Not a bit of shame about him. He said something to Clive and sort of smirked and then he was gone.'

'Can you remember what he said to your brother?' Kitty helped herself to an iced bun.

'Something like, "It's up to you, old man. Try it and see how far you get."' Lavinia's hand clenched into a fist around the napkin. 'Clive was really angry. I can always tell, his neck goes red. He slammed the office door again and refused to speak to me for a good half an hour.'

Kitty refreshed their teacups. 'Did the inspector question you as well as your brother?'

Lavinia nodded. 'I had to tell him all of this, of course. He was asking me if Clive could have had any opportunity to go out to Thomas King's car or if I had gone anywhere near it. Well, of course we hadn't. It was such a horrid day, who would want to be outside in that terrible fog.' A delicate shiver ran through Lavinia's ample frame. 'I know it's been reported in the papers as an accident, but I don't think it could have been, Miss Underhay, do you?'

Kitty set her delicate china cup and saucer down on the table. 'It seems unlikely to me,' she admitted. From what Matt had told her, it was definitely murder but she wasn't going to say that to Lavinia. She could have been covering for her brother but that seemed unlikely or why have this conversation now?

'That inspector asked if we had heard or seen another car or anyone prowling about outside at the time Mr King was in the office with Clive but you couldn't see a hand in front of your face and, well, one of the bulbs has failed at the front of the hotel,' Lavinia admitted.

'You poor thing. It all sounds perfectly awful. How far had Mr King travelled from you when he had his accident?' Kitty offered a plate of meringues to Lavinia. She supposed Lavinia could have tampered with the car but it seemed unlikely. Lavinia was scared of her own shadow.

'Not terribly far. The lanes are quite narrow to reach the hotel, as you know. We didn't hear anything until Mr Potts, our meat supplier, turned up in a dreadful state asking to use the telephone. Well, he made the call and Clive returned to the accident with him to wait for the police. The poor man was in such a state about it. There is quite a nasty bend about a quarter of a mile down the road and it happened there at the crossroads. There have been accidents there before but never as bad as this one.' Lavinia shook her head sadly before biting into one of the meringues. The raspberry filling staining her lips red as she continued to look mournful.

'Gracious, I hadn't realised it had occurred so close to you,' Kitty said. 'How terrible. Poor Mrs Everton, to lose her husband and her nephew.' She waited for Lavinia's reaction.

Lavinia's carefully pencilled eyebrows arched upwards. 'It is quite awful, but I don't think there was much love lost between Mrs Everton and Mr King. Or between him and Daphne for that matter. I'm not normally one to gossip but Mrs Everton dropped it out at that dinner that it was Mr Everton's suggestion that Thomas come to live with them. I think that it had put Daphne's nose quite out of joint. Apparently, Mr Everton had always wanted a son and he doted on Thomas. That's why he gave him the job working for him.'

'I must admit, I had heard the same as you.' Kitty leaned forward in a confidential manner. 'Like you, I'm really not one to gossip, but I heard a rumour that Marigold Everton was a little too close to Ivor Silitoe.' She wondered what Lavinia would say to that suggestion.

Mrs Craven had seemed so certain about an affair after her conversation with Gladys Silitoe, it would be interesting to discover Mrs Braddock's thoughts on the matter.

Lavinia pursed her lips. 'I must admit I hadn't thought about it, but it would explain a lot. Marigold Everton was certainly hanging on to Mr Silitoe a lot at the inquest. At the time I put it down to the shock of the event but thinking about it now, she was very clingy. Mrs Silitoe definitely didn't appear too pleased about it. You would have expected her to cling to Daphne or Thomas King really. She more or less hinted as much to me when we walked out of the town hall together. Yes, I can see how it would appear.' She nodded her head sagely.

Kitty drew back a little. Lavinia was very fond of oil of patchouli perfume and it was rather overpowering at close quarters. 'I heard she had been telephoning Mr Silitoe at all hours over the slightest thing.' She felt a little guilty at gossiping in such a manner, but she wanted to induce Lavinia to feel comfortable with her confidences.

Mrs Braddock clicked her tongue and tutted. 'I can't say I'm surprised. Mrs Everton struck me as being quite a clinging vine. I heard that the daughter, Daphne, was engaged. She had a ring on when she came to the inquest. I don't know if you noticed it. A small sapphire on a white band. I presumed the young man accompanying her was the fiancé. Shocking so soon after her father's death.'

'I understand that Councillor Everton had opposed the match.'

Lavinia shook her head again. 'Goodness.'

There was a comfortable silence for a moment as they finished their tea. Lavinia gazed through the window at the view of the river and the embankment.

'Forgive me if I'm speaking out of turn, but a horrid thought has just occurred to me.' She turned to face Kitty with round, frightened eyes.

'Whatever is the matter?' Kitty could see that the woman looked genuinely scared.

'It suddenly occurred to me, Miss Underhay. If Mr King was murdered, which seems most possible, then one of those people who were at our table must be the murderer. And that as Councillor Everton had said he wished to consult your friend, Captain Bryant, then his life could be in danger too. The murderer might think Councillor Everton had told him something.'

Kitty stared at Lavinia. She hadn't considered Matt to be in danger. She, like Matt, had assumed that the killer had acted to try and prevent the councillor from speaking to him. But what if now, with this latest death, the killer thought Matt might be on their trail?

'I hadn't considered that possibility.' Kitty felt slightly sick. Had she and Matt been complacent? She couldn't believe she hadn't thought of the idea herself.

'I do hope I haven't worried you. It was just, well, looking out at this lovely view with everything seeming so normal on the surface, and all the time these terrible things are happening. I thought, what if we are all unsafe?' Lavinia's pleasant face crumpled.

'I'm sure Inspector Greville is on the case and will make an arrest soon. It is frightening though, I agree. I shall warn Matt to be on his guard.' Kitty tried to reassure the woman and made a mental note to telephone Matt as soon as Lavinia left to ask him to take care.

'I really wish I had not allowed Clive to persuade me to leave Southend to come here. It was a huge mistake. I was quite comfortable with my little B & B. I had friends there.' Tears gleamed in Lavinia's eyes. 'Clive was so unhappy in his last job though and, after I lost my husband, I was so low. At the time it made sense, now I wish I had stayed put.'

Kitty sympathised with the woman. It seemed the move to Cockington had been ill-judged and it was obvious to her that they were out of their depth.

'I think this time of year makes things feel worse. The weather is cold, and the business is quiet,' Kitty said.

Lavinia dabbed at her eyes and blew her nose. 'You are right, Miss Underhay. I dare say things will improve after Christmas.' She managed a watery smile, but Kitty could tell her voice had little conviction.

After Lavinia had thanked Kitty warmly for the tea and been waved off back to Cockington Kitty returned to her office to telephone Matt.

CHAPTER NINETEEN

When his telephone rang again later that evening Matt assumed that it must be Kitty again. She had called after her tea with Lavinia Braddock and had seemed unusually rattled by Lavinia's suggestion that his life might be at risk.

He had done his best to reassure her, while feeling a little pleased that she obviously cared so much for his safety. He had never been very good at judging women, despite his marriage to Edith. He had worked in a masculine world and Kitty was a very modern young woman. She was no clinging vine or helpless housewife, as she was keen to remind him.

At times they had seemed very close but then events would overtake them, and the old insecurities would rear their head in his mind. He was older than Kitty, thirty-five, battle-scarred physically and mentally. There were things in his past, in his work. His mother had pointed out to him that the bad dreams which haunted him and sometimes led him to destroy the room that he slept in might make a marriage dangerous.

He sighed as he picked up the receiver. He needed to talk to Kitty about his visit to Edith's grave the other Sunday.

'Captain Bryant? I'm sorry to disturb you at this late hour.' Matt blinked in surprise at hearing Father Lamb's gentle voice.

'Father, is everything all right?' Matt glanced at the bronze clock on his mantelpiece, it was after ten thirty at night.

'I just received a visit from two young urchins who gave Miss Underhay's name. She mentioned in her thank you note to me that she had asked them to bring me any news relating to the Glass Bottle.' Father Lamb's voice held a note of wry amusement. 'She is in debt for a couple of sixpences.'

Matt smiled to himself. 'Thank you, Father, what news did the boys have?'

'Ha, it seems that earlier this evening smoke was seen coming from the roof of the building. The fire brigade attended and when they entered the pub, they sent word for the police.' Father Lamb's voice had taken on a sombre tone.

'Arson?' Matt asked. He could see no other reason for the building suddenly catching alight.

'I'm afraid so, and worse. Murder. The body of the landlord's half-brother, Mr Denzil Hammett, was discovered with his throat slit in one of the upstairs rooms. I presume the police will be seeking Ezekiel Hammett.' The grim tone of the priest's voice underlined the horror that must have greeted the firemen.

'Good Lord! Sorry, Father.'

'Forgiven, my son. I can understand your reaction. The boys had run all the way to the presbytery to pass on the news. I have made a few enquiries of my own and an Inspector Pinch is in charge of the investigation. I dare say your Inspector Greville will know him if Miss Underhay desires any further information.'

Matt wondered what Kitty would make of this strange turn of events. 'Thank you, Father. Do you know if the pub has been badly damaged? Is it accessible?'

The priest chuckled. 'The boys said the roof has gone and the firemen have just finished hosing the place down. I don't know if Inspector Pinch will allow anyone inside. I presume you are thinking of obtaining access to the cellars to check out Miss Underhay's theory of a passage?'

'Not much escapes you, Father, does it? Yes, that is what I was thinking. Miss Underhay can be very determined,' Matt said.

'Well, if I hear anything else I shall let you know. Give my regards to Miss Underhay.' The priest bade him goodnight and ended the call.

Another possible source of information was gone. The landlord of the Glass Bottle had been the last link Kitty had to try and obtain information about her mother's disappearance all that time ago. Now, Denzil was dead and his half-brother, Ezekiel, missing.

Kitty was somewhat surprised to see Matt shortly after breakfast.

'I wasn't expecting you so early. Has something happened? Has the inspector made an arrest?' She indicated the empty seat opposite her desk in the office where she had been busy sorting out the receipts from the refurbishments to the hotel.

Matt's demeanour was unusually sombre, and she felt a little frightened.

'Father Lamb telephoned me late last night. You owe him a couple of sixpences.' He gave a small smile.

'Oh, the young boys. They had some news? Is Hammett back?' Her pulse speeded.

'There was a fire at the Glass Bottle last night. It's been badly damaged. Worse still, there has been a murder.' He told her what had happened.

Kitty was horrified by the news. 'Do they know when it happened? Oh, Matt, he could have been lying inside there dead when we stopped by in the taxi the other day.' He could even have been there ever since the pub was shut up. The very thought of it made her feel sick.

'I spoke to Inspector Greville about it this morning. I explained your interest in the pub. He has said he will speak to his colleague, an Inspector Pinch, who is in charge of the investigation.'

Kitty's mind raced. 'Do you think it might be possible to access the cellars?'

'It may not be safe, Kitty. I don't know how badly damaged the pub is. Father Lamb said the roof had gone but I don't know if any walls have collapsed or are in danger of collapse.'

Kitty jumped up from her seat and reached for her hat and coat from the small stand in the corner of the office.

'Come on, we have to go and take a look for ourselves.' She tugged on her coat and picked up the telephone.

'Mary, please ask Mr Potter to bring his car. I need to go to Exeter as soon as possible.'

'Kitty, do you think this is wise? The pub will be a crime scene and this Inspector Pinch may not be too happy at us simply arriving to gape at it.'

Kitty couldn't judge if Matt was alarmed or amused by her actions. Very probably a mixture of both.

'I know, but I have to go and see it for myself. Plus, I can repay Father Lamb his sixpences.' She put on her hat and collected her gloves and handbag.

She opened the drawer of her desk and pulled out a torch. After checking that it lit, she dropped it in her bag.

'Better to be prepared,' she said.

'You're determined to do this, then?' Matt asked.

She nodded.

'Hell's teeth,' he muttered, running his hands through his hair.

Mary knocked on the office door. 'Begging your pardon, Miss Kitty, but Mr Potter has just pulled up.'

'Thank you, Mary.' Kitty turned to Matt. 'Are you in?'

He groaned, then gave her his familiar lazy smile and the dimple quirked in his right cheek. 'Someone has to rein you back. Lead the way, Miss Underhay. Let's go and see what's afoot in Exeter.'

She smiled back at him, relieved she didn't have to go alone despite her bravado. 'Perhaps by the time we get back Inspector Greville will have made that arrest.'

He followed her out of her office and waited while she locked the door. 'Perhaps. He was speaking to Mr Silitoe again today.'

Kitty quickly told Mary where they were going and left her instructions before venturing out into the weak wintry sunshine. She hoped the inspector would make an arrest soon. Lavinia Braddock's suggestion that Matt might be in danger had somehow unnerved her.

Kitty stayed silent for most of the journey to Exeter. Various scenarios running through her head. She couldn't have told Matt what she was thinking even if he'd asked. She wasn't sure herself quite what she expected to do or see. She just knew, deep in her bones, that she had to go to the Glass Bottle and see it again for herself.

Matt helped to guide Mr Potter through the narrow maze of unmade up alleyways scarcely big enough to take the car. A rat's nest the other driver had called it. Today, in the pallid light of a winter morning, she could see what he meant even more clearly.

Mr Potter's shoulders were hunched in disapproval when Matt instructed him to stop and drop them off. Kitty could smell the stench of charred wood and gasoline even from inside the taxi. Someone had liberally doused the building to set it ablaze.

She scrambled out of the taxi and stared at the remains of the Glass Bottle. The roof had indeed completely gone. Only a few spars of blackened wood stuck up from the shell of the building. The walls, grubby before, were now dark grey and streaky with an ominous outward bulge as if the force of the blaze had been too much for them to contain.

Broken glass was strewn on the pavement and someone had made a half-hearted attempt at reboarding the windows, although the door itself still stood. As she drew nearer she could see the heat of the fire had caused the paint to bubble and crack in little blisters.

Matt joined her, the glass crunching under the soles of his shoes as they stared at the building.

'Quite a mess, old thing,' Matt observed.

'I thought there would be a constable here.' Kitty frowned. She had expected to see someone patrolling or guarding the door.

'Nipped off for a cup of tea, he has.' The voice came from behind her.

Kitty whirled around to discover the two urchin boys who had taken the message to Father Lamb had reappeared. It must have been the younger boy who had spoken out as the older one nudged him with his elbow as if to indicate he should keep his mouth closed.

'Hello, boys, thank you for taking the message to Father Lamb. Do you know if the policeman will be back soon?' Kitty asked. She noticed the boys' clothes were quite thin and patched and the younger lad's fingers were blue with the cold.

'He won't hurry, miss. He's gone to the workman's stand down near the Mermaid Yard.' The younger lad spoke out again and the older one glared at him.

Kitty delved in her bag for her purse. 'Thank you, that's very meaningful information.' She found some coppers and dropped the coins into the eager hands of the two boys.

The younger one gave the older lad a triumphant smile.

'Can you do me a favour? There will be more money in it for you if you do.' Kitty looked at the lads.

'What you want, miss?' The wary expression was back on the face of the older boy.

'I need to get inside the pub for a few minutes.'

The boys exchanged glances.

'Can you keep watch and let me know if the policeman is returning?' Kitty looked at the lads. She heard Matt mutter an oath under his breath.

'Best be quick though, miss. T'es Constable Tate and he's a right grumpy old so and so,' the elder boy cautioned.

'I promise.' Kitty smiled at the boys hoping she looked more confident than she felt.

The lads melted away and Kitty sucked in a breath. 'Now to find a way inside.'

Matt fumbled inside his trouser pocket and pulled out a small bunch of strange metal objects attached to a leather fob.

'This is madness, Kitty,' Matt warned as he selected one of the instruments and slid it into the lock on the front door of the pub. 'Better hope there are no bolts on the other side.'

'Why, Captain Bryant, are there no ends to your talents?' Kitty watched as the lock clicked and the door cracked open, swinging easily as if the scorching from the fire had warped it on its hinges.

Blood pounded in her ears as she peered into what remained of the dank interior of the pub. She pulled her torch from her bag and shone it around. Part of the ceiling had caved in just in front of the bar allowing a patch of light to filter down from where the roof had been.

Water dripped from the ceiling onto the stone flagged floor. Heat from the flames had caused the bottles and glassware which had stood behind the bar to explode and more glass shards reflected the beam of her torch back at her.

A shiver ran down her spine as she thought of the grisly find made by the firemen in the upstairs room. The pub stank of smoke and gasoline and she tugged her woollen scarf up to cover her nose and mouth as she ventured cautiously inside.

'Have a care, Kitty. We don't know how safe this structure is,' Matt warned as he followed behind her.

She noticed his quick, assessing gaze as he took in the charred remains of the tables and chairs. The fragment of velvet drapery hanging from the side of the window, faded with age and now a tattered flag of what had once been.

'Where is the access to the cellar likely to be found?' Kitty asked as she played the beam of the torch around the remains of the bar area.

'Judging by the layout and the dray delivery doors in the pavement outside, I'd say there should be a hatch at the back of the counter, set in the floor.' Matt's expression was sombre in the dim light, his mouth set in a grim line.

Kitty walked carefully forwards trying to dodge the drips of water still raining down from the ceiling above their heads. She knew Matt hated every moment of this. The darkness and the increasingly confined area behind what was left of the wooden counter that must once have served hundreds of pints of ale.

She shone the torch down on the floor looking for the trap. The broken glass was thick where the pint mugs had shattered and fallen to the floor. The smell of gasoline was especially strong now, acrid in her nose and throat making her feel dizzy. She guessed that the arsonist must have soaked the bar with fuel before lighting a match.

She moved some of the glass shards aside with her foot until she spotted the metal hasp of the trapdoor.

'Found it.'

'Watch the glass, Kitty,' Matt warned as she carefully used her gloved hand to release the catch and lift the door.

Fetid air, wet and noxious swirled up at her making her cough.

'You don't have to come down with me.' Kitty glanced at Matt. His face was white in the faint light and she could see beads of perspiration at his hairline.

'Make sure it's safe to go down,' he directed, ignoring her suggestion that he stay behind.

A row of stone steps led down into the darkness. The light of her torch was feeble as she started a careful descent into the gloom. Her heart pounded against the wall of her chest and the building groaned like something in pain. Ahead of her in the darkness beyond the reach of her torch she heard scratching sounds. She prayed it was only mice and not rats. Mice she could cope with but rats, she suppressed a shudder. How had they survived the fire? Or had they entered the cellar from elsewhere?

Once safely on the dirt floor of the cellar she flashed the torch around. Much to her relief she didn't see any sign of rodent life. A thin rim of light above their heads in the far corner indicated the dray delivery hatch set on the pavement outside. The body of the cellar though was extensive, high and with arched vaults made of red brick badly painted with whitewash.

The earth floor was sodden and muddy where the water from the firemen's hoses had trickled down through the hatch and the stone flags to run down the walls. A few ancient barrels stood to one side and a pile of wooden crates containing bottles of ale were stacked carelessly in a corner.

Kitty played her torch slowly along the walls looking for any sign of a concealed entrance or exit. She was conscious of Matt close beside her.

'Over there, Kitty, behind that cask. See where the water is running down the wall? There's something different in the surface.' Matt tugged at the sleeve of her coat to show her where he meant.

She saw that where the water was running down the rough, once white limewashed wall it had washed away some of the paint and plaster. A faint outline of what could be a door was now just visible.

Matt made his way over to it and took out his set of instruments once more. 'Shine the torch on this edge, old thing, I'm going to try and get this open.'

Kitty held her breath and directed the light from the torch on the spot where Matt was working. It was clear that that entrance had been sealed shut for some time.

'It's just painted board,' Matt grunted as he applied his weight to the widening crack.

There was a splintering sound and the board fell forward with a crash causing Kitty to skip neatly backwards to avoid it from falling on her feet.

Matt let out a low whistle as she directed the beam of light into the opening. 'You were right, Kitty. Here's the passageway and I'm willing to wager it links up with the old water conduit passages.'

The opening was narrow and low, and the sides were lined with more of the local red brick.

'I'm going in to take a look.' Kitty darted inside the gap before Matt could protest. She didn't expect him to follow her. She wasn't sure if what she was doing was safe or wise, but she had to take a look.

'Kitty! For God's sake be careful.' Matt's voice echoed around the narrow space.

She sucked in a breath, conscious of a sickly, rotting smell from further along the tunnel. She steadied her grip around the torch and hoped a rat didn't suddenly run out over her feet.

To her disappointment she wasn't able to get very much further when she was faced with a pile of earth and brick blocking her way where the tunnel had obviously collapsed. She played the torchlight all around the fall hoping it was an old one and the tunnel wasn't about to drop in on her trapping her underground.

She was about to retreat back the way she came when something small and shiny caught the light on the floor. She stooped carefully to retrieve it, turning it around in her fingers to dislodge the dirt that had collected on it where it had been trodden into the ground.

Her hand shook as she recognised the purple green and white colours on the broken and crushed enamel pin. She had seen that pin every day of her life before her mother had vanished. Pinned with care on the collar of whichever coat her mother chose to wear.

She bent down and played the light again closer to the surface of the tunnel wall where the bricks had come away leaving the bare crumbly earth. There was something else. Something in the wall of the tunnel next to the cave-in. She rubbed at it with her glove, fearful of causing more earth to fall. A shower of dirt fell onto her from the ceiling.

Somewhere in the distance she heard a whoop and whistle.

'Kitty, come back, we've got to get out,' Matt's voice was urgent.

A fragment of fabric, dirty and rotting in soft pink, and the leather toe of a shoe. Kitty retched in horror and started to stumble back through the narrow passage towards Matt. She would have fallen onto the dirty floor of the cellar if he hadn't caught her.

'Kitty, what is it? What did you find?' Matt gripped the tops of her arms holding her upright. 'Come on, the constable is returning to his post. We have to go.'

Kitty shook her head. 'We need the constable, Matt. We have to get the police down here.' She was trembling now from head to foot. 'We have to get them now, Matt. She's down there. My mother. I found her. I have her pin.'

CHAPTER TWENTY

When they emerged from the interior of the Glass Bottle, dirty and dishevelled, it was to find Constable Tate holding the eldest of their lookouts by his ear. Kitty was as white as milk, her blue-grey eyes huge in her pale face.

'Oi, what's your game? It's dangerous in there. Crime scene that is. You newspaper people are all the same.' The constable puffed up the street towards them, his broad face red with indignation.

Kitty escaped from Matt's grasp to quietly be sick in the gutter.

'Let go of the boy, Officer. We need him to take a message back to the police station,' Matt said. He looked anxiously at Kitty who was wiping her mouth with her handkerchief.

'I'll be the one to give the instructions around here. What's going on? What were you doing in there?' The constable glared at them.

'Release the child, please, Constable.' Kitty wobbled on her heels and Matt rushed forward to steady her, concerned she might faint.

The policeman puffed up his ruddy cheeks, his moustache trembling in indignation. 'I'll be the one giving the instructions around here, missy. I caught this one up to no good as usual, him and his brother, and then I finds you two.'

Matt circled his arm around Kitty's slender waist. 'Constable, we need to get an urgent message to Inspector Pinch. You can surely see for yourself, man, that my fiancée has had a terrible shock. There is another body in this building.'

The policeman's mouth fell open and he released the boy's ear. The lad immediately skipped smartly out of reach of the constable and was joined by his brother. Matt let go of Kitty and scribbled two notes as quickly as he could on pages torn from his pocket notebook.

'Boys, take this one to Inspector Pinch at the police station. Tell him Captain Bryant sent you and it's urgent. Then deliver the other one to the presbytery to Father Lamb and return here as quickly as you can.' He gave the boys the notes ignoring the constable's indignant splutterings.

The lads beamed at him and sprinted away on their errand.

'What's going on? What's your game? What body?' The constable glowered at Matt.

Kitty swayed and Matt instantly ignored the man to go to her support. 'There is a low wall just there. Darling, you need to sit down before you fall down.'

'Oi, come back here.' The man huffed after them as Matt led Kitty to a crumbling fragment of a garden wall and made sure she was seated. Once he was certain she was safe he turned to face the now furious policeman and in a low voice quickly appraised the man of their reasons for entering the Glass Bottle and the significance of Kitty's find.

The officer's expressions changed from angry to astounded to confused and finally to understanding by the time Matt had finished his explanation. The sound of a motor engine cut the air and a black police vehicle swept to a halt further down the narrow street.

A tall, rail thin man in a black overcoat and Homburg hat accompanied by another uniformed constable got out and began to walk towards them.

'Best look lively then, sir, the inspector is here.' The constable drew himself up taking on a more official air.

Matt could see Kitty looked slightly better but was still ashen. He stepped forward to greet the inspector and gave him the same briefing he had given the constable.

'One moment, sir.' Matt left the police standing in a small huddle looking at the Glass Bottle and returned to Kitty.

'How are you, old thing? May I borrow your mother's brooch to show the inspector?'

Kitty sniffed and nodded. 'I'm all right.' Her teeth chattered as she spoke and Matt's anxiety for her went up a notch. She was cold and in shock.

She opened her hand and he took the brooch. 'I'll bring it straight back.'

He returned to Inspector Pinch and showed him the broken pin, explaining the significance of the find.

The sight of some tangible evidence galvanised the inspector into action. His mouth set in a grim line and he began to instruct the constables to break open the dray delivery door set in the pavement to provide more light and better access into the cellar.

The men then began to knock on the doors of the nearby houses requesting tools and within minutes the unseen watchers from behind their curtains were out on the pavement forming an interested crowd of onlookers at this strange turn of business.

Matt went back to Kitty and held her close to him, trying to warm her.

'Miss Underhay, Captain Bryant, oh my goodness, I came as speedily as I could.' Father Lamb came puffing towards them, his pleasant face creased with anxiety. The two urchins trotted at his side.

'Father, thank you for coming.' Matt was relieved to see the elderly priest. 'Kitty is in a bad way, sir. It's been a horrible shock for her, as you can imagine.'

The priest nodded and uncaring of the dirty rough pavement he dropped to his knees in front of Kitty to take her hands in his.

'My dear child, we need to take you somewhere warm and comfortable. I will speak to the inspector. Our paths have crossed before on other matters. Courage, my child, your quest is at an end.' He squeezed her hands and rose as tears started to flow down Kitty's pale face.

'I shall speak to Inspector Pinch. Wait here,' Father Lamb said to Matt before trotting off towards the thin, crow-like figure of the inspector who was peering into the cellar.

Matt watched as the small cassocked priest spoke to the inspector. Kitty was still shivering against him. Dirt from the cellar streaked her cheek where she had absent-mindedly dashed the tears from her face.

He realised the two lads were still hovering nearby and he reached into his pocket for some coins.

'Thank you, lads. You have done well today.'

'Is it right, mister, as there was another body in there?' the oldest boy asked as he took his share of the spoils.

'Sadly, yes.' Matt's tone was clipped, unwilling to distress Kitty further by revealing details.

The lads exchanged excited glances and ran off to join the group of onlookers.

Father Lamb returned. 'Come, my daughter, Inspector Pinch has given us the use of his car to take you to the presbytery. He will join us there in a while.' The priest took Kitty's one arm and Matt steadied her on her other side. Between them they got her into the back of the police car. A uniformed constable took the wheel and they set off down the alleys away from the Glass Bottle to the warm serenity of Father Lamb's drawing room.

The two men got Kitty onto the sofa and the housekeeper took her hat and coat tutting over the streaks of mud that had attached themselves to her garments. A tartan rug was wrapped around her and the fire stoked.

'Have a sip of this,' Father Lamb instructed offering Kitty a small crystal glass of a dark, plum coloured liquid. 'Madeira and a splash of extra brandy. I find it an effective remedy for these kinds of situations.'

Her hands shook as she accepted the drink, her teeth chattered against the lip of the glass. The liquor warmed her mouth and hit the back of her throat making her cough. Ever since she had scraped away the dirt in the wall of the tunnel to expose her grisly find she had felt detached from all reality. As if everything was happening to someone else and she, Kitty, were stood to one side like a spectator at a movie watching the action from afar.

'Take another sip.' Matt's fingers, lean and strong, closed gently around her hand, guiding the glass back to her mouth. She sipped obediently. The drink warmed her stomach and started to drive some of the terrible chill from her body.

Matt's eyes, bright blue and intense, locked with hers. 'It'll be all right, Kitty. Inspector Pinch will sort everything out.'

She tightened her grip around her mother's brooch. She had refused to release it ever since Matt had returned it after showing it to the inspector. Even when she had handed over her gloves to be cleaned by Father Lamb's housekeeper. The broken part of the clasp pressed into the flesh of her palm, grounding her, returning her slowly back to herself.

She closed her eyes and fragmented memories of her mother swirled about her mind. The violet scent of her perfume, the sound of her laugh.

'Kitty, do you need a doctor? Shall I ask Father Lamb to telephone?' Matt's voice was anxious, penetrating the fog of inertia that had her in its grasp.

She kept her eyes closed for a moment longer until the last of her memories had dissipated away to be replaced by a slow-burning ball of anger deep inside her. She opened her eyes to meet Matt's concerned gaze.

'No, I shall be all right. I will find them, Matt. If it takes me until the day I die I will discover who did this to my mother. I will track down Hammett and he will answer for this.'

She saw relief on his face at her words and the corners of his mouth tilted upwards in a small smile. 'That sounds more like my girl.'

She frowned, a ghost of a different, more recent memory filtering back into her consciousness.

'And since when have I been your fiancée, Captain Bryant? This morning I was not even your girlfriend,' she asked with some asperity.

Father Lamb made a sound that could have been a cough or a chuckle. 'I shall leave you two alone for a moment. I need to organise some tea for us all.' He slipped from the room leaving a somewhat abashed Matt sitting next to her on the sofa.

'Ah, so you heard that?' he muttered.

'Well?' She waited for his explanation. At the same time, she realised that if he did ever ask her to marry him, she would very likely say yes.

'Um, it seemed simpler to say that than give some convoluted explanation of our relationship.'

Kitty raised an eyebrow. Matt looked sheepish and raked his hand through his hair.

'Dash it all, Kitty. I don't know how you feel about me, about us. Not getting married or anything, I mean us walking out together. You know what I mean. Hell's bells…' He spluttered to a halt.

'Are you asking me to be your girl?' Kitty asked. Her heart raced at the thought.

He took her free hand in his. 'Yes, Miss Underhay, I suppose I'm asking if you will walk out with me.' His gaze tangled with hers and he dipped his head, his lips brushing hers.

There was the discreet sound of a cough from the doorway and the ostentatious clattering of a tea trolley as Father Lamb returned to the room. Matt sprang away from Kitty and she was amused to see a dull flush on his cheeks.

'You look a little better, my dear.' Father Lamb smiled benignly at her, his eyes twinkling as he took his place on the armchair nearest the fire.

Kitty's own face heated. 'Thank you, Father. I do feel more myself now. I still have to break the news to my grandmother, however.' Anxiety hit afresh as she thought of how her beloved Grams would take the news that Elowed had finally been found.

'Inspector Pinch will be here in a little while. He wishes to speak to you before you return to Dartmouth. I am more than willing to accompany you, my dear, if you feel it would help when you break this sad news to your grandmother.' Father Lamb poured tea for all of them as he spoke.

'That's very good of you, Father. I fear we have been the most terrible nuisance to you.' Kitty felt quite guilty as she accepted her cup and a generous slab of home-made gingerbread. They were not even members of Father Lamb's faith and his goodness and generosity of spirit humbled her.

'Not at all, my dear,' the priest reassured her.

The jangling of the front doorbell echoed along the hall and was swiftly followed by the sound of voices. A moment later and Inspector Pinch's lean figure entered the room.

'My dear Inspector, come and have a seat.' Father Lamb ushered his latest guest to the other armchair and pressed a cup of tea upon him.

'What news do you have for us, sir?' Matt asked.

The inspector coughed and peered at Matt and Kitty. 'My men have managed to enter the tunnel and have shored up the sides and roof with boards. It's in a very unstable condition as I'm sure you can appreciate. They are excavating as we speak but the process is slow. I anticipate that the… erm, remains will be out in the next few hours providing things go as planned. I have to say, Miss Underhay, that based on what we can see so far, and the description Captain Bryant gave us, I am inclined to believe the remains are that of Mrs Elowed Underhay.'

Kitty released the breath she had been holding. She had known from the moment she had discovered the broken pin what the outcome would be. It was simply strange to have it confirmed in Inspector Pinch's flat, official tones. Sadness washed through her.

'What will happen next, sir?' Matt asked.

'Once the… erm, remains are removed they will go to the morgue for our doctor to try and establish a cause of death. That may prove difficult given the amount of time that has passed. A definitive identification will be made, and the date of an inquest set. After the formalities are completed then a funeral can be arranged.' The inspector looked at Kitty. 'I must warn you, Miss Underhay, that it will prove very difficult after this length of time to gather evidence to secure a conviction. If indeed the perpetrator is still alive. We are seeking Ezekiel Hammett in connection with the murder of his brother and now, of course, the death of your mother. At the very least, we need to know how she came to be interred there.'

Kitty placed her plate on the tea trolley. 'I understand, Inspector. I know you will do everything in your power to get justice for my mother. Hammett must know something. He would have been a young man at the time of her death and has always lived at the pub.' The little pin concealed in her palm seemed to burn in her hand as she spoke. 'I have to return to Dartmouth to break the news to my grandmother. I also need to send a telegram to my father in America.' She wondered if he would wish to return for the funeral.

'Of course. I understand that I can contact you at the Dolphin Hotel?' The inspector nodded.

'Yes, my grandmother and I both reside there,' Kitty said.

*

An hour later Kitty found herself seated next to Matt in the back of a taxi on their way back to Dartmouth. She had declined Father Lamb's kind offer to accompany her, suspecting that her grandmother would wish to be alone once she knew about Elowed.

She had placed her mother's pin carefully inside her purse when she had freshened up in the cloakroom at the presbytery. Father Lamb's housekeeper had cleaned her gloves and sponged her coat. With the streak of mud washed from her face and after pinching some colour back to her cheeks she had felt more herself once more.

Her hand rested inside Matt's, and despite the horrible events of the day she now felt surprisingly at ease. The light was already slipping away, and Kitty wondered what time it was. Apart from the gingerbread she had eaten nothing since breakfast, and she had brought most of that up outside the Glass Bottle.

Inwardly she was steeling herself for the task ahead. A moment she had been bracing for over the last seventeen years. The length of a lifetime. What had Father Lamb said? The end of her quest. Maybe, but now she had a new one, to get justice for her mother.

Matt seemed to sense her need for silence. She glanced across at him. His expression was blank, and he too appeared deep in thought. Wearily, she closed her eyes and allowed the rumble of the car engine and the wheels on the road to lull her into a half sleep.

The lights were already coming on when they pulled to a stop near the Boat Float. Kitty was jolted awake as the engine stopped and Matt moved, disturbing her from where her head had been resting on his shoulder.

She realised they were disembarking a short distance from the Dolphin, just as they had done before when they had returned from Exeter.

'I wanted to talk to you for a moment, before you go to be with your grandmother,' Matt said.

She nodded and they paid the driver, watching the taxi pull away before walking together toward the embankment. Kitty shivered in the cold, damp air coming from the river. She huddled into her coat and wondered what it was that Matt wanted to talk to her about.

They halted by unspoken common consent at the railing and looked across the Dart towards Kingswear. In the distance she heard the mournful hoot of a departing steam engine and the glug and gush of the river only a few yards away.

'What is it, Matt?' She turned to face him.

'You didn't answer the question I put to you earlier at Father Lamb's. Before you do there are things I need to tell you that I want you to know before you reply.' He shifted his feet and leant forward, resting his elbows on the rail. The brim of his hat cast a shadow on his face so she couldn't make out his expression.

An icy chill ran along her spine that had nothing to do with the wintry weather or the task that lay ahead of her. 'Matt?' She went to place her hand on his arm, to reassure him, but something about his stance held her back.

'You asked me where I went the other Sunday while you were at One Pine with Marigold Everton. I told you I took the bike towards London. I rode to a small churchyard, St Margaret's Church. I go once a year, every year, for Edith's birthday.'

Kitty nodded. She could understand that, but why not tell her? What was it about this visit that had been different? Yet she knew that something was changed.

'You remember that when my parents were here a few months ago you told me you had that strange conversation with them when they came to see you at the Dolphin?'

Kitty remembered it clearly, every embarrassing detail. She had shared the gist of it with Matt later on, making light of his mother's hints and inferences that Matt was not a suitable match for her, that he was too scarred, too damaged mentally by the war for a relationship with a girl like her. She was too young and naïve. He needed someone closer to his own age, worldly-wise and experienced.

'I remember,' she said.

'When we married, I promised Edith that I would never tell another soul the truth about our marriage. Only the two of us knew and she is long gone.' Matt's gaze was fixed on some point across the river, but she could tell he was back in the past.

'Edith was my nurse when I was wounded, you know that much. She was older than me. A lot older, thirty. I suppose that's why my parents never liked her, one of the reasons anyway. They thought she had taken advantage while I was recovering. I had been sent to one of the large houses that were made into temporary hospitals. She was different from the other nurses. They were mainly younger, chatty, flirtatious. Edith was quiet, restful. She liked books, poetry, music.' He paused for a moment.

Kitty tried to picture a much younger Matt. He would have been nineteen or twenty then at most.

'She had been engaged to another officer. A couple of weeks before I arrived at the hospital, she received word he had been killed. To make matters worse, she didn't receive the news officially. She received it in a letter from someone who had been serving alongside him, who knew about Edith.'

Kitty's heart went out to Edith, she could envisage how awful it must have been.

'She was always unlucky. Then, one day, just before I was due to be discharged from the hospital, I found her in tears. She had reached out to his family only to discover that they knew nothing of her. It seems he was already married with a child.'

Kitty gasped.

The Adam's apple bobbed in Matt's throat as he swallowed and continued his story. 'She had no one to turn to. Her father was frail, and the disgrace would have killed him. She couldn't return home and she couldn't stay in her post.'

Understanding of the girl's plight slammed into Kitty like a shock wave. 'She was pregnant? Betty?'

Matt nodded. 'We married a couple of days later by special licence. I suspect my parents guessed that Betty might not be mine by the dates. They didn't approve of the match, of course.' He pulled out his cigarette case and lit up. The light from the match illuminating his face for a brief moment.

'But why Matt? I can see why Edith might have agreed to the marriage but why did you offer?' Kitty tried to make sense of it.

Matt blew out a thin stream of smoke. 'I gave Edith respectability, a home and, if anything had happened to me, she would have had a widow's pension. It wasn't love, for either of us, not at first. That came later when we got to know one another better. She gave me an anchor. A point to return to. Betty and Edith helped to tamp down the spirit of recklessness that had increasingly possessed me. She and Betty were something to live for. Something to return to.'

Kitty thought she understood.

'I promised her that she and Betty would be safe. Nothing bad would happen to them. Whatever else happened during that terrible war they would be taken care of.'

Kitty blinked to hold back the fresh round of tears that threatened to fall. Except Matt had been wrong. He had been the one to survive. Edith and Betty had been in the wrong place at the wrong time and their lives had been brutally cut short.

'When the war ended that old recklessness was still there, except now it was fuelled by grief and anger at the injustice of it all. I've been to places, Kitty, seen things and done things that no one should ever have seen and done. It haunts me. You know that the demons surface sometimes at night, in my sleep.' His voice cracked.

She stayed silent, not wanting to break the spell or say the wrong thing. All the pieces of the jigsaw were clicking into shape.

'So, you see I went to see Edith and Betty. To tell them about you. And now you know about them, about me. I don't put down roots easily, Kitty. You saw that in me I think when I first arrived. Until I came here, met you, I didn't know if it would ever be possible again. I carry a lot of baggage, old girl. More than you could imagine. It seemed only fair that you knew.' He extinguished his cigarette, grinding the remains beneath his heel.

'You need to go and send a telegram to your father and be with your grandmother. This day has been hard enough. If our friendship is all you want, Kitty, then I'll abide by that. We can go back and stay just as friends. I'll make no pleas or ties on you.' He glanced along the embankment towards the Dolphin. 'I'll be here tomorrow at the tea rooms at Bayards Cove at twelve. You can give me your answer then.'

Before she could stop him, or even think about going after him he had gone and, a moment later, she heard the sound of his motorcycle heading towards the far ferry station.

CHAPTER TWENTY-ONE

Kitty stayed rooted to the spot for a moment trying to take in everything Matt had just shared with her. It had certainly been a day full of surprises. She took in a breath and lifted her chin before briskly walking the short distance to the Dolphin.

Mary gave her a curious look when she entered the lobby.

'Miss Kitty, I've a pile of messages for you.' The girl blinked as Kitty approached. 'Begging your pardon, miss, is everything all right? You look as if you've been in the wars.'

Kitty glanced downwards realising that the bright lights of the reception area were revealing the splashes of mud on her shoes and the tear in her stockings.

'It's been a difficult day.' She took the slim sheaf of papers from the girl. 'Is my grandmother in her salon?'

'Yes, miss.'

'I need to send a telegram too, urgently, to my father. Can Albert, the kitchen boy, run a message to the post office?' Kitty already had a pencil in her hand and was busy scribbling the message and directions for the lad.

'Of course, Miss Kitty.' Mary picked up the telephone and dialled the kitchen extension while Kitty found some money from her purse.

The boy came hurrying into the lobby just as she finished. She entrusted him with the money and message and sent him on his way.

'I'm going up to my grandmother. I have some bad news for her so I would appreciate it if we were not disturbed.' Kitty gathered up her messages, gloves and bag before heading to the elevator. She didn't feel as if she had the energy left to climb the stairs.

'Very good, miss.'

Kitty entered her grandmother's apartment, her heart heavy with the task before her.

'Darling, whatever has happened to you?' Her grandmother put down her magazine from where she had been reading beside the fire. She frowned, clearly perplexed by Kitty's dishevelled appearance.

'Grams, I have something to tell you.' Kitty delved inside her bag and took out the broken pin from inside her purse. She handed it across to her grandmother.

She knelt down next to her grandmother's chair. The colour drained from the older woman's face as she looked at what she held in her hand.

'Elowed.'

Kitty woke the next morning with puffed and swollen eyes. She had stayed with her grandmother for a while before retiring to her own room to telephone her cousin, Lucy, with the news. Her aunt and uncle had been shocked by the discovery and Lucy had immediately offered to come and stay.

Her father had telephoned as soon as the telegram had reached him, and he had booked his passage back to England on the first ship leaving New York. The heartbreak had been evident in his voice even after all this time.

There was a tap at her door and Alice appeared carrying a tray.

'Mrs Treadwell asked me to bring you up some tea and toast. She said she's expecting Mrs Craven in a little while.'

Kitty peered at her clock. She had slept for longer than she'd intended. 'Thank you, Alice.' She sat up and took the tray.

'I'm sorry about your mum, miss,' Alice said, her expression sympathetic. 'Your grandmother told all the staff first thing this morning. Mickey and Mrs Homer was proper sad.'

'Thank you. It all feels rather unreal right now.' She took a welcome sip of tea and realised how hungry she was. She hadn't eaten much at all yesterday. By the time she'd left her grandmother and had taken a bath, the kitchen staff had gone home. She'd made do with a large cup of cocoa and jam sandwiches for her supper.

'Mrs Treadwell said to tell you to come and see her when you're dressed, miss, and then you're to take the rest of the day off,' Alice said.

Kitty smiled at the little maid. 'Very well. I won't be long.' She finished her cup of tea.

'Can I do anything for you, miss? Help you with your hair or run you a bath?' Alice asked.

'No, thank you.'

Alice collected the tray and left Kitty to dress. A small pile of papers on her dresser caught her eye. The messages from yesterday. She hadn't even looked at them last night. She had been much too preoccupied with her grandmother.

She dressed quickly in a dark blue two-piece with a pale blue silk blouse. After tidying her hair, she dabbed some of her favourite rose perfume on her wrists and picked up the messages.

Most of them were from tradespeople wanting instructions or approval for various aspects of the refurbishment. Only one message made her pause. It was an application for employment letter.

'I wonder,' Kitty muttered and tucked the folded application into the pocket of her jacket.

Mrs Craven was already with her grandmother when she entered the salon.

'Kitty, darling, come and have some breakfast. Millicent came straight away as soon as she heard the news about your mother.'

Her grandmother still looked pale but was composed. She had selected a dark grey suit with a rose-pink blouse.

It had felt wrong to Kitty to dress in black and she assumed her grandmother had felt the same way. Mrs Craven was in dark brown tweed with a jade green blouse, her diamond brooch glittering on her lapel. The two women were seated at the small table in the bay window which overlooked the river. Weak wintry sunlight glinted on the glass dishes containing the selection of jams, marmalade and honey.

Kitty took a seat and helped herself to toast and marmalade.

'I've informed the staff, Kitty. The older staff, Mickey and Mrs Homer, who remember your mother, were quite distressed. Have you heard anything from your father yet?' her grandmother asked.

Mrs Craven gave a small sniff at the mention of Edgar Underhay.

'He telephoned and said he has a passage on a ship sailing today. I called Aunt Hortense and Lucy has offered to come here and stay but I said it was quite all right. Uncle has said he will attend the inquest.' Kitty started to feel better with some food inside her.

'That is very good of him,' Grams conceded. 'I shall speak to the vicar today about planning the funeral once the inquest is concluded.'

'I shall be happy to assist you, my dear,' Mrs Craven said.

Kitty was happy to leave the planning to her grandmother and her friend. She was still not feeling quite herself after yesterday's events. It was bizarre. It was as if whatever had been anchoring her down had been removed and she was bobbing aimlessly like a fishing float adrift on the sea.

'I see there was nothing in the papers about an arrest being made for Councillor Everton's murder,' Mrs Craven observed as she sipped her coffee. 'I bumped into Mrs Silitoe yesterday. She said her husband was assisting the police with the inquiry.'

'I really thought Inspector Greville would have made an arrest by now,' Mrs Treadwell said.

'Mrs Silitoe seemed quite unperturbed that her husband might be suspected of murder. Some strange deposit in the bank account had set the police back on his trail apparently. Then again, she was always an odd fish. She's much cleverer than him, of course. She runs his office with frightening efficiency. I swear she knows as much about the law as he does.' Mrs Craven finished her coffee and set down her cup.

'Gracious, I hadn't realised she acted as his secretary,' Kitty said. This was something new.

'Oh, only for a few hours a day at his office. They have no children, so I suppose it keeps her busy. That's why she joined the flower arranging guild, to occupy her time. She's terribly house proud too, quite unlike Marigold Everton. She made some very disparaging remarks about that lady's standard of housekeeping. She's had to assist Marigold with the papers to sort out Mr King's estate as well as Mr Everton's,' Mrs Craven said.

Kitty puzzled over this latest piece of information. Lavinia had said Marigold and Gladys were not on friendly terms. The application form in the pocket of her jacket crackled as she moved, reminding her of its presence.

'Are you certain you don't need me today, Grams?' she asked.

'No, darling, you run along. Millicent and I will deal with the arrangements. We can catch up this evening at supper.' Her grandmother smiled and patted her hand.

Kitty left the ladies to finish their coffees and hurried downstairs to her office. An idea had begun to form in her mind, and she wanted to dig a little deeper. She took the application letter from her jacket pocket and spread it out on the desk.

She had not been mistaken. The letter was from a Miss Anne Bennett, parlourmaid, currently in employment at One Pine. Daphne and Marigold hadn't dismissed her, and she had listed them as one of her references. Her other reference was the servants' employment agency offices in Paignton.

Kitty tapped the letter thoughtfully with her finger. Why was Bennett seeking new employment? The furore over the councillor's death was dying down and Thomas King's death was still considered an accident in the minds of the public. The maid had been happy enough to remain there before.

Her mind made up, she telephoned the agency number given as the other reference.

'Hello, my name is Kitty Underhay and I'm calling from the Dolphin Hotel in Dartmouth to check a reference for a woman called Anne Bennett.'

'One moment, Miss Underhay, whilst I consult our records.'

Kitty waited whilst the brisk female voice on the other end of the line looked up Anne Bennett's employment details.

'I'm sorry to have kept you, Miss Underhay. Ah yes, Miss Bennett has been in the employ of Mrs Everton of One Pine Torquay for the last six weeks. I have received no complaints from them about her work. Before then she was in a number of short-term positions.'

'Thank you, do you know her reasons for wishing to leave her current employment? I know there was some kind of tragedy amongst the household?' Kitty held her breath as she waited for the response.

'Oh yes, it was very sad. I believe Mrs Everton is intending to move abroad imminently and the daughter of the house is getting married and setting up her own establishment.'

Kitty thanked the woman and rang off. So, Marigold planned to move abroad soon. Presumably, this would take place after the funerals of Mr Everton and Mr King. She wondered when Daphne intended to marry. The girl certainly wasn't letting the grass grow under her feet.

Marigold must be planning to leave soon after the funerals and Daphne's wedding if her staff were seeking new employment now. And was she intending to travel abroad alone? That didn't sound like Marigold. How had she been described? A clinging vine. The kind of woman who always needs a man.

She glanced at her wristwatch; she had an hour before she was due to meet Matt at the tea room. Her hand hovered over the telephone receiver, perhaps she should call him. This new information was important, she knew it. It was as if all the pieces of the puzzle were in front of her and she just needed to fit them together.

Matt tidied up the papers on the desk in his office in Fore Street. He'd gone in early to light the fire to drive the chill from the rooms. There were invoices he needed to send and a couple of enquiries for his services that he needed to respond to.

He was due to meet Kitty in just under an hour back in Dartmouth. Would she meet him? And if so would she want to continue just as friends or would she feel that they might have a future together as a couple? It had been a strange and emotional day yesterday. Seeing Kitty's reaction to the discovery of her mother's remains had been devastating. He had feared she might completely collapse when he had got her out of that wretched pub.

It had confirmed for him what he already knew, that Kitty was too important to him for them to continue as they were without telling her the truth about Edith and Betty. It wouldn't have been right or fair. If he were to finally free himself of the past, then it had needed to be done.

When the telephone on his desk rang, he was tempted to ignore it. He wanted to get to the post office to drop off his mail and then set off for Dartmouth. Business was business, however.

'Hello, Torbay Private Investigative Services.'

'Is that Captain Bryant?' A woman's voice, vaguely familiar.

'Speaking, how may I help you?' He picked up a pencil in his free hand and prepared to scribble any notes on the pad he kept next to the telephone.

'Oh, Captain Bryant, I'm so very glad I caught you. I don't know what to do. I really need some advice and assistance. It's Gladys Silitoe, I don't know if you remember me from that dreadful incident at the Imperial Hotel?'

'Of course, Mrs Silitoe. You and your husband were friends of Councillor Everton's.' Matt could tell from the woman's voice that she sounded quite distressed.

'Yes, well, that's the thing. My husband is Mrs Everton's solicitor and I assist him with a few small jobs in his office. Oh dear, Captain Bryant, I really don't know what to do. My husband is at the police station with the inspector and I'm at Mrs Everton's home. One Pine, near Torre Station, I came to sort out some papers of Thomas King's. Mrs Everton and Daphne have gone to finalise the funeral arrangements so I'm here alone and I'm so frightened, Captain Bryant. You see I've found something, and I don't know what to do about it.'

'What have you found?' Matt frowned. The woman wasn't making sense, she sounded quite distressed and panicky.

'Please can you come? They will be back soon, and I need to show someone.' Before he could answer the line went dead.

Matt muttered a curse under his breath. He would be late meeting Kitty. He dialled the Dolphin and was surprised when Alice answered the phone.

'Alice, is Kitty there?'

'No, Captain Bryant, she's stepped out just for a moment with Mary. Can I take a message? She'll be back in a minute.' Alice was using her best telephone voice.

'Can you tell her I might be late. I had a strange call from Mrs Silitoe at One Pine. I'll be at the tea rooms to meet her as soon as possible.'

'Very good, sir.'

Matt picked up his keys and hurried out of the office. He had a good idea of where One Pine was situated. It bothered him that the line had gone dead before Gladys Silitoe could enlarge on what she had discovered that had worried her so much.

'Miss Kitty, Captain Bryant just telephoned for you.' Alice waved to attract Kitty's attention as soon as she entered the lobby.

Kitty's pulse quickened. Had he called to cancel their meeting? Was he already regretting having shared so much with her yesterday?

Alice relayed the message. 'He sounded as if he were in an hurry, miss.'

'He said he'd gone to One Pine to meet Mrs Silitoe?' Kitty asked. It didn't make sense. What would Gladys Silitoe be doing at One Pine?

She hurried the few steps to the reception desk to where Alice was standing, picked up the telephone receiver and asked the operator to try Marigold Everton's number.

'I'm sorry, madam, there appears to be a fault on the line,' the operator informed her.

'Is something wrong, miss?' Alice looked bewildered.

Kitty frowned. 'I'm not sure but I think Captain Bryant may be in trouble.' Lavinia Braddock's warning that Matt might be in danger resonated around her head. There were a lot of things all coming together in her mind and she didn't like the conclusions she was drawing. Gladys Silitoe at One Pine. What had Mrs Craven said? Gladys was the brains.

Alice's eyes widened. 'What makes you say that, miss?'

A shiver raced along Kitty's spine. 'I think he may have just walked into a trap.'

Mary returned to the lobby.

'Mary, call Mr Potter, I need to leave for One Pine immediately.' Kitty dived back inside her office to retrieve her hat, coat, handbag and, for good measure, her stout umbrella.

'He's out with someone, miss. Mr Robert says can he help?' Mary had the receiver in her hand as Kitty locked her office door.

'Has he any transport?' Kitty asked.

'He says if it's urgent there's the Daisybelle.' A frown puckered Mary's brow and she clearly considered that Kitty had lost her mind.

'The Daisybelle will be fine. Please ask him to hurry.' Anxiety knotted inside Kitty's stomach. She was certain now. It had to be.

Mary complied with her request. 'He's pulling her out now, miss. You need to go along aways to board her.'

'Call Torquay Police Station next, Mary. Tell them that I've gone to One Pine near Torre Station. Ask for Inspector Greville and ask him to send his men there as soon as possible. I believe Captain Bryant is in danger.' Kitty tugged on her hat.

Mary gaped at her. 'Very good, miss.'

Kitty started for the door only to find Alice hard on her heels.

'I'm coming with you, miss. You might need some help.'

'Very well, but your mother will kill me.' Kitty rushed along the street with Alice accompanying her still wearing her apron and cap.

The Daisybelle was waiting for them with Robert at the wheel. Kitty scrambled aboard the elderly bright green and yellow painted motor coach with its daisy logo with Alice following behind her.

'Thank you, Robert, as fast as you like to One Pine,' Kitty said. The sooner she could learn to drive and buy herself a car, the better it would be.

They were lucky there was no queue for the ferry and Robert persuaded the ferrymen to take them over to the other side of the Dart without waiting for more traffic to join them. Kitty gave them a generous tip.

'Why do you think as Captain Bryant is in trouble, miss?' Alice asked as Robert coaxed the Daisybelle into a faster pace as they exited Kingswear.

'He said he'd had a strange telephone call asking him to go to One Pine and now the telephone line has gone dead. The woman who asked him to meet him there is not the lady who lives there, and her husband is being questioned by Inspector Greville about the murder of Councillor Everton.' Kitty gripped her seat tightly as Robert took the corners as quickly as he dared in the Daisybelle. 'Of course, I may just be making the most frightful fool of myself,' she added, even though her gut feeling told her that she wasn't. No, she was sure she had worked it out. She knew who had killed Councillor Everton and Thomas King and why.

'No, miss, that doesn't sound right at all,' Alice said loyally, as Daisybelle groaned her way over the common and on down the hill towards Torquay.

CHAPTER TWENTY-TWO

Matt's motorcycle rumbled to a halt at the top of the gravel drive outside One Pine. The house looked unprepossessing in the gloomy winter light. No other vehicles were parked there and everywhere appeared silent and deserted. Even the birds were still with no gulls calling overhead or birdsong from the bedraggled and neglected shrubbery.

He walked to the front door, the fine hairs at the nape of his neck prickling. Something was very amiss. The door was slightly ajar, and rather than call out or ring the bell, he pushed it slightly more open to peer inside.

The skeletons of a pile of long dead leaves swirled suddenly about his feet. The hall looked dark and miserable with no sign of the house's occupants. Still feeling uneasy, Matt stepped into the hall and walked carefully towards what he assumed was the drawing room door.

Another door further along the hall creaked. Matt turned to see Gladys Silitoe staring at him clutching a laden tea tray with a frightened expression on her face.

'My word, Captain Bryant, you scared the living daylights out of me. I never heard you come in. I was just taking this into the drawing room. There's a fire in there and it's a little warmer.' She led the way through to the door that Matt had been about to enter.

'Where are the servants?' Matt asked as she bustled inside, placing the tray down on the coffee table beside the fire. The room appeared unkempt, dust lay on the polished surfaces of the china cabinets and side tables. A long dead vase of flowers scented the air with rotting vegetation. The room felt abandoned and deserted.

'Marigold has dismissed them, I think. She's intending to leave immediately after her husband and nephew's funerals. Daphne and her fiancé plan to marry by special licence and are to sell this place.' Mrs Silitoe gave a shudder and looked at her surroundings with distaste.

'What happened to the telephone line?' Matt asked as the woman seated herself on one of the armchairs and began to set out teacups.

'I really don't know. It was most odd. I assumed the fault must have occurred at your end.' She continued to busy herself with the tea things. 'Do have a seat.'

Matt tried to tamp down the irritation rising in his gut as he took the chair opposite her. 'You said you had discovered something and wanted me to come here urgently. You sounded quite distressed?'

'Yes, oh dear me, yes, I did. Please have a seat, Captain Bryant, I'll just fetch the notes. They were with Mr King's papers.' Mrs Silitoe bustled out of the room and returned a moment later with a small carpet bag in one hand and a few documents in her other hand.

She resumed her seat, dropped the bag down by her side as she passed across the papers. 'They seem to be a list of names and payments. Oh, Captain Bryant, I didn't know what to do. Councillor Everton was planning to consult you about something, wasn't he? Do you think this is important?'

Matt glanced at the papers she had given him. There was something in the tone of her voice that didn't sound quite right. The prickly feeling that he was in danger increased. 'I'm not sure, Mrs Silitoe. I think perhaps Inspector Greville should take a look at these. I believe there may be some question of fraud in his line of enquiry.'

'Yes, of course. That must be why he keeps questioning Ivor and why he looked at Ivor's bank account and the one for the business. Do have a cup of tea, Captain Bryant.' Mrs Silitoe urged.

She placed the strainer over the cup and poured the tea before he could decline.

'Mrs Silitoe, I really must get going. I'm late for a meeting.' Why had she got him to Marigold Everton's house to show him the documents? He could see nothing in the documents that didn't confirm what he had already pieced together for himself.

'Oh, dear Captain Bryant, I feel terrible that I've inconvenienced you. I do hope the meeting isn't something very important?'

Something in Gladys Silitoe's voice made him lift his head. She was staring at him in a very odd fashion, her eyes were hard and bright as if she were expecting something from him.

'Quite important,' he said.

'I really do suggest you stay and drink your tea.' Her voice was now as hard as her eyes.

Startled Matt looked up and realised that a small but deadly looking gun rested on Gladys Silitoe's lap with the barrel pointing right at him.

'I can only assume you've made an addition to my tea, in the same way you added to Councillor Everton's medicine?' He made no move to touch the teacup. He kept his gaze fixed on her face as he tried to think how he could make good his escape.

'Of course. I had prepared the sachet beforehand when I first heard that Harold was suspicious. The poison was easy to get hold of and Marigold's bag was open next to mine at the hotel. It was the work of an instant to pop it into the box while she was fiddling around with her furs. You see, my dear husband intends to leave me and go abroad to the Riviera with Marigold Everton. That really won't do at all, Captain Bryant. It would be much better if they were caught and convicted of Harold and Thomas' murder. I gathered from Ivor that the police think Thomas was murdered as well. Finding your body here with dear Marigold's fingerprints over everything, the servants dismissed, and her bags already packed, well, that would tie things up nicely, don't you think?'

'Is that what this is about? Revenge on Marigold and your husband?' Matt asked.

A movement outside in the garden behind Gladys Silitoe caught his attention and he schooled his face to remain expressionless as he realised it was Kitty creeping around the shrubbery towards the back door.

Gladys gave a harsh laugh. 'You disappoint me, Captain Bryant. No, I couldn't care less about those two and their tawdry assignations. Men are all the same, not very bright. Ivor didn't even realise that I'd put that money into his account and tipped off the police. Anonymously, of course.' Her eyes gleamed.

Matt looked at her. 'Councillor Everton, I think, thought there was fraud in his department. People were paying Thomas King for so-called legal advice to uncover loopholes that would permit their plans to go ahead.'

The smile on her face broadened. 'Do go on.'

Matt hoped the woman had left the back door unlatched and that Kitty had called Inspector Greville. The longer he could keep her talking, the better. Something Kitty had used to her advantage when she had been the one in the tricky situations. 'Thomas King was the go-between, making the contacts and collecting the payments. Councillor Everton knew something was amiss. He argued with your husband on the night he died but Ivor didn't know anything either, did he? You were the one who had the legal knowledge and you primed your husband with the notes for the committee.' Matt shifted slightly in his chair to try and cover the faint sound he thought he had detected in the kitchen.

Gladys immediately raised the gun. 'Don't get any bright ideas, Captain Bryant. I assure you I am a very good shot. I learned when I was a girl, my father taught me. It would suit me better if you drank the tea, less messy, but I'm not particular.'

'Thomas King got paid handsomely for his part, didn't he? But he was becoming a liability. His uncle had become suspicious of the flashy clothes and his spending habits. He started to change his routine and open his own post. Meanwhile Thomas King had become greedy. Instead of those carefully chosen cases which you knew you could get through the committee he went into business for himself and the complaints began to surface. People like Clive Hendricks and Lavinia Braddock.' He was sure now that Kitty was in the hall listening to the conversation. He had to try and warn her about the gun.

'Thomas was an idiot. A greedy idiot,' Gladys said.

'I take it you were the one who tampered with the wheel on his car when he called at your house before driving out to Cockington,' Matt said.

Gladys sniffed. 'I learned a lot about cars and car maintenance from listening to Thomas drone on about his beloved motor. I'd watched him fix it the one day when there was a problem, so I knew what to do. It was the work of a few minutes while he was dropping off Marigold's papers and waiting for a signature on some documents. I slipped out of the back door with a wrench.'

'He'd definitely become a problem, then? I'm surprised you didn't just shoot him with your gun.' Matt hoped Kitty had heard the hint.

'An accident was much more appropriate. It would have taken more planning to shoot him and then to plant the gun on dear Marigold or Ivor.' Gladys sneered.

'I presume you decided to get rid of me because you didn't know for certain what I knew already or what Councillor Everton had said to me before he died,' Matt attempted to appear composed.

Gladys levelled the gun at him once more, the barrel glinting in the light from the fire. 'I'm afraid your tea will be cold, Captain Bryant.'

Matt picked up the cup and willed Kitty or someone to make a move. He couldn't stall for very much longer.

'Do drink up.' Gladys' voice was sharp.

*

Kitty was braced against the wall outside the drawing room door. Her pulse pounded and she was scarcely able to breathe. Gladys Silitoe must have a gun trained on Matt if she had understood his hint correctly. For she was certain that he had seen her sneaking past the drawing room window.

She glanced at her watch. She'd given Alice and Robert strict instructions to create a diversion seven minutes after she had left them to creep around the back of the house. Thank heavens the back door had been left unlocked. Probably for Gladys to make her getaway.

The bell outside the front door clanged and, at the same time, Kitty flung the door to the drawing room open with her umbrella. She dived low along the floor and prayed Gladys would miss if she attempted to shoot. Mrs Silitoe leapt from her seat with her gun at the ready startled by the unexpected commotion coming from two directions at the same time.

Kitty swung her furled umbrella at Gladys' ankles as hard as she possibly could; the metal handle gave a loud crack as it made contact with its target. Matt took advantage of the confusion to hurl the contents of his teacup into Gladys' face. He made a grab for the gun, wresting it from Mrs Silitoe's hands as she crumpled back onto the armchair reeling in pain at Kitty's assault on her ankles.

There was a loud bang as the gun went off and a cascade of plaster fell from the ceiling onto Kitty's head temporarily blinding her and making her splutter. A stream of abuse emanated from Gladys Silitoe as she riled around on the armchair clutching her ankles.

Kitty looked up from her prone position on the floor coughing and spluttering from the plaster dust. Matt had hold of the gun and had it firmly trained on Gladys Silitoe who now looked a sorry sight with the remains of Matt's tea dripping from her hair.

'I was becoming concerned, Miss Underhay. You took your time.' Matt extended a hand to help her up from the floor, while still monitoring Gladys Silitoe. The dimple in his cheek flashed and she thought she caught more than a hint of relief in his smile.

'You were certain that I'd come then,' she observed drily as she picked chunks of plaster from the shoulders of her black woollen coat.

'I never doubted you.' His tone became serious.

The hammering at the front door increased before finally crashing open and Alice rushed into the room wielding a wrench. Robert Potter accompanied her, rosy faced with the drama of it all, bearing a walking cane.

'Oh, you've got her,' Alice said in a disappointed voice, staring at Mrs Silitoe. 'We were frantic when we heard a shot.' Her eyes grew even rounder when she saw the gun in Matt's hand.

'The police have just arrived,' Robert Potter observed as the sound of running feet came from the hall.

Inspector Greville entered the drawing room accompanied by two uniformed constables. His moustache quivered slightly when he took in the tableaux before him.

Kitty guessed they must present a strange sight with Gladys covered in tea and herself smothered in grey plaster dust.

'I presume there is an explanation for this?' Inspector Greville remarked in a mild tone. His eyebrows raised when he saw the gun in Matt's hand.

Matt calmly explained the gist of events to the inspector as Gladys scowled at them from her position on the armchair. Inspector Greville gave the nod to one of the constables and they secured Gladys Silitoe. Kitty's shoulders sagged in relief that the woman could do no more damage to anyone.

'I can see you have disposed of much of the tea. Is there enough left for testing?' the inspector asked, peering at the cup which lay miraculously intact on its side on the carpet.

One of the constables retrieved it with care. 'A dreg, sir.'

'Excellent. I've no doubt we will discover more potassium cyanide in its contents.' He turned to Gladys Silitoe. 'It had struck me as rather queer that throughout all our questioning of your husband, he seemed a little afraid of you.'

Mrs Silitoe lifted her chin. 'Ivor was always a weak man. Weak, ineffectual and vain. He dyes his hair, for heaven's sake. I am much more his superior in intellect, wealth and everything. Why should I have lost my good name and lovely home just so that miserable worm could run off with Marigold Everton? Marigold, of all people. I should have married Harold Everton you know. I was the one that introduced him to Marigold in the first place. The worst days work I ever did.'

'And yet you murdered him,' Kitty said.

'I had it all planned. I have my house and a nice sum of money. With Harold gone so I could be safe and Thomas out of the way, then Marigold and Ivor would have swung. I'd have kept everything. It was perfect, quite perfect. Then Captain Bryant came along, and you, Miss Underhay, asking questions, poking around.' She tried to hobble towards Kitty but was restrained by the constable.

Matt placed a protective arm around Kitty's waist, and she was glad of the solid reassurance of his presence. Gladys Silitoe's face was contorted in a mask of hatred.

'I think that is quite enough of that.' The inspector nodded again to the constables, and they led the limping figure of Mrs Silitoe away.

More footsteps sounded on the hall floor and Marigold and Daphne Everton arrived in the drawing room.

'Whatever is going on? Why was that woman in my house?' Marigold looked around at them all.

'I suggest, Mrs Everton, that we leave this room for my men to collect the evidence we require to charge Mrs Silitoe with the murder of your husband and nephew. Captain Bryant, may I relieve you of your firearm?' Inspector Greville took the gun from Matt and opened it to remove the bullets, dropping them in a small empty tobacco tin which he produced from the inner pocket of his overcoat.

'Gladys Silitoe killed my father? And Thomas?' Daphne stared at the inspector before falling to the floor in a dead faint.

Robert Potter and the inspector got her to the sofa where she came round slowly with the aid of some smelling salts that Alice found in the kitchen drawer.

'Miss Underhay and Captain Bryant, I shall of course require statements from you both, although Mrs Silitoe appears to have already made a confession.' The inspector looked at Matt and Kitty.

'Of course, sir.'

Marigold perched on the edge of the sofa next to her daughter. 'Goodness, I can't quite believe it. Ivor always said that Gladys was not a person one should cross, but murder, I can hardly believe such a level of wickedness.' She swallowed hard.

More constables arrived and they were all gently but firmly ushered from the house, while the inspector issued his instructions. Marigold and Daphne went upstairs to pack up their things.

'Well, that was an adventure and no mistake. Just like one of the films that was. My heart was going like the clappers,' Alice said as they stood on the gravel drive.

'I should get the Daisybelle back to Dartmouth. Father will wonder what's gone on.' Robert Potter glanced towards his beloved motor coach.

'Can you take Alice back with you, please?' Kitty could see her maid was shivering in her thin black uniform. 'I'll settle the bill with you later. Thank you so much for acting so bravely and promptly, Robert.'

The lad's broad pleasant face turned dark red. 'Not at all, Miss Kitty.'

Alice and Robert trotted away leaving Kitty and Matt temporarily alone together on the driveway.

'Are you all right, Kitty?' Matt asked as he picked another small piece of plaster from her shoulder.

'I seem to have skinned my knees and ruined another pair of stockings. My hat is, I suspect, beyond repair, and even Alice's ministrations may prove to be insufficient to save my coat. Oh, and I have spoiled another perfectly good umbrella.' She blinked to stop her eyes from unexpectedly filling with tears. 'Yes, I'm all right. It's you I should be asking. You were the one who ended up staring down the barrel of a gun.' She shivered as a sudden blast of wintery air swirled around her.

'I'm fine, thanks to your quick thinking. It was a tight squeak for a few moments though. What made you realise that I might be in trouble?' Matt asked.

'Mrs Craven remarked at breakfast that Mrs Silitoe was Mr Silitoe's secretary and that she was much cleverer than he was. Then when you left your message, I tried the telephone number for One Pine and the line was dead. Everything started to slot into place, especially after Lavinia Braddock's warning the other day. Then I knew it was Gladys.'

'I hadn't realised you had pressed the Daisybelle into service, a most unlikely vehicle for staging a rescue,' Matt mused as he guided her further away from the icy draught coming around the corner of the house.

'Mr Potter was already out with the taxi. I had little choice. Another point towards my obtaining a car of my own,' Kitty said.

Inspector Greville came towards them. 'Mrs Everton and her daughter are going to stay at The Grand for a few days. You look as if you have been in the wars, Miss Underhay.' He regarded her dusty hat and coat with a quizzical smile. 'Still, good thing the bullet went up into the ceiling instead of either of you. Quick thinking of yours with the umbrella.'

'Thank you, Inspector,' Kitty said.

'Mr Silitoe has been released. I don't know if he will wish to represent his wife. I very much doubt it under the circumstances. I shall be busy here for some time, so I'll telephone you both to arrange to take your statements probably tomorrow.'

'Very good, sir.' Matt nodded his agreement and the inspector disappeared back into the house.

Matt looked at Kitty. 'What now?' he asked.

Her lips suddenly dried. 'What now indeed?'

CHAPTER TWENTY-THREE

They made their way by mutual accord away from One Pine and towards the taxi rank near the station.

Kitty peeped up at Matt from under the brim of her hat. 'You haven't asked me what my answer was,' she said.

They had stopped near the cream and brown painted entrance near the taxi rank. A small kiosk stood nearby selling newspapers, sweets and penny dreadfuls. All around them people were entering and leaving the station and climbing in and out of motor cars. The air smelt of smoke mingled with the faint tang of brine from the sea.

'Very well, Miss Underhay, are we to remain just friends, or are we, as we keep being asked, walking out?' His lips were curved upwards in a smile, but she could see his eyes were dark and serious.

Her heart rate sped up. 'I think we could try walking out and see how it goes,' she replied demurely.

His grin widened. 'You realise that we shall be the talk of Dartmouth?'

She grinned back at him. 'And your parents do not really approve of me?'

He lowered his head to press a kiss firmly on her lips. 'Will that concern you?'

A small giggle escaped her. 'What do you think?'

'I think you should probably take a taxi back to the Dolphin and change. I'll collect my motorcycle from One Pine and come to meet you. I think a late lunch is in order?' Matt suggested.

'That sounds very acceptable, Captain Bryant. I shall, of course, expect many lunches, teas, flowers, chocolates and trips to the cinema.' Kitty bit her lip to stop herself from laughing.

'I am deeply wounded, Miss Underhay. Do you not find our outings exciting enough?' The dimple in his cheek deepened.

A taxi pulled into the rank next to them and Matt opened the rear door to allow Kitty to clamber inside.

'The Dolphin Hotel, Dartmouth, please,' he instructed the driver. 'I'll see you shortly,' he said to Kitty as he gave her another fleeting kiss and closed the door behind her. A smile played on her lips as she watched him stride away back towards One Pine.

'The Dolphin, then, miss?' the driver asked, and at her confirmation, he pulled out of the rank into the traffic.

Mary let out a horrified gasp at her appearance when Kitty entered the lobby a short time later. She had stayed in the taxi for the ferry crossing rather than disembarking at Kingswear and crossing as a foot passenger as she usually did. She had not wanted to draw attention to her dishevelled appearance. Gossip spread far too swiftly around the town for Kitty's liking and she knew her appearance would be a nine days' wonder.

Alice was standing by the side of the reception desk and had no doubt been regaling Mary with the story of their adventures. A small dog of indeterminate parentage ran towards Kitty, greeting her with licks and enthusiastic yips.

'Muffy!' She bent down to fuss the happy little dog before straightening to see her cousin's smiling face. 'Lucy! When did you arrive? Oh, and I look such a state.'

She was sharply aware of her slender brunette cousin's smart wine-coloured coat and hat compared to her dust-covered appearance.

'Best give me your hat and coat, Miss Kitty, and I'll do my best with them. If you run up and change your stockings and have a bit of a brush up, you'll soon be right as ninepence,' Alice suggested, suiting her words to her deeds and relieving Kitty of her outdoor garments.

'Darling, I had to come when you told me about your mother. I'm so very sorry.' Her cousin embraced her in a fierce hug. 'Whatever have you been up to, Kitty? Mary had just told me you were called out on an emergency to help Captain Bryant.' Lucy's face was alive with interest and Kitty realised how very glad she was to see her.

'Matt will be here soon so if you've not yet had lunch then you can join us, and we'll explain everything. You have come to stay, haven't you?' Kitty asked.

'If you'll have me. Mary was going to find me a room, and Muffy, of course.' The little dog wagged her stumpy tail at the sound of her name.

'Of course. Mary ask Mrs Homer to make up the room Captain Bryant used up on my floor.' Kitty turned back to her cousin. 'It's not as nice as the hotel rooms but it's more private and it will be so nice having you next to me. My room has just been redone and I have a little sitting room now so we shall be very snug.'

Lucy laughed. 'That sounds perfect. You'd better run and change your stockings before your beau arrives. Matt is your beau now, I assume?' she asked archly.

'You are impossible. I'll be right back.' Kitty grinned at her and ran off up the stairs.

By the time Kitty had changed her ripped stockings, bathed her knees and tidied her hair and face Matt had arrived and was in the lobby talking to Lucy. Muffy continued to do an excited little dance all around them.

Kitty had taken time to don one of her favourite hats in pale beige and had dug her second-best winter coat out of the wardrobe.

Luckily it was a dark caramel colour and teamed up nicely with her beige kid gloves and handbag. At least now she would feel more respectable next to her very chic cousin.

They were about to set off for the tea rooms when the telephone rang at the reception desk.

'Captain Bryant, it's for you, sir.' Mary passed the receiver to Matt.

Kitty waited, her arm linked through Lucy's, for him to come and join them.

'I see, sir. Yes, thank you, I'll tell Miss Underhay.' He replaced the handset.

'What is it, Matt?' Kitty asked. His face was grave, and she could tell that whoever it was had not given him happy news.

He joined the girls and they set off together along the embankment, Muffy trotting happily ahead of them.

'That was Inspector Greville.'

'Oh.' Kitty wondered what the inspector could have said to make Matt look so severe.

'I'm afraid that Gladys Silitoe is dead.'

Kitty halted in shock. Lucy and Matt paused with her. 'What happened?' Kitty asked. Gladys had been carted off kicking and spitting invective at everyone just an hour or so ago.

'Suicide. It seems she had another sachet of poison concealed about her person. Once she was alone in her cell, she swallowed it in a glass of water,' Matt said.

Kitty gasped, her hand flying to cover her mouth with the horror of it all.

'Heavens, how awful!' Lucy exclaimed, her eyes rounding.

'I suppose she couldn't face the trial and, inevitably, given what she'd done, the noose.' Kitty shuddered and her cousin patted her arm in sympathy. It didn't bear thinking about. A vision of Councillor Everton's dead face flashed into her memory.

'Dreadful,' Lucy said.

The sombre mood was broken by Muffy attempting to interrogate a seagull that had the temerity to land right in front of her.

By the time they were seated inside the tea room, with a chastened Muffy lying at their feet waiting for titbits, the atmosphere had lightened a little.

'Will Uncle Edgar be here in time for the inquest, do you think? I must confess I am eager to meet my rogue relative. Papa is not so keen. He keeps making noises about shotguns again.' Lucy laughed.

'No, his ship will arrive too late, but he will be here for the funeral though, Grams and her friend are busy making arrangements. Inspector Pinch is to confirm all the details from the coroner,' Kitty said.

'What shall you do next?' Lucy asked, looking at Kitty.

She knew exactly what her cousin meant. 'Father Lamb said my quest had ended, and I suppose in one way he was right.' She paused and glanced at Matt. 'But I want to know what happened. I need to at least try and find out. I want justice for my mother.' Her voice wobbled.

'Oh, you poor darling.' Lucy took hold of her hand and her eyes filled with sympathetic tears.

'So, I've decided that once the inquest is over if Inspector Pinch hasn't managed to find Ezekiel Hammett, then I intend to place an advertisement with a reward for information.' Kitty looked at Matt.

The waitress came to take their orders.

'And a pot of tea for me too, please,' Lucy said. 'Anyone else?'

Kitty glanced at Matt. 'I rather think Matt is off tea at the moment.'

Lucy grimaced. 'Yes, how silly of me.'

The waitress left and they resumed their conversation.

'Papa will be there at the inquest, of course. He felt someone should be there from Uncle Edgar's side and these things are not pleasant. But, Kitty, will it not be rather dangerous? This man, from what you have told me, is a vicious murderer.' Lucy drew off her black kid gloves and stowed them in her handbag.

'Grams and I are very grateful that Uncle will be attending to support us. I will, of course, have to be careful how the advertisement is worded.' Kitty was fond of Lucy's father, Lord Medford. She liked his kind, bluff nature.

If the police had found Hammett by then, she might even get her answers as to how her mother had died, by whose hand and why. If not, then offering a reward might help to find either Hammett or others who might be prepared to speak out.

'Are you determined on this, Kitty?' Matt asked.

'Yes.' Her gaze tangled with his.

'Then I'll help you with the wording and sift out the replies with you. I agree with Lucy that we must be careful. Hammett is dangerous and there may be many false trails. We also have to be careful not to undermine the police. We need them onside.' He smiled at Kitty and her heart lifted.

'I know I may never discover anything more, but I have to try.' Kitty looked around at her companions.

'Of course, darling, we understand completely. Anyway, I am rather getting off the point for the other more pleasant reason why I'm here.' Lucy wiggled in her seat with excitement.

The waitress returned and placed their plates of hot golden crispy fish in front of them.

'This looks delicious, I'm starving.' Kitty sprinkled vinegar over the fat fluffy chips and waited for her cousin to continue. Breakfast seemed like a long time ago and adventuring took it out of a girl.

'I am here to invite you and Matt to stay for Christmas. Please do say you'll come. I'm being entirely selfish, otherwise it will be me and a houseful of random people that Mother and Father have invited. Aged distant relatives and waifs and strays. I shall be so bored I will have eaten myself to death with figgy pudding and mince pies by the day after Boxing Day.' Lucy turned limpid eyes on Kitty.

'I'd need to speak to Grams, I know she wants a quiet Christmas at the hotel. Great Aunt Livvy is coming from Scotland to stay for a month or so to attend the funeral and to stay for Christmas.' Kitty didn't look at Matt, she wasn't sure what his plans were. Would they be changed with her new status in his life?

'If Kitty can be spared from the hotel then I'd love to accompany her. My parents always go to Yorkshire for Christmas to visit an aged relative of Father's so I shall not be missed. Thank you, Lucy. I hope our stay will be more peaceful than last time.' Matt poured some water from the decanter into a tumbler for each of them.

Kitty shivered a little at the memory of her last stay at Enderley Hall when three people had died and she and Lucy had been taken prisoner.

'No murders, I promise,' Lucy said.

'I'll drink to that.' Kitty raised her glass and chinked it against the others. 'Here's to a nice quiet uneventful Christmas.'

'Woof,' Muffy added.

A LETTER FROM HELENA

I want to say thank you for choosing to read *Murder on the Dance Floor*. If you enjoyed it and want to keep up to date with all my latest releases, just sign up at the following link. Your email address will never be shared and of course you can unsubscribe at any time.

www.bookouture.com/helena-dixon

If you read the first book in the series, *Murder at the Dolphin Hotel*, you can find out how Kitty and Matt first met and began their sleuthing adventures. I always enjoy meeting characters again as a series reader, which is why I love writing this series so much. I hope you enjoy their exploits as much as I love creating them.

I hope you loved *Murder on the Dance Floor* and if you did, I would be very grateful if you could write a review. I'd love to hear what you think, and it makes such a difference helping new readers to discover one of my books for the first time.

I love hearing from my readers – you can get in touch on my Facebook page, through Twitter, Goodreads or my website.

Thanks,
Helena Dixon

nelldixonauthor

@NellDixon

www.nelldixon.com

ACKNOWLEDGEMENTS

My thanks as always go to the wonderful residents of Torbay who generously allow me to fictionalise their beautiful towns. Many thanks to everyone who supplied me with old photographs of Paignton, Cockington and Torquay.

Many of the places named in the book are real places. You can walk those streets, take a drink at the gorgeous art deco bar at the Imperial Hotel and catch a train along the coast.

You can also visit the underground passages at Exeter and take a tour, and I recommend a visit to the historic quayside, especially on Sundays. You might find a band playing, an open market, swans on the river and wonderful artisan shops in the arches.

Much of the area I describe near the cathedral was lost during the Second World War and my thanks go to everyone who supplied me with old maps showing the area pre-blitz.

My thanks as always go to the coffee crew, Elizabeth Hanbury and Phillipa Ashley for their unstinting support. My hard-working agent, Kate Nash. To everyone at Bookouture, my incredible editor, Emily Gowers, my very patient copyeditor, Jane Eastgate, my fabulous proofreader, Shirley Khan and talented cover designer, Debbie Clement, plus all the many unseen people who do so much to help 'birth' these books.

Printed in Great Britain
by Amazon